THE
BOWMAN BOYS

The Sultan Saga

Book One

D.W. ULSTERMAN

This is a work of fiction.

To Elmore Leonard for helping me to talk less
and say more.

And to Sultan and the Sky Valley—it was a hell of a time.

1.

"Killing is easy. It's the forgetting that's hard."

That was the spoken wisdom of the man with the dark eyes and salt-and-pepper mustache named Levi Bowman. He was the patriarch of the Bowman clan, a family of some notoriety among the rag-tag, dirt-road survivors of Sultan, a tiny mining and logging town on the outskirts of Snohomish County in the rain-drenched watershed of Washington State. The year was 1923. Sultan's appearance hadn't changed much since before the Great War, but its people were different. Their former rugged nobility had devolved into something more hard-edged and sinister. Out of poverty came desperation, and from desperation arrived a willingness to do just about anything to survive.

Prohibition added fuel to that degenerate fire. Whenever government attempts to forbid something, opportunity fills the void. Sultan was no different than other parts of the country in that regard. People wanted to drink, and opportunists like the Bowmans were there to profit from that demand.

And profit they did.

"Dig it deep," Levi said.

It was eighteen-year-old Chance Bowman's first grave. He was the youngest of the four Bowman boys and had been demanding he be allowed to help more with the family business. Tonight, his father decided to give him his first real taste of the kind of commitment that sort of help required.

Chance kept shoveling. His muscular arms burned, and his back ached, but he didn't show it. The last thing he wanted was for his father to see him as weak. That was the curse of being the youngest. No matter how tall and strong Chance grew, he was still the baby. He hated it.

Levi lit a cigarette and looked up at the moon. It was nearly midnight. It had taken an hour to drag the body of Roy Coon through the woods to the clearing at the end of the dirt road at the top of the Sultan Basin—a large hill that loomed above the little town below.

Chance paused to catch his breath. "Pa, why are we burying Mr. Coon?"

Levi took a deep drag and then blew the smoke out through his nose. "Because he's dead."

"I know that. What I mean to say is... why'd you have to kill him?"

"Just dig."

"Didn't you like him? I remember before the war watching you two joking like you were the best of friends."

"Liking him had nothing to do with what happened. It was business—had to be done. That's all you need to know. Now hurry up. Rain's coming."

Chance glanced up at the same clear night sky his father had been looking at. "Rain?"

Levi pointed at the unfinished hole in the earth. "Keep going--needs to be deeper."

At the very moment the grave was finally finished, Levi held up a hand and crouched low. "Someone's coming," he whispered.

Chance pulled himself out of the hole. He heard rustling from the woods that surrounded the clearing. Levi was holding his pistol–the same one he had used to put a bullet into Roy Coon's chest just a few hours earlier.

"Is it Fenner?" Chance asked. Sixty-two-year-old Fenton Fenner was the town's only lawman.

Levi shook his head. "Not likely. It's past his bedtime."

Fenner was on the Bowman family's payroll. Levi paid him twenty dollars a week to look the other way, an amount which nearly doubled Fenner's regular salary.

"Then who the hell is it?"

Levi's eyes narrowed as he tried to see into the forest. "Hold tight. We'll find out soon enough."

A bear cub walked out of the woods and into the clearing. Levi's face tightened. He put a hand on Chance's shoulder. "Stay still and keep real quiet."

Father and son watched the cub as it shuffled through the grass. The little bear made whimpering noises as it zig-zagged its way toward them.

"I think it's lost," Chance said.

Levi didn't reply. He wasn't even looking at the cub. His eyes remained fixed on the tree line. The cub stood up on its hind legs, opened its mouth wide, and let out a wail that echoed across the clearing.

Its cry was answered by a deep groan from its mother. She emerged from the woods, stood up on her hind legs, and bellowed. The cub ran to her. Both Chance and Levi watched the mother bear sniffing the air. She appeared to be staring right at them.

"Shit," Levi said. "The wind is at our backs. She knows we're here."

The mother bear dropped onto all fours and moved further into the clearing. Levi pushed Chance back. "Get behind me. She's gonna charge."

"Why do you think that?"

Levi's mouth was a hard slash as his jaw clenched tight. "Because I know rage when I see it, and that there is about three-hundred-pounds of rage staring us down."

Both mother bear and human father were focused on the same thing—protecting their child.

The bear charged.

Levi took aim and pulled the trigger.

10

The bear kept coming. Levi fired again. Chance dove to the side while his father stood his ground. Man and beast fell backward in a tangle of arms, legs, and fur and then disappeared. A savage roar came from inside the dark pit. Chance couldn't tell if the sound was from his father or the bear. There was another gunshot. The grave was suddenly quiet.

Chance scrambled to the edge of the grave and looked down. All he saw was the outline of dark fur.

"Pa!"

Chance had already lost his mother to cancer when he was just a child. He feared his father was now gone as well.

A cough. A groan. Then a flash of light and the smell of fresh-burning tobacco.

Levi Bowman sat nearly crushed by the weight of a dead bear at the bottom of a grave dug for a man he had just killed. The irony of it all made him chuckle.

"What's so funny?"

"Life, death, all of it," Levi answered. "Now help me out of here."

Chance took hold of his father's hand and pulled. Levi stood, turned around, and looked down. He was contemplating something. Chance waited to hear what it was.

"The rope around Roy's feet—we're gonna need it."

Chance handed the rope to his father. Levi jumped back into the hole.

"What are you doing?"

Levi looked up. "Either we haul this bear out of here, or you dig another grave. It's not deep enough to fit two bodies. Besides, this is good meat—more than enough to help a lot of people enjoy a decent meal. Wouldn't be right to waste it."

It took some time for the two of them to pull the bear out. Both their faces were covered in sweat. They rolled Roy Coon's remains into the pit. Chance shoveled dirt until the body was buried. Levi clapped his son on the back.

"You did good. Kept your head."

Chance grinned. Getting a compliment from his father was a rare thing. It meant a lot. The grin faded. Levi scowled.

"What is it?"

Chance leaned against the shovel. "I guess I'm sad about Mr. Coon. With that hole covered up, well, it's like he never was. And then I wonder...."

Levi stood up straight, cocked his head, and arched a brow. "You wonder *what*?"

"I wonder if we're bad people. I know some around here think so, but I never paid that much mind. But tonight, I buried a man. Maybe those people are right."

"You're suffering some kind of moral crisis. Is that it?"

Chance shrugged. "I don't know about all that. I just know I feel bad for Mr. Coon."

Levi ran a hand through his thick, gray-streaked black hair. "Do you think I'd lie to you?"

Chance shook his head. "What? No!"

"Earlier tonight I told you that what happened to Roy Coon had to be done. I had no choice. You remember?"

"Sure."

"Okay, then that's it. You know I'm not one to lie, especially to family. If I say that's how it had to be, then that's how it had to be."

"But *why*?"

Levi pointed toward the woods. "When that bear was charging, was I right to try and kill it, or should I have just let it take us both? Which death would you have chosen—the bear's or yours?"

"The bear of course. But what does that have to do with—"

"There's your answer. I made the same choice with Roy Coon as I did the bear. It was either him or us. He owed our family a lot of money. He was a drunk. He should have kept his mouth shut, but instead he started to talk about that debt to others, boasting about how he was gonna ride it out for as long as he wanted. Now what do you suppose happens when people start to think you can owe money to the Bowmans and not have to worry about paying it back? I'll tell you. The whole enterprise collapses. We lose everything we've worked so hard for. This is a cruel and dangerous world. I take no pleasure from taking a life, but sometimes you have no choice. It must be done. Our own survival requires it. If others around here sense weakness, they'll come for us. They'll take what's ours and make it their own. I'm not about to allow that to happen. Are you?"

Chance shook his head. "No."

"Good, because if you really want to be a part of this thing we do, then there will come another time when the bear will charge, and you'll be the one to have to pull that trigger. And

I hope on your momma's memory that's exactly what you do. *You pull the goddamn trigger.*"

Chance felt something hit the tip of his nose. He looked up. His father's prediction of rain was right. From miles away came the sound of a lone train whistle.

"Pa, how'd you get to be so smart?"

Levi flicked another spent cigarette away and shook his head. "I ain't so smart. I just try and learn quicker than most."

The two dragged the bear corpse back to the car. Levi did his best to hide a limp. The bear attack had hurt him more than he was letting on. Each step was a jolt to his lower back. He whispered a 'thank God' to himself when they finally reached the road. Levi knew the car's trunk was too small, and he didn't want the bear stinking up the leather interior. That left just one other option. They lay the body over the hood and tied it down. Levi tugged on the rope to make sure it was secure and then nodded.

"That'll do."

Chance looked back toward the woods. "What about the cub?"

Levi shrugged. "That cub can fend for itself. It's big enough."

"I hope so."

Levi attempted a reassuring smile, but it didn't look right. Smiles weren't his thing.

"It'll be fine. Now let's get back to town and see what your brothers are up to. In fact, how about you drive?"

"Really?"

"Sure. I'm beat tired. She's all yours. Just don't grind the gears."

Chance ground the gears. If it bothered Levi, he didn't show it. The headlights illuminated the way back to Sultan as the sky opened and the rain fell.

Though it was late, the night was still far from over.

2.

A hand-painted sign that read THE SILO hung at an angle above the door of a single-story brick structure. It marked the entrance to the Bowman family's small-town business empire. The Silo was surrounded by a gravel parking lot and located at the very end of Sultan's Main Street. A few automobiles were parked out front. Levi told Chance to drive to the back entrance.

The second youngest of Levi's sons, Bennett Bowman, leaned against his car smoking. He looked up at the sound of Levi and Chance's arrival, took a long drag, and then flicked the cigarette away. He was the shortest of the four Bowman boys but powerfully-built with broad shoulders and a muscular chest. Like his father, he had a head of unusually thick, dark hair which he wore slicked back. He also had a mouth that always appeared to be on the verge of telling a joke.

"You let the kid drive, huh?" Bennett teased. "Looks like he hit something and forgot to clean it off the hood." Chance ignored the slight.

Levi winced as he slid out of the passenger seat and closed the door. Bennett asked if he was okay.

"I'm fine. Sore is all."

Bennett looked around to make certain no one was nearby listening. His voice lowered. "I'd have taken care of it."

Levi gripped Bennett's shoulder. "I know. It got done. Chance was a big help. The bear was an unexpected addition. So, what's the action like inside?"

"A little slow. A few guys at the poker table. A few more at the bar."

"Just locals?"

"Mostly, but there's this big fella from, uh, Bellingham, I think. Apparently visiting family in Monroe. He's been losing at poker most the night."

Monroe was a larger town located eight miles west of Sultan. They were connected by U.S. 2, a route that began as a wagon trail that linked the western and eastern halves of Washington State. Unlike Sultan, Monroe was an aggressively dry municipality that fully conformed to the federal prohibition laws. Its longtime mayor was a man by the name of Bill Brown. Mayor Brown was another one receiving regular payments from the Bowmans. It was his job to keep Monroe a dry town to ensure all its residents who wished to enjoy the occasional drink had no choice but to make the trip to The Silo in Sultan. Mayor Brown made that trip often.

Levi opened the back door and went inside. Bennett and Chance followed. A short hall led to a small office with a desk and chair and a steel safe bolted to the floor. A second door opened into The Silo's main room.

Levi collapsed into the chair behind the desk, opened a drawer, and withdrew a bottle of whiskey. He uncorked it, took a long drink, put it back, and then stood up with a freshly-lit cigarette hanging from his lips. "Okay, let's go to work."

The Silo's windowless main room had a low ceiling, pine floors, a bar, and a card table and chairs. The electric chandelier that hung from the center of the ceiling provided the only source of light. The place smelled of tobacco and aged wood. Levi tipped his head toward the attractive, stern-faced woman on the other side of the room who stood behind the bar.

"How's Laney's mood tonight?" he asked.

Bennett grinned. "Pretty good. She's hasn't had to throw anyone out yet–including me."

Laney Lorne had been pouring drinks at The Silo since it opened some twenty years earlier. She was a widow who came to Sultan by way of Seattle, bringing with her considerable restaurant experience and the no-nonsense attitude such experience required. It had been many years since the Bowman boys lost their mother, and Levi lost his wife. Laney had gradually come to fill both those roles. She was as much a Bowman as they were. Levi owned The Silo, but the bar was Laney's kingdom, one she ruled with an iron fist. Foolishness and disrespect were not tolerated. If those basic rules were broken, the offender was warned just once via a withering glare. A second offense would get them thrown out for the rest of the night. A third offense was banishment for a month. None of the Bowman boys had yet witnessed what happened to a four-time offender. They wondered, only half-jokingly, if the sentence for that was death by firing squad.

Levi walked to the bar and sat down in front of Laney. She poured him a drink. When Chance and Bennett sat on either side of their father, she poured them drinks as well.

"You look tired," she said.

Levi emptied his glass with a single gulp. "I am." He glanced behind him at the poker table. His oldest son Dalton was dealing cards to two other men. One was a local. The other one he didn't recognize. He nudged Bennett with an elbow. "That the fella from Monroe?"

Bennett nodded. "Yeah."

"You're right," Levi said. "He's big."

"Big or not, he can't play poker for shit. Dalton's about ready to clean him out."

Dalton Bowman was the oldest of Levi's sons. When he went to France in 1917 to fight in the Great War, he left Sultan an idealistic young man confident he was going off to help save the world. What returned two years later was barely recognizable to those who had known him before. He spent weeks inside his room either lying in bed or in a chair staring at the wall. He hardly spoke a word. This was partly due to the scarring of his vocal cords from the mustard gas he repeatedly inhaled while crawling for months through rat-infested trenches overrun with rotting corpses, shit, and blood.

Six months after his return home, Dalton finally walked outside. The Bowman property included a large farmhouse on twenty acres of land on the outskirts of town. There was a big red barn, a hen house, a pen for the pigs, and a trout pond. Dalton cleaned out the horse stalls, moved bales of hay, fed the pigs, collected the chicken eggs, and then went back into the house, walked upstairs to his room, and closed the door.

He repeated that exact routine for nine weeks. One day after finishing the farm chores, for reasons known only to him, Dalton walked the two miles from the house to The Silo. It was late afternoon. He went inside, sat down at the card table, and started to play poker. Laney brought him a whiskey. He looked up, smiled, and in his sandpaper-whisper voice, told her thank you.

Dalton had been playing poker there nearly every day since. He had a knack for it and made decent money. He remained a quiet, sulking, intimidating presence, but something of the old Dalton had returned. Though he didn't know it, the hoarse laugh Dalton unleashed recently one night after winning an especially good hand was overheard by Levi as he sat inside his office. After a long and troubled recovery, his war veteran son was finding a way to enjoy life again. It was a sound that made Levi's eyes fill with grateful tears.

"You're a goddamn cheat!" The big man from Bellingham knocked his chair over when he got up. He pointed at Dalton. "I want my money back. Right now. All of it."

Dalton continued to count his chips.

"Hey!" The man slammed the poker table with his hand. "I'm serious. You're a cheat, and I want my money."

Laney cleared her throat. "Sir, I assure you we don't allow cheaters at our tables. If you'll calm down, I'm happy to get whatever drink you like--on the house. What do you say?"

"Unless you're the one who's gonna get me my money back I say mind your own business, you nosy bar bitch!"

"Uh-oh," Chance muttered.

Levi put out his cigarette, slid off the bar stool, and walked over to the poker table. "I understand you're not from around here. The lady tried to make nice. You insulted her. That means you insulted me. I think it's best you leave."

The man from Bellingham puffed out his chest. He was younger, bigger, and nearly half a foot taller than Levi. "And who the hell are you?"

"I'm the owner. This is my place."

"You mean the place that cheats at cards and serves *illegal* alcohol?"

Levi's dark eyes flashed a warning. "Careful."

The man poked Levi in the chest. "Or what?"

There were few things more dangerous to someone's personal well-being in Sultan than threatening a Bowman. As soon as that finger touched his father's chest, Dalton Bowman flung the poker table aside and charged. At nearly the same time, Chance and Bennett Bowman were on the move as well. Dalton's fist smashed into the out-of-towner's mouth while the other two brothers grabbed him from behind.

22

With his lips pulled back in a feral snarl, Dalton glared at the man, pointed at his father, and croaked his outrage. "Nobody touches him! Ever!"

The man strained to get free from Bennett and Chance. "You act real tough when it's three against one. And what's with your voice? You sound like you swallowed a pile of frogs."

Dalton nodded at his brothers. "Let him go."

Bennett and Chance held tight. Dalton's eyes flared.

"Let him go! I'll handle him."

Levi stepped close to Dalton. "You sure?"

"Really?" Dalton said. "You don't think I can?"

"Okay, he's all yours." Levi pointed to the exit. "Drop this sack of shit outside. I won't have him leaking blood on my floors."

Chance and Bennett pushed the man out the door. Everyone else followed. The rain had stopped. Never one to pass up a chance to make a quick buck, Bennett announced he was taking bets. He put ten dollars down on his brother. A local regular put ten on the big man from Bellingham.

Dalton rolled his head from side to side, took a few practice swings, and waited. Levi pointed the out-of-towner. "You ready?"

The man nodded. He was about the same age as Dalton, but taller, and slightly bigger.

"Yeah, I'm ready."

Dalton threw the first punch. It missed. The man countered with a glancing blow off the top of Dalton's head. Dalton ducked low and grabbed hold of the man's waist and tried to fling him to the ground. The man spread his legs wide, lowering his center of gravity. His knee smashed into Dalton's chest.

Bennett leaned over to whisper to Chance. "This guy knows how to handle himself."

"You regretting that ten-dollar bet?"

Bennett shook his head. "Hell, no. Dalton hasn't even flipped the switch yet."

Dalton's 'switch' was something his brothers had seen go off in him since they were boys. It was that moment when his anger turned to something else–something uncontrollable and impervious to pain.

A hard uppercut snapped Dalton's head back. His knees buckled. The man from Bellingham appeared to think he had the fight won.

He didn't. Dalton sent a hard jab into the man's nose and followed that up with another punch to the stomach. The man doubled over, gasping for breath. Dalton paused. There was a metallic flash. Dalton looked down and saw a thin line of crimson where the front of his shirt had been slashed open. The man held a knife with one hand and motioned at Dalton with the other.

"You want more? That was just a warning. Next time I spill your guts."

The switch went off.

Dalton bent down, scooped up a handful of dirt, flung it at the man's face, and tackled him. The man fell back. Dalton pounced. Chance stepped on the man's wrist and kicked the knife away as Dalton used both fists to pummel the out-of-towner's face. Each blow was a heavy wet smack.

"That's right!" Bennett yelled. "You give him the business, Dalton!"

"You two better pull your brother off him," Levi said. "Or we're going to have a dead man in our parking lot."

Bennett and Chance attempted to grab hold of Dalton. He shrugged them off and kept punching. Levi crouched down and clasped Dalton's chin.

"That's enough. It's finished."

Dalton blinked. He looked down at the mess that was the man's face and then nodded.

Levi and Dalton got up together. Dalton's knuckles were drenched in blood. Some of that blood was his. Most of it wasn't. Levi put his arm around him.

"C'mon, let's get you cleaned up."

Dalton didn't say anything as he let his father walk him toward The Silo. Right before opening the door, Levi turned around. The man from Bellingham was holding his face and groaning.

"Make sure he gets on the road back to Monroe."

Bennett collected his ten-dollar winnings. A pair of lights illuminated the parking lot. The two brothers looked up to see

Dylan, the second-oldest of the Bowman boys, getting out of his car.

Dylan was tall and lean with reddish-brown hair. He had been given the nickname 'Professor' on account he was the only one of the four Bowman boys to go off to college. He had done so in search of a teaching degree. That search was cut short when he was arrested for taking the university president's new Ford on an impromptu joyride that included an hour-long police chase through two counties. Dylan was promptly banned from the university. When he returned to Sultan after spending three days in the county jail, Levi looked at Dylan and declared, "Way to go, Professor." The nickname stuck.

"What's this about?" Dylan asked as he watched Chance and Bennett straining to push the man into his car.

"Isn't it just like you to show up after all the work is done?" Bennett replied.

"What work is that? You robbing this guy? And what the hell happened to his face?"

Chance gave the man a final shove and closed the door. "Dalton happened to his face."

Dylan's brows lifted. "Oh, I see. Looks like it was a hard lesson."

Bennett held up the man's knife. "They were fighting fair and square before he decided to cut Dalton with this."

Dylan's lips pressed tightly together. He had become very protective of his older brother since Dalton's return from the war. "What? Is he okay?"

Bennett nodded. "He's fine. Pa and Laney are cleaning him up."

Dylan grunted. "I take it this guy isn't from around here. He's lucky all he got was a beating."

"You don't know the half of it," Chance said. "He even called Laney a nosy bar bitch–*to her face*."

"And he also put his hand on Pa," Bennett added.

Dylan clicked his tongue and shook his head. "Give me the knife."

Bennett scowled. "What?"

"I said give me the knife. Hurry, before he gets the car started."

"Pa wants him on the road."

Dylan nodded. "Yeah, fine. Now give me the damn knife."

Bennett dropped the knife into Dylan's outstretched hand. "You kill him and there'll be hell to pay with Pa."

"I'm not going to kill him." Dylan grabbed hold of the man's ear and with a flick of the blade snipped off half an earlobe. When the man started to scream, Dylan clamped his hand over his mouth.

"Stop crying, or I swear to God I'll cut your tongue out next. Nod if you understand."

The man nodded. Dylan grinned, but his green eyes were ice. He dropped the piece of ear into the man's lap.

"Good boy. Remember, this is all your fault. You don't *ever* pull anything on one of us. Next time I might not be in such a forgiving mood. Now get out of here."

The man started the car, pulled out onto the main road, and drove away. Bennett rolled his eyes at Dylan. "Jeez, you laid it on a bit thick don't you think? We're not the goddamn Pinkertons."

Chance pulled on Dylan's tie. Dylan was always buying new ties to go along with the custom-made suits he loved to wear. "Looks like you got some of that fella's blood on you."

Dylan looked down. "Dammit! I just bought this one today."

"Cheer up, big brother," Chance said. "We still have time for some drinking."

The three brothers walked into The Silo together. Levi looked up from his seat at the bar. "Ah, there you are, Professor. Nice of you to join us. I'm afraid you missed all the excitement."

Chance shook his head. "Not quite. He decided to cut off a piece of the guy's ear."

Laney, who was about to pour Dylan a drink, set the whiskey bottle back on the counter. "Dylan Bowman, why on earth did you go and do that? This family is a lot of things, but we're not animals."

"I was told by my dear younger brother here that the man, among his many other offenses tonight, disrespected you. I was merely defending your honor."

Laney shook her head and smiled. Her love for each of Levi's boys ran very deep. She found it impossible to stay mad at them for long. "I see. Well in that case, I guess you actually deserve this drink."

Glasses were filled, emptied, and filled again. Stories were shared, and jokes were told, most often ones that came at another brother's expense. Chance begged Dalton to show everyone the shallow cut on his stomach. Dalton glared at him and refused. Levi snuck a glance at Laney. She smiled back. They were both experienced enough to know that, as time moved on, such moments with all of them together were likely to become fewer and farther between. Nobody was getting any younger, and life had a way of becoming more and more complicated with each year that passed.

Levi lifted his glass high. "A toast to my sons."

"To the Bowman boys," Laney added as she raised her glass.

"That's right–to the kings of Sultan!" Bennett declared. "May long we reign."

Everyone drank. Everyone laughed.

Even Dalton.

3.

Levi Bowman began the morning as he normally did—in his bathrobe at his kitchen table with a cigarette, a cup of coffee, and a slice of buttered toast. Laney joined him. They sat together by themselves until the boys made their way downstairs. The small kitchen with the flower-pattern wallpaper and the circular glass table then became a crowded mix of elbows, forks, and fingers as breakfast was hungrily consumed. It was the only meal the family regularly ate together. A long-standing rumor around town was that nothing of importance was done in Sultan until it was first discussed inside the Bowman kitchen.

There was a knock at the back door. Bennett instinctively reached for the pistol that was always kept at the end of the kitchen counter. With Bennett distracted, Chance jabbed his fork into the last piece of sausage on Bennett's plate and ate it. Laney stood up, went to the door, and peeked through the curtain.

"It's Pastor Jim."

Pastor Jim Flores was primarily known in Sultan for two things. The first was his height of six-foot-seven. The second was the stutter that inexplicably disappeared when he stood behind the podium at the front of the church during his Sunday sermons. Each of those sermons was viewed by many in his congregation as proof of a weekly miracle. They would sit listening to a man who at any other time struggled to speak a complete sentence.

Levi had been among the first to welcome Pastor Jim to Sultan. He also helped to raise the initial funds that made the construction of the new church possible. Levi viewed religion much like politics—as something that could be good for business so long as it was controlled and contained.

Laney opened the back door. The pastor ducked under the doorframe and stepped into the kitchen holding his hat in his hands.

"It's been a while Pastor," Levi said. "If you're looking to save some more souls, I'd ask that you wait until I finish this next cup of coffee. Then I'll be more awake. Otherwise, it wouldn't be a fair fight."

The pastor appeared unusually nervous as he shook his head. His face showed the strain of trying to get the words out without it taking too long. "That's quite all right Mr. Bowman. I'll stand."

"Can I get you some coffee, tea, or something to eat?" Laney asked.

"I'm fine. Thank you."

Levi lit a cigarette. "Well, Pastor, you best get to it. Whatever has you showing up unannounced on my back porch must be important."

The pastor cleared his throat, licked his lips, and then explained how a woman in Monroe had recently been meeting with several of the ladies of the church regarding the need to eradicate, once and for all, the evil that was illegal drinking in Sultan. Her name was Noretta Saul. She had called out the Bowman family directly as the primary cause for much of what she felt ailed the Sultan community. She described Levi as a willing tool of the devil, his sons a horde of demons, and The Silo a pit of sinful carnage. That last description caused Levi to chuckle. He said he might actually put it on a sign.

"This woman is no joke, Mr. Bowman. She means to destroy you."

"I don't doubt you, Pastor. She sounds like serious business. That said, she wouldn't be the first one to try and bring trouble my way, and I doubt she'll be the last. What's important to note, and it's something I'm sure you're already aware of, is that those who have challenged me are all gone, and I'm still here. Isn't that right boys?"

Levi's sons nodded their heads. "That's right, Pa," Chance said. "We're the ones still standing."

The pastor shifted on his size-fourteen feet. "I just wanted to make sure to let you know, Mr. Bowman. You've always been a good friend to the church."

Levi stood and shook the pastor's hand. "I appreciate that. I truly do. Here, why don't you add this to the collection box?" Levi held up a crisp ten-dollar bill.

The pastor shook his head. "No, thank you, Mr. Bowman. I didn't come here for money. I'm just hoping to avoid trouble for the town."

"You sure? I recall hearing something about the church being long overdue for a new roof."

"I'm sure, Mr. Bowman. Thank you."

Levi watched the pastor step off the back porch, get into his car, and drive away. Laney put her hand on his shoulder.

"I know that look. You're worried about something."

Levi returned to his seat at the table and stared down into his coffee cup. When his head lifted all eyes were on him. "He didn't take my money. That was a first."

Dylan folded his hands on the table and leaned forward. "The pastor didn't take your money because he wants to put some distance between you and him. That means he thinks this woman, whoever she is, has some real power. He's not sure who would win if there's to be a war between you two. So, he makes the trip here to let you know about her."

"He's hedging his bets–covering both sides," Bennett added.

Levi nodded. "That could be right. We'll just have to keep our ears to the--"

They all heard another car pulling into the driveway. A frowning Laney again looked to see who it was. "It's Grand Central Station around here this morning." She opened the door. Her thin smile conveyed her annoyance.

"Hello, Officer Fenner. What brings you out this way?"

Fenton Fenner took off his police cap. Strands of thin, gray hair were plastered across his damp forehead. "Sorry to interrupt your breakfast."

Levi motioned for the others to make room at the table. "Have a seat, Fenton. That foot still bothering you?"

Fenton grimaced as he sat down across from Levi. "It sure is, Mr. Bowman. The doctor says my circulation ain't right. Old age, I suppose." Laney put a coffee cup in front of Fenton and filled it. He gave her a grateful smile. "Much obliged, Ms. Lorne."

Levi waited while Fenton took a sip from the cup and then set it down. "There's been a complaint filed against you Mr. Bowman. Actually, it's against all of you."

Levi scowled. "Complaint?"

"Well, uh, apparently there was an altercation during the early morning hours at The Silo. A man was beaten and had a piece of his ear cut off. According to the complaint, it was Dylan who did the cutting. Now I'm not saying any of this is true. I'm just letting you know what the complaint outlined."

Dylan opened his mouth to say something. Levi held up a hand to signal he wanted him to keep quiet. "Was this complaint filed by a man from Bellingham?"

Fenton's face tightened. "Well, not exactly. He was a party to the complaint, but the one who actually filed it is a woman who stated she's a cousin to the alleged victim. She showed up at the station early this morning with an attorney, a fella named Broadmoor--Joseph Broadmoor. He's out of Monroe.

Pretty sharp fella, and I believe he's also good friends with Judge Thompson. I know you're familiar with him."

Levi grunted. "I would hope so, given the amount of money I've donated to his campaigns over the years. What's the name of the woman who filed the complaint?"

"Her name is Noretta Saul. Apparently, she was married to some big shot lumberyard owner up in Bellingham. He died last year. She turned around and sold the business for a small fortune and ended up buying a place in Monroe. Since arriving there, she's been quick to become rather well-connected. Not someone I'd cross if I could help it."

Levi arched a brow. "I'd like to think people still say that about me."

Fenton shifted in his chair. "Well, yes, of course, you're plenty formidable in your own right, Mr. Bowman. I'm not denying that one bit. No, sir. The thing is... uh...."

Everyone at the table waited for Fenton to complete his thought. "The thing is, the attorney that came with Ms. Saul, he, uh... he mentioned something about possibly forwarding an illegal sales of alcohol complaint to federal prohibition agents in Seattle. Now as you know, I can slow-walk the assault complaint until it dies of old age. You have no worries there. But should this woman and her attorney manage to get the attention of the federal government, that goes well beyond my authority as the law here in Sultan. I know the last thing you want, the last thing *any* of us wants, is to have the damn feds sniffing around our backyard."

Levi added more cream to his coffee. "Indeed. You know anything else about this Noretta Saul?"

"I do. She's become a frequent guest at Pastor Jim's Sunday sermons. I've seen her there myself. Drives up in her new fancy car and sits right down in the front row. Has a whole gaggle of ladies hanging on her every word. In fact, the pastor has her scheduled to speak to the entire congregation this coming Sunday. I'd wager the subject of her talk is going to be *you*, Mr. Bowman."

Cigarette smoke swirled around Levi's head. "You don't say?"

Fenton finished his coffee and rose from his chair. "I just thought you should know. If I hear anything more, I'll be sure to tell you."

Levi stood. When he shook Fenton's hand, he placed into it the same ten-dollar bill Pastor Jim had refused. Fenton promptly put the money into his shirt pocket, thanked Laney for the coffee, and left. Levi sat back down.

"What's the plan, Pa?" Chance asked.

Levi traced circles on the glass table with the tip of his finger. "This Noretta Saul is obviously very confident, but should she be? She has a few friends in high places and some coin to throw around. She's coming right for us—and in the open, no less. That said, it's business as usual, boys. Nothing is different until Sunday."

Bennett cocked his head. "What happens on Sunday?"

Levi stopped tracing circles and looked up. "We go to church."

4.

Murmurs rippled through the congregation when Levi strolled into the Sunday sermon with Laney and the boys. They sat in the back and watched and waited.

The church had twelve rows of wooden pews—six on each side. There were also twelve stained glass windows that bathed the congregation in multi-colored morning light. Levi knew exactly how much each of those windows cost when the church was first constructed. It was his donation that had paid for them.

When Pastor Jim stepped onto the stage, he wore an especially wide smile as he surveyed the crowd. Then he saw the Bowmans, and his smile faltered.

"I don't think he was expecting to see us here," Laney whispered.

Levi scanned the room trying to locate Noretta Saul. Dylan pointed to a woman seated on the left side of the front row. "I don't recognize that one," he said.

She had an abnormally lean face with a downturned mouth comprised of almost-not-there, lips. Her gray hair was cut short. Despite the warmth inside of the church, she wore a heavy dark coat that covered most of her scarecrow body down to the knees. Levi recognized the large man with the ear wrapped in gauze who sat next to her. He was smartly dressed in a suit and tie and looked every bit the respectable gentleman and not the belligerent card player who had accused Dalton of cheating.

The man whispered something to the woman. She turned her head, stared directly at Levi, and smiled. Levi nodded back.

"You think she's dangerous?" Laney asked.

"Yup," Levi said.

"I don't know why, but this is starting to feel like an ambush."

Levi rested his hand on top of Laney's. "We'll be fine."

"What a glorious morning it is!" Pastor Jim declared as he took his place behind the podium and spread his long arms wide. He spoke loudly and clearly. The stutter was gone. "Let us pray."

Everyone in the church but Levi bowed their heads. He kept his eyes locked on Noretta Saul. He didn't hear a word of Pastor Jim's prayer. That is, until the pastor finished and then announced he was pleased to be able to introduce a guest speaker as part of that day's service. When Noretta stood, several of the other women in the church applauded loudly. She stepped onto the stage as Pastor Jim shuffled to the side.

"Thank you, everyone. Thank you so very much. For those I haven't yet met, my name is Noretta Saul. I wish I was here to speak about more positive things, but as anyone who has read the Good Book knows, people of faith have had to deal with challenge and adversity for as long as we can remember.

I come to you today as a Christian woman in fear of what is happening to a beloved neighbor. You see, my home is in Monroe, but the more time I spend with all of you here in this wonderful church, the more my heart resides in Sultan. The town has such potential. Such possibility. And yet, there is also evil among us. Yes, I said evil. Sadly, that is not an exaggeration. In fact, that evil sits here in this very church right now. It has arrived with its full complement of heathen offspring."

Noretta paused, slowly raised her hand, and pointed at the Bowmans. "There."

Everyone in the church turned around. Most then quickly looked away. Some eyes lingered, though, and there was an unspoken challenge in their stares. Without meaning to do so, Levi's hand gripped Laney's more tightly.

"Don't let her bait you into a confrontation," Laney whispered.

"You all see how Mr. Bowman glares at me? Can anyone here truthfully say they don't see the murderous intent in those midnight eyes of his? The Bowmans are a plague upon this community. We all know it. For far too long, far too many have allowed it to continue. That must end—now."

Noretta turned to face Pastor Jim. "What about you, Pastor? Whose side are you on in this battle of good versus evil?"

The pastor's eyes blinked rapidly. "Uh...I...uh, we are all here to serve God, Ms. Saul. Please, this is not the place for confrontation."

The stutter had returned.

Noretta wagged a finger while looking out at the congregation. "Oh, I disagree. What better place is there than the House of God to battle evil? And what better time than now? Can everyone see the man sitting there with the injured ear? Yes? He is my younger cousin, Robert Saul. Robert would you please let everyone look at you?"

Robert stood. Noretta smiled at him lovingly and then appeared to be on the verge of tears. It was a remarkable performance.

"Robert was playing cards at The Silo. You all know that establishment. Just as you all know who owns it and what they do there. Well, Robert discovered he was being cheated during that crooked card game. He rightfully demanded to be given his money back, and for that, the Bowman family nearly killed him. He was beaten within an inch of his life and part of his ear was cut off."

Some of the women in the church gasped. Dalton stood. The corners of his mouth twitched, and his eyes burned hot. His voice was a low, croaky snarl.

"I...don't...cheat."

Noretta stuck out her chin and smirked. "Is that so? Do you also deny you attacked Robert outside The Silo and that with the help of your brothers beat him senseless and then took a knife to him?"

Dalton grabbed hold of his shirt and pulled it open with such force the buttons flew off. The sound of them clattering across the floor echoed inside the church.

Chance rose up out of the pew and pointed at Robert. "That fella was the one who turned a fair fight into a knife fight–not Dalton. You all see the mark on Dalton's stomach. The man she calls Robert, he cut him. I was there. And another thing, there was no cheating at poker. People around here know how well and how fair Dalton plays at cards. Anyone who says different is a rat-faced liar and will need to answer to me and my brothers."

Noretta grunted. "Ah, there we have it. One of the Bowman boys threatening me, a little old lady. How very brave of him. Ladies and gentlemen, what more proof do you need? This is a family that thrives on threats and intimidation to support their criminal enterprise. That time must come to an end. I ask that you join me today in calling for a new era in Sultan. A better and more Christian one that is free from the fear and intimidation of the Bowmans."

Many in the church nodded their agreement.

"Shut up, you sanctimonious bitch!" Laney stepped into the aisle and began walking toward the stage as Pastor Jim, his eyes wide with panic, pleaded for calm. "Ladies, please! This is a house of God!"

Laney nodded. "That's right! And who helped to make this church possible, Pastor? You know. You *all* know. It was Levi Bowman. Yet, here you are listening to the words of some out-of-towner who casts stones against a family that has *always* been there to help others when that help was needed. We aren't perfect. We would never claim to be. What we are, though, is loyal. We don't turn our backs on our own when someone makes baseless allegations against them. NO–we stand *with* them. That thing on the stage claims to be a good

Christian woman. Really? Based on what? Her own inflated self-importance?"

The pastor cleared his throat. "Well, actually, Ms. Saul did make a generous donation to the church recently."

Laney put her hands on her hips. "Oh, I see. So *that* is what makes her worthy of this church's approval, huh? Well, if that's the case you best get out your money clip, Levi. Seems you really *can* buy your way into heaven."

Noretta clicked her tongue. "Such shameful words, Ms. Lorne. Have you no dignity? Though coming from a woman living in sin with this town's equivalent of Satan, perhaps none of us should be surprised."

Laney's lips drew back as she hissed her next words between tightly-clenched teeth. "Don't you dare think to judge me or this family. You want a war with the Bowmans? Fine—YOU GOT IT!"

Pastor Jim stepped off the stage and moved toward the back of the church, waving his hands in front of him. "No-no, there will be no war. Everyone, please, we are better than this."

Laney shook her head. "Too late Pastor. You've clearly chosen sides. Don't you act like you haven't. This family has nothing more to say to you." Laney whirled around and headed for the exit.

Levi waited in the pew with his sons as Pastor Jim again pleaded for peace. "Please, Mr. Bowman, it doesn't have to be like this."

Levi shrugged as he lit a cigarette. "Doesn't it? You brought that woman here. You helped to give her a voice, which means you're also helping her to turn the town against me and my own. Seems *this* is exactly how you wanted it. Fair enough. Every action has a consequence, Pastor. You should remember that. No worries, though. I look forward to reminding you."

"Mr. Bowman, is that a threat? Here? Now? In this church?"

Levi got up. "We'll be in touch. Let's go boys."

The Bowmans walked outside. They found Laney leaning against Levi's car smoking a cigarette. Her face was flushed. "That damn woman," she said. "The pastor, those people, our so-called friends–they can all go to hell."

Levi leaned in and gave her a peck on the cheek. He was grinning. Laney frowned.

"What?" she asked.

"I seem to recall a warning in there about not getting baited into a confrontation."

Laney put her cigarette out and nodded. "That's right. She wanted you, a man, to go after her, to make you look bad. She's playing the victim. That left *me* to stand up for this family."

Levi was still grinning. "Well, you certainly did that."

"Yeah, but what now?" Bennett asked.

"We wait to see what her next move is," Levi answered.

Dylan folded his arms across his chest. "You think that's wise?"

Levi arched a brow. "You have a different idea?"

"Yeah," Dylan said. "I was thinking a couple of us drive up to Bellingham and ask around about who this Noretta Saul really is. We should also do the same in Monroe. She's clearly done her homework on us. That gives her an unfair advantage."

Dalton looked at his father. "Dylan's right. We can't just sit and wait."

"Does everyone else feel the same?" Levi asked.

Laney, Bennett, and Chance all nodded.

"Okay," Levi said. "Dylan and Dalton, you two go to Bellingham. Bennett and Chance, you ask around Monroe. In the meantime, Laney and I will hold down the fort here in town."

Levi opened his jacket to reveal the gun he kept in a shoulder holster. "And anywhere that anyone in this family goes, they go armed—no exceptions. We may not know the how or the why of it yet, but Laney's right. We're at war."

5.

It was the first time since returning from France that Dalton drove a car on the open road. Dylan leaned over to look at the speedometer. They were doing just over forty miles-an-hour. It was a 1921 Dodge Brothers Roadster Dylan had purchased from a Seattle dealer last summer.

"You've got a bit of a lead foot, don't you?" Dylan shouted over the din of the air that pummeled the vehicle's canvas top.

Dalton smiled like a kid on Christmas morning as he mashed the gas pedal to the floor. The flat farmlands of Skagit County passed by in a green blur. It took them another hour to reach Bellingham, a sprawling trees-and-shores metropolis of some twenty-five thousand residents. Money was plentiful there, the result of the thriving coal, logging, and fishing industries. It was the kind of place people came to make their fortunes, not run away from them, which added another layer of mystery to Noretta Saul's sudden arrival in the far more limited markets of Monroe and Sultan.

"Where should I park?" Dalton asked.

Dylan pointed to a space in front of a three-story bank building in the center of the city's bustling Fairhaven District. "That should work."

It was just past noon on the Monday following the Bowman family's dramatic appearance at church. The brothers got out of the car and stretched. Dalton stood on the sidewalk and watched the procession of cars, trucks, and people going by. He looked over at Dylan.

"What now?"

"Noretta is supposedly a pretty big name around here. We shouldn't have too much trouble finding someone who knows something about her so long as you let me do the talking."

Dalton grunted. Between the two of them, he would never have been mistaken for being the more talkative one. He extended his hand toward the door.

"Lead the way."

The bank's interior was a gleaming mix of marble floors, pillars, and walls. An attractive young woman looked up from her seat at the lobby desk and smiled. "Can I help you?"

Dylan smiled back. "Perhaps. We're hoping you might know the address for the Saul lumberyard. We're not from around here but heard they might be hiring."

"Do you mean the Lemkee yard that's down by the waterfront?"

Dylan shrugged. "I'm not sure. We were told it was the Saul lumberyard."

"Ah, you must be talking about another lumberyard that was bought out last year by Titus Lemkee. The one you're thinking of is somewhere on the other side of town. I'm not sure exactly where, but I think you're right–it used to be owned by a man with the last name Saul. I wouldn't know anything about them hiring, though."

Dylan kept smiling. "Can you tell me where we'll find the Lemkee yard, then? The one by the waterfront? We can start there. They'd likely know where the other lumberyard is located."

The woman nodded. "Of course! Just head down the hill, take a right, and follow the road that goes along Bellingham Bay. It's about two miles from here. Look for the big blue-and-green sign that says LEMKEE LUMBER. You can't miss it. Most the ships you see heading out of the harbor during business hours are leaving with loads of Lemkee lumber. He has really become quite the businessman around here in just the last few years. I would never have guessed there was so much money to be made from cutting down a bunch of trees. Some of us joke that pretty soon we'll have to replace the name Bellingham with Lemkeeville!"

"Thank you so much. You've been a great help."

The woman beamed. "That's what I'm here for. Oh–and good luck finding work!"

"We'll do our best."

Once they were both outside, Dylan noticed Dalton looking him up and down. "What is it?" he asked.

Dalton tugged on his beard. "You need to show me how to do that."

"Do what?"

Dalton turned away. "Nothing," he mumbled.

"Hold on. What do you want me to show you?"

Dalton lit a cigarette and then looked out at the shimmering blue waters of Bellingham Bay. He closed his eyes and lifted his head, enjoying the sun's warmth on his face. Dylan stood behind him waiting for an answer.

"Since I got back...I haven't been with a woman."

"*What*?" Dylan said. "But that's been..."

Dalton sighed. "I know—more than two years. I want to be with someone again, but I don't know how. I see their fear when they look at me–when they hear my voice."

"Well, that's because you're a disgusting, hairy brute."

Dalton turned around and glared at Dylan who then started to laugh. "I'm kidding! It's just that you are kind of intense. You tend to capture people in your eyes and rough them up a bit before they've even had a chance to say hello. Fact is, you do come off as unapproachable. I get it, though. What happened to you in France, what you saw, what you did... it couldn't have been easy. And now you're dragging that experience behind you like a stone. My advice? Cut the rope. Free yourself. Move on. Quiet the screams of the past so you can finally enjoy the present and have a shot at a decent future. You could have died over there. You didn't. You're a survivor–a tough son-of-a-bitch. You always have been. That's a good thing. Use it.

"I tell you what. The Silo's stock is getting low. I'll need to do a booze run up to Chan's in a few days. He has women there and some of them aren't half bad. You should come with me. Clean out your pipe and get you back on your game."

Dalton shook his head as he stomped out his cigarette. "This isn't a game to me. I'm lonely. I don't want a whore. I want a woman. Someone who's with me because they want to be not because I've paid them."

Dylan gave his brother a playful shove. "Hey, there'll be none of that. We have a job to do. There'll be plenty of time for you to be depressed once we get back home. Until then I need you focused."

"You really want me to go with you to Chan's?"

"Yeah. Absolutely."

Dalton almost smiled. "Okay. I'll do it. Now what?"

"We find that lumberyard, try and track down this Lemkee, and see if he'll tell us what he knows about Noretta Saul."

"Even if he knows something, why would he want to tell us anything?"

"I don't know. Maybe he won't, but we're going to find out."

The brothers located the lumberyard and parked in front of a small building near the entrance. Three rickety steps led to a door with a sign on it that indicated it was the foreman's office. Dylan knocked twice and then went inside where he found a desk and phone. A large map of Bellingham and the surrounding area was stuck to the wall. Parts of the map had been circled in red ink. The room was dark and smelled of mud, oil, and woodchips.

The door was flung open. A short, heavyset, middle-aged man with a handlebar mustache stepped inside. He wore jeans and a heavy flannel shirt with the sleeves rolled up over large forearms. Sawdust covered his hair and clothes. "Who the hell are you?" he asked.

"My name is Dylan Bowman. This is my brother Dalton. We're looking for a Mr. Titus Lemkee. We thought we might find him here."

The man brushed past Dylan and sat down at the desk. "Really? Whoever told you that didn't know a damn thing about it. Mr. Lemkee isn't around. What do you want with him?"

"Just a few questions," Dylan said. "We won't take up much of his time."

"Mr. Lemkee is busy and so am I. You see that map behind me? Those red circles? Each one represents a work crew I need to check in on before the end of the day. Now get out of here so I can get to it."

"Could you tell us where we can find him? It's important."

The man's eyes narrowed as if he was suddenly seeing Dylan and Dalton for the first time. "You're persistent. I'll give you that. Who the hell are you? Feds?"

Dylan shook his head. "No-no, far from it. We're just looking for some answers and hoping Mr. Lemke can provide them to us."

"What was your names again? Where you from?"

"Dylan and Dalton Bowman. We drove up from a little town called Sultan."

"Your brother doesn't say much. At least not with his mouth. Where the hell is Sultan?"

"It's couple counties south of here."

"Uh-huh. So, you want to speak with Mr. Lemkee, and you don't plan on leaving here until you do?"

"That's right."

The man picked up the phone. "It's me. Is Mr. Lemkee at the dock? Okay, tell him I have a couple uninvited strangers here who want to speak to him. They seem pretty determined. That's right. Good. I'll walk them down myself." He looked up and smiled. "Congratulations, you have your meeting. Now before we go I'll need you to leave your weapons on the table here."

Dalton scowled. Dylan held up a hand. "It's fine."

They placed their guns on the table.

The man got up and walked out of the office. "Follow me."

Dylan and Dalton had to almost jog to keep up as the man headed toward the water. The air was thick with the smell of saltwater and seagulls. Bellingham Bay stretched out for miles in front of them. The man's boots struck the dock with a heavy thump while the water licked the bottom half of the creosote-soaked pilings. At the very end of the dock, which extended out over the bay like a long, wooden finger, was a rusty tin shack.

"Mr. Lemkee is right this way. Hurry. You don't want to keep him waiting."

Dalton slowed down and gripped his brother's arm. "I know," Dylan whispered. "You still have your knife?" Dalton nodded. "Good. Be ready."

The man reached the shack and knocked on the door. "I'm here with the two men who want to see Lemkee. They're unarmed."

"Let 'em in!" bellowed a deep voice from inside.

The door opened. The man moved aside. "After you," he said.

Dalton stepped in front of Dylan. His arms hung loose at his sides as his eyes peered into the shack's dark interior.

He was ready.

6.

"Boys, need I remind you I'm the mayor of Monroe? You can't just walk up in here snapping your fingers and making demands of me."

"I don't care if you're the mayor of the goddamn world, Mr. Brown. If we wanted to sit here and get our wires yanked, we'd have made the drive out to Chan's. But we're here. With you. And we *will* get the answers we came for."

Bennett appeared amused by Chance's outburst. "What my little brother means to say is that we're here on behalf of our pa. The answers you give us are the answers you're giving him. If you refuse, then you're refusing him as well. Is that the situation you really want, Mayor Brown?"

At nearly sixty, Bill Brown wasn't a man who scared easily. He had first been elected Monroe's mayor twenty-seven years earlier. The Bowman boys were just part of long line of characters that kind of experience accumulated. He rocked back in his chair and stared up at the ceiling of his office on the top floor of Monroe Town Hall.

"You know I've worked with your daddy for many years. Yes, sir, he's been in this very office more times than I could count with all our hands together. I've *always* looked forward to those visits. You want to know why?"

The mayor quickly answered his own question. "Because he has the good manners to bring me something for my trouble. A show of respect. So far, the only thing you two have brought in here is a bunch of demands, some puffed out chests, and little else. I'm sorely disappointed."

Bennett leaned down, pulled up his pant leg, and withdrew a pint bottle. "You mean something like this? It's the last of the gin Pa had come in from Canada last year. Apparently, the ladies love the stuff–can't get enough of it."

Mayor Brown's eyes lit up as his hands reached across the desk. "That's more like it. Why didn't you give it to me when you first came in?"

Bennett kept the bottle just beyond the mayor's reach. "I was hoping you'd tell us what you know right off, and then I'd get to keep the gin for myself. Like I said, the ladies love it."

"Before you get the gin," Chance said, "we'd like your word that you really do have information to share with us about Noretta Saul."

Mayor Brown nodded. "Of course! I know something of everyone who lives in my town, and I've certainly taken note of her recent arrival."

Bennett slid the bottle across the desk. The mayor grabbed it up with the speed of a striking cobra, unscrewed the top, and took a long swig. He closed his eyes and sighed.

"Ah, that's better. Tell your father thank you. I've had too many poor attempts at gin before, but this here is the real deal. My compliments. It's very good."

Mayor Brown opened a drawer and dropped the gin inside. "So, you're here to pick my brains about Ms. Saul?"

The brothers nodded. The mayor adjusted the gold ring on his pinkie finger, folded his hands together, and leaned forward. "Might I ask why?"

Chance shifted on his feet. "That's none of your business. Just tell us what you know."

The mayor wagged a finger. "There you go again. Rudeness. Impudence. That's not how this works. You've come to me asking for something you don't have. You're sitting in my office. I've had a long-standing agreement with your father to officially keep Monroe a dry town. That agreement has been beneficial to us both. Out of respect for him, I was willing to take this meeting with the two of you. Your attitude, though, it doesn't sit well with me. Not one bit. Good day gentlemen."

Chance's mouth fell open. "*What*?"

Bennett wasn't nearly so diplomatic. He pulled a gun.

"We're not going anywhere until you give us what we came here for. I'll ask you just one more time, Mr. Mayor. What do you know about Noretta Saul?"

The mayor rolled his eyes and then leaned over and cracked the window blinds. "That's *my* police station right across the street. There are two armed officers sitting in there. Do you really plan on making this day your blaze of glory demise? I don't think so. You two are overly bold but not completely stupid. I have friends on the county government. Friends in Olympia. If I wanted your family business shut down for good, it wouldn't take more than a phone call, you ignorant little Sultan hicks. Now get that fucking thing out of my face and get the hell out of my office."

Chance's hands balled into fists. "I'm gonna beat the shit out of you in the next few seconds if you keep talking without actually telling us what we came here for. I won't be the one to kill you, though. I'll leave that to Bennett."

Mayor Brown's eyes widened, and his jowly cheeks quivered. He pushed away from the desk until the back of his chair hit the wall. His voice was a warbling yelp.

"Now hold on. There's no need for threats of violence. Christ, Chance, you're supposed to be the kinder and gentler of your brothers. Please, we're all friends here."

Bennett grinned as he twirled his gun a few times and then put it away inside his jacket. "Is that what we are, Mayor? Friends?"

"Of course, we are. You both know that. So, let's start over. I fear we all got off on the wrong foot. Let me tell you about Noretta Saul."

Chance leaned over the mayor's desk and smacked his palm with his fist, nodded, and then sat down. "About damn time. Now get to talking."

The mayor brought out the bottle and had another swig. This time, he offered the brothers a drink. They both declined. He put the bottle back and cleared his throat.

"Yes, regarding Ms. Saul. Well, she arrived here sometime last year. Lives in a home not more than three blocks from this office with that brooding cousin of hers. The address is 218 Fourth Street–a little blue single-story with a white picket fence. She has some money and has been unusually generous in sharing it with the right people–including myself and the three members of the town council. Clearly, there's something she wants, and I do believe I now know at least partly what that something is."

The mayor paused. Chance looked like he was ready to jump out of his skin. "So, spill it!"

"There's a property in the county about three or four miles east of our town limits–off Woods Creek Road. It's this little valley about forty acres or so. Used to be a dairy farm years ago. The only thing of value there now is a big barn–one of the biggest barns in the county. Word is the newly-arrived Ms. Saul is trying to buy the place. There's not much timber, and the soil has been flooded regularly over the years, which means a person would have a hell of time growing any kind of crops."

"Then why would she want to buy it?" Bennett asked.

"That's a bit of a mystery, isn't it? Why would Noretta Saul, a seemingly well-to-do woman from a city like Bellingham, suddenly take an interest in forty acres of wasteland here in Monroe?"

"It's not just the forty acres," Chance added. "Why is she also going to war with my family at the same time?"

"I'm afraid don't know," Mayor Brown replied.

Bennett's eyes narrowed. "How much is she paying you?"

"What do you mean?"

"You told us Noretta Saul had been unusually generous with her money. How much of that generosity has been going into your pockets? Is it more than what my father pays you?"

"Are you implying I'm no longer loyal to the Bowman family?"

"No, I'm asking how much she's paying you."

"I assure you the money from Ms. Saul has been a nice bonus but not nearly enough to risk my relationship with your father."

Bennett's head lowered slightly as he stared into the mayor's eyes. "Is that the message you want me to take back to Sultan?"

The mayor shrugged. "You tell Levi what you wish. If he should ever need to speak with me directly, he knows where I am. For him, my door is always open."

Bennett stood. "That door sure as hell didn't feel so open for us today. Fair enough, Mr. Mayor. I'm sure one of us will be in touch. Enjoy the rest of your gin."

Chance followed his brother out of the office and down the stairs. "What now?" he asked.

Bennett lit a cigarette as he watched the cars and horse-drawn carriages pass by them on the street, marveling over how busy Monroe's Main Street was while also looking disgusted by it. He had never cared for city life.

"How about we drive by her house? The mayor gave us the address."

Chance grinned. "That's right. He did. Okay, let's do it."

They found the house just as Mayor Brown had described it. There didn't appear to be anyone home. Bennett drove another block and parked on the side of the road. He glanced at Chance.

"You up for a little breaking and entering?"

The brothers were soon standing on Noretta Saul's back porch. Chance peered into a window. "Don't see anyone inside," he said.

Bennett turned the handle. The door was unlocked. He pushed it open a few inches, waited, then pushed some more. He looked up to find Robert Saul pointing a shotgun at his face.

"Hey," Bennett said smiling, "your ear is looking a lot better!"

Robert thumped Bennett's chest with the tip of the shotgun barrel. "The both of you back up."

Chance turned to run and then froze. "Shit."

Two Monroe police officers stood in the backyard with their guns drawn. One was older; the other younger. "Well, well, well," the older one said. "I've heard so many stories about the Bowmans. I always hoped I'd have a chance to meet one of you. Must be my lucky day–a two for one deal! Get those hands up where I can see them. We can take it from here, Mr. Saul."

"If it's okay with you, I'll keep my gun on them until they're cuffed."

The older officer shrugged. "Suit yourself. That won't take long."

It didn't.

Chance and Bennett sat unarmed inside Monroe's windowless ten-by-ten jail cell. The older officer was the one who processed them. His name was Chief Moyer. He had pale blue eyes, a downturned mouth, and a pair of hands slightly bent from arthritis. After he shut the cell door with a loud clang, he leaned against the outside of the bars and shook his nearly hairless head.

"You two done messed up bad. You don't get the benefit of dealing with crooked old Fenton Fenner and his one-man operation. No, sir. This here is a whole different thing entirely. Now you're dealing with *me*. This is Monroe. We do things different. We do them right. There's no daddy here to save you. Come tomorrow, I'll have the both of you standing before Judge Thompson on armed robbery charges. I'd say you two are absolutely and undeniably on your way to taking it up the ass *real* hard. Won't even give you the courtesy of some spit. They say it only hurts real bad the first few times, so you got that to look forward to. Until then, enjoy your stay here in my jail. Don't ask me for anything because you won't get it. Your hard time starts now."

The chief shut out the lights and closed the door. The brothers sat atop their slab bunks in the dark. Chance bumped the back of his head against the concrete wall.

"Was it the mayor who set us up?"

"Seems about right," Bennett said. He lay down and put his arms behind his head. "Try and get some rest. Pa will be wondering where we are soon. If it was the mayor who screwed us, and Pa finds out, there'll be hell to pay."

The brothers lay quietly for nearly an hour before Chance broke the silence. "Bennett, why'd Pa have me help bury Roy Coon?"

Bennett sat up. "Ssshhh! Keep it down. Don't be using names like that in here."

Chance lowered his voice to a whisper. "I want to know. Why me? When we got back to The Silo that night, you told Pa you could have helped. He didn't have you do it, though. He picked me. Why do you suppose that was?"

Bennett rubbed his eyes and sighed. His hand went to the pocket where he kept his smokes, but it was empty. Moyer had confiscated them.

"Did Pa say anything to you that night? You know, when you two were out there?"

Chance nodded. "Yeah. He said that killing was easy. It was the forgetting that was hard."

Bennett drew his knees up toward his chest and rested his arms over them. "That sounds like Pa. It's also your answer."

"What do you mean?"

"Think about it. Have you killed anyone yet?"

"No."

"And why's that?"

"Because...because I don't want to. Why would I?"

Bennett leaned forward. "Exactly. None of us should *want* to kill. Killing is wrong. It should always be a last option. Pa wants you to understand that. He let you see a dead body, someone we knew, to make that point. And he's right. Killing isn't easy, but it's a lot easier than having to live with that killing for the rest of your life, so whenever possible, *don't do it*. That's the kind of men he wants us to be. The kind who would only kill when there's no other choice."

"But Pa killed Mr. Coon."

"Yeah, he did. What's the problem?"

"You just said killing should be the last option."

"Okay, so I'll ask you again. What's the problem? You know what happened right?"

"Pa told me Mr. Coon owed him a lot of money and that he was telling people he wouldn't have to pay it back. That he needed to be dealt with for the good of the family."

Bennett nodded. "Uh-huh. That was the reason for Pa going up to Coon's place. He didn't go there to kill him, though. Scare him, sure, but not kill him."

"But Mr. Coon is dead."

"No shit. Pa didn't have a choice. Coon drew on him. He came out on the front porch all drunk and wild-eyed, said he didn't care about nothin' or nobody, and pulled a gun."

"He pointed it at Pa?"

"No—*at me*."

"You were there?"

"Yeah," Bennett said. "I was there. I was the one Coon aimed for. You know how fast a draw Pa is–and how accurate. It all happened so fast. Pa fired just once. That's all he needed. Coon dropped dead. And let me tell you something. Pa was busted up about it. He felt awful. He didn't speak it, but I saw it in his eyes. Killing Coon like that–it shook him up. They'd known each other a long time."

"Why didn't he tell me you were there?"

"I don't know. Maybe he wanted me to be the one to decide what I share with my brothers. What I *do* know is this. If Coon had pointed his gun at Pa, I don't think Pa would have been nearly so fast to pull the trigger. He was protecting me, just the same as he tries to protect all of us. Even when killing someone is the right thing, it's gonna haunt you. Just look at Dalton and what it's done to him. That's what Pa wanted you to understand that night. If two people take something that far, there's always a price to pay for the one left standing."

"Pa's been the one left standing for a long time."

Bennett lay back down. "Yeah, he sure has. Now try and get some sleep."

Chance closed his eyes, but he had never been more awake.

7.

Dalton and Dylan lay face down on the shack floor with their hands tied behind them. The place smelled of seaweed, mud, damp wood, and seagull shit. Dalton turned his head to check on his brother.

"You good?"

Dylan winced when he went to answer. "I'm still breathing despite the crack my skull took. I thought I told you to be ready?"

Dalton struggled against the rope that bound his wrists. "Thought I was."

"Is that a chicken?" Dylan asked.

Dalton looked up at a small, mesh wire pen in the corner of the room. A white chicken bobbed its head as it stared back at him. "Huh, that can't be good."

"Why's that?"

Dalton gritted his teeth as he continued to try and break free. "We're tied up in a shack with a caged chicken. That's so weird it's got to be trouble."

There were voices outside. The brothers recognized one of them as the foreman they met earlier–the one who had led them into an ambush. The shed door was flung open. Heavy footsteps made the floor creak.

"Stand them up," the foreman barked. Two men grabbed the brothers and yanked them onto their feet. The foreman stood in front of them. He stared at Dalton for several seconds then did the same to Dylan.

"I need you both to understand something, so please listen very carefully. You're gonna die today. It can either go quick, or real slow and painful. The choice is yours."

Dalton spit out a thick, frothy wad that landed on the foreman's boots. "Fuck you."

The foreman looked down. He sighed, looked up, and then punched Dalton in the face. Dalton's head rocked back then fell forward. He licked the blood off his lips and grinned. "That all you got little man?"

The foreman rubbed his knuckles and shook his head. "No, not by a mile. There's more–a lot more. Have a look."

He bent over and grabbed hold of a brass latch and pulled open a three-by-three cutout in the floor. A whoosh of saltwater air filled the shack. The foreman pointed at Dylan.

"That one. Bring him here."

Dylan was shoved forward until the tips of his shoes hung over the opening. He glanced down and saw the dark surface of Bellingham Bay below. The foreman reached across the opening and poked Dylan's chest.

"Is your name actually Bowman and is the other one really your brother?"

Dylan didn't answer.

The foreman nodded. "Fine. I'll start. My name is Titus Lemkee. Yeah, I'm the one you came looking for. I don't like visits from people I don't know. Before you die, you're gonna explain why you came here asking to see me."

Dylan rose up to his full height and straightened his shoulders. "Good to meet you, Mr. Lemkee. I wish you'd have been more honest with who you really were at the start. Could have saved you all the trouble of bashing us in the backs of our heads and tying us up like this."

"Oh, it wasn't any trouble. You already told me your names. Now I want to know why you're here."

"I don't respond well to threats."

"Threats? I'm sorry if you think that's what's going on. You're way out of your element here, boy. You have no idea who I am, what I've done, and what I'm gonna do to you two. Tell me something. You know what a mud shark is?"

Dylan glanced down at the water and shook his head. "No."

"I didn't think so. You're about to find out. You see, this bay, it has a mud bottom–the kind of bottom this particular shark thrives on. Hence the name–mud shark. These things, they're not so big. A few feet or so but their teeth will slice through a man's skin like a hot knife through butter. I've seen it. There are plenty of fisherman around here, you look at their hands, they're all scarred up, tips of fingers missing—mud sharks. They're also called a dog fish because they run in packs. Hundreds and hundreds of them swimming around looking for a next meal. Add just a bit of blood and flesh, and they swarm. I've seen them churn the water like it's boiling when that happens. When I was a boy, I'd slash them open and throw them back into the water, and you know what happened? They'd go crazy feeding on their own entrails. Biting, tearing, swallowing–it's all these little beasties know how to do. I admire them. How they go about killing and consuming without thought. It's a beautiful thing."

Dylan's brows drew together. "Your idea of beauty is a whole lot different than mine."

"Perhaps, but does it really matter? You'll be dead soon. Here, let me show you."

Lemkee opened the pen, grabbed hold of the chicken, and broke its neck. He cut open its breast, and then tied a weighted rope around the body.

"The weight keeps it on the bottom. That's where all the action is."

The chicken hit the water with a splash and sank. Lemkee freed Dylan's hands and then handed the other end of the rope to him.

"If you let go of that rope, I'll have your brother's head blown off, understand? Boom. Gone. Just like that."

Dylan nodded. Lemkee beamed. "Good! You *do* know how to take an order. The rope will get tighter in your hands. It shouldn't take long. Remember, *don't let go.*"

Five minutes passed. Then ten. Dylan flinched when he felt the first tug. This was quickly followed by a stronger pull. He tightened his grip and drew the rope toward him a few inches. He cried out and almost fell over into the water when it was nearly ripped from his hands.

Lemkee took out a flask from the inside of his jacket and took a long swig. "There we go. You feel how powerful they are, don't you? It's quite a hungry horde down there. All those mouths and those thousands of teeth; imagine how excited they'll be when it's your brother's body I toss into the drink. I'm going to make you hold the rope for that as well. Don't think I won't."

The rope went slack. "Pull it up."

Dylan pulled. The end of the rope was torn and frayed, the tips red with blood. Nothing of the chicken remained. Not even a feather.

Lemkee took another drink, returned the flask to the inside of his jacket, and levelled his eyes on Dylan. "Why'd you come here?"

"If you're going to kill us either way, why should I tell you anything? What's in it for us? Why not just tell you to go to hell and keep quiet?"

"Because I gave you the choice of dying quick or dying hard. Here's how it will go. I can put a bullet into your brother's head and throw him into the water, or I can put one in his leg. That leg will be messy. It's going to bleed an awful lot. He'll sink to the bottom just like the chicken did, but his instinct will be to hold his breath. That'll give him a good three or four minutes of full awareness. The mud sharks are down there right now circling, waiting... hungry. He'll feel every bite, and you'll feel every tug on that rope. They go for the softer bits first. He'll be looking at his own guts being torn out and devoured right in front of him before he finally loses consciousness. That's why you should answer. It's the difference between being a dead meal for the sharks or a live one. Of feeling everything or nothing. So, I'll ask just one more time. What do you want?"

Dalton stepped forward, ignoring the gun at the back of his head. "You talk too damn much. If you're gonna do it just fucking do it!"

Lemkee looked at Dalton, looked at Dylan, then nodded. "Fine, but it'll be him first. Go ahead. Shoot him in the leg."

Dylan was thrown against a wall and a gun jammed into the top of his thigh.

"Wait!" Dalton cried out.

Lemkee held up his hand. "Hold on. Let's see what the big one has to say."

"We didn't lie about our names. I'm Dalton Bowman. That's my brother Dylan. It's like we said from the beginning—we're here about a woman named Noretta Saul."

Lemkee blinked rapidly several times at the mention of Noretta. Dalton continued.

"We were told you bought the Saul lumberyard. That's why we came here looking for you. We just want some information. That's all."

"Did Noretta send you?"

Dalton shook his head slowly. "No."

"Then why are you here asking about her?"

"It's business."

"Business, huh? And what sort of business would that be? I know Noretta ended up in some little shithole called Monroe."

"Our business is the same as the one you have in your coat pocket. It's the drinking kind."

"Really? That's interesting because I imagine that's the very same business Noretta is most likely involved in given that was her specialty here in Bellingham even after she married up."

Dalton and Dylan shared a quick glance. Lemkee scratched the stubble on his cheek.

"You didn't know that? It's true. She ran a downtown saloon before that kind of thing was made illegal. Sold spirits, drugs, women, whatever a paying customer wanted, and I do mean *anything*. At least that's what the rumors said."

"I take it you're not a fan of hers?" Dylan asked.

"I've always respected her survival instinct but knew she was trouble. My old friend and mentor Jacob saw it different. For reasons I'll never understand, he loved her, and despite all my warnings made her his wife. I watched that man fade into nothing starting on the day they wed. She's a goddamn succubus. He had a bad ticker. Troubled him since he was young. With her claws in him, Jacob went downhill fast, but before he died, he made me promise I would do no harm to Noretta. I made that promise to my friend, and I've kept it even when she took the lumberyard that had made Jacob Saul a successful and respected man in this community and drove it into the ground. I bought her out–everything. The house, the lumberyard, her bar. Gave her more than a fair price. My only requirement was that she leave Bellingham for good. I didn't want that snake in my backyard or to see her face and be reminded of my friend. She took the money and left, and when she did, I gave a loud and heartfelt good riddance to her."

Dylan cleared his throat. "Mr. Lemkee, I have a proposition, but before I share that with you I also have a question."

"I don't need propositions, and I'm in no mood to answer your questions. I'm already behind schedule. We have boats to load up this afternoon. Can't do that while I'm standing here. It'd be a whole lot easier to just dump the both of you into the water right now, so I can get to it."

"You're not going to harm us, Mr. Lemkee," Dylan said.

"I'm not?"

"That's right. And you want to know why? Because you're not a stupid man."

Lemkee slammed the trapdoor shut and stepped over it. He stood in front of Dylan with his hands on his hips. "Careful what comes out of your mouth next. I'm in no mood for games. Explain yourself. No lies, or I swear I'll cut your brother's throat from one ear to the other while you watch. Then it'll be your turn."

"Can I ask my question?"

Lemkee leaned forward and looked up. When he spoke his hot and sour whiskey-breath washed over Dylan's face.

"Sure. Let me hear it."

Dylan took a deep breath.

Lemkee took out his knife.

8.

"Boys, let me assure you I'd have been here a lot sooner had I known you were locked up. I'm here now, though, so let's work on getting you out."

Mayor Brown didn't really appear too concerned about the Bowman's well-being. Chance gave Bennett a look that let his brother know he thought Brown was likely putting on just enough of a show to keep their father from making the trip to Monroe himself.

The mayor stood in front of the cell door with his hands stuffed into the pockets of his slacks. "The thing is, breaking and entering? Armed robbery? Those are *very* serious charges. Keeping this mess under wraps, well, I'm going to have to really pull some strings."

Bennett got up and put his face between the bars. "Bullshit. You are the strings. Let us out. Send us on our way. We never went into the house. There was no robbery."

"That's right," Chance said. "Sure, we were checking out her place because *you* all but told us to. And when we arrived, Robert Saul was waiting there–like he knew we'd be coming. Now I wonder how that was?"

"I had nothing to do with you going to that house. I certainly had nothing to do with any gun being pointed at you, and frankly, I resent the implication. As I already said, I can make this go away, but...."

Bennett sighed. "How much?"

The negotiation was underway. The mayor smiled. "Yes, well, perhaps you could remind your father of the important part I play in his business ventures? You two locked up and facing serious charges of wrongdoing should remind him how invaluable having a friend like me can be to your family's continued success."

"And what *invaluable* amount should we tell our Pa is a fair price for your friendship?" Chance asked.

Mayor Brown crinkled his nose. "There's no need for contempt. Let's keep this simple. I'll set the amount of your release at $47 with the expectation your father will give some serious consideration regarding what fair compensation is for my ongoing service to him."

Bennett wrapped his hands around the bars. "Chief Moyer already took our money."

Mayor Brown grinned. "Did he?"

"Yeah, and the amount he took from us just happens to be $47," Chance added.

"What a remarkable coincidence. Fortune continues to smile on you boys. Be grateful! I'll have you out of here within the hour. You'll be home in time for supper, and we all know what a fine cook Laney is. I envy the many meals you likely take for granted."

The mayor made good on his promise. Bennett and Chance were soon released. They stepped outside and found Chief Moyer on the sidewalk leaning against their car. He flicked a spent cigarette at their feet.

"I'll be seeing you two again. You can count on that."

Bennett fired up his own cigarette. "C'mon, Moyer. We both know you can't count."

Moyer pushed himself off the car and knocked the cigarette from Bennett's mouth. "Don't you *ever* talk like that to me again. Not here. This is my town."

Chance pointed at City Hall. "Your boss is likely in his office across the street looking down on you right now. He personally said we were free to go. Seems to me you're all fired up and ready to make a liar out of him. I seem to remember a word for that. Wish my brother Dylan was here. I'm sure he'd know it."

"Insubordination," Bennett said. "That's the word for it–insubordination."

"Why, brother, I do believe you're right! That was a lot of syllables. Well done. There you go, Chief. You're dangerously close to insubordination. I bet the mayor would consider that a firing offense. I'm sure he could easily give your job to one of those other two fellas on your crew. In fact, I should march on over there and tell the mayor that right now."

Moyer's hand reached out and grabbed hold of Bennett's shirt. "You're gonna shut up, get in your car, and drive away." His other hand hovered over his sidearm. Bennett and Chance had no weapons. Though the mayor had given them back their freedom, the Monroe cops had kept their guns.

"Go ahead," Moyer seethed. "Say something with that smart mouth of yours."

The brothers kept quiet.

Moyer let go and stepped back. "Good. Get back to that shithole you call home."

Bennett slid behind the wheel. Chance got in the passenger side and slammed the door shut. Moyer stood staring at them as they drove off.

"I'm don't think he likes us much," Chance said.

Bennett shrugged. "I learned a long time ago our family can be an acquired taste." He leaned forward and looked up through the windshield. "We still have a couple hours of daylight left. How about we go take a look at that forty acres out on Woods Creek Road the mayor was telling us about?"

Chance's eyes nearly doubled in size. "Have you lost your damned mind? That's the same kind of thing that just got us thrown in the hoosegow."

"Exactly."

"Exactly *what?*"

"That's exactly the last thing they'd think we'd do. Besides, Woods Creek is way outside of Chief Moyer's jurisdiction. There's nothing to worry about. All we have to do is look for a big barn out in the middle of nowhere. Remember what the mayor said? It's about three miles outside the Monroe city limits. Shouldn't be too hard to find."

"We're unarmed."

Bennett used his thumb to point behind him. "Flip up the back seat."

Chance looked under the seat and found a hunting rifle hidden there. It was the old Winchester that all the brothers had been taught to shoot with when they were boys.

"See? We still have some firepower."

"An old rifle isn't much."

The car creaked and rattled its way down the backwoods passage that was Woods Creek Road. It was little more than a tree-lined wagon trail. After fifteen minutes of difficult driving, Chance spotted a massive barn sitting in the middle of a field at the bottom of a gently sloping hill.

"Take a left here."

Bennett turned and then accelerated. "The mayor was right. That's one big barn. This place must have been home to a lot of cattle back in the day."

Almost all the property's fence had fallen over or rotted away. The field grass stood nearly three feet high.

"Stop!" Chance yelled.

Bennett slammed on the brakes.

"That's a bridge up ahead."

Bennett squinted as he looked through the dirty windshield. "Really? You sure?"

Chance was already getting out. "We should have a look. It's just as likely to be falling apart like everything else around here."

The brothers pushed back the brush and found the remnants of a wood bridge that had once allowed wagons to cross over a narrow, pebble-strewn creek that dissected the property.

Bennett inspected the area around the creek more carefully. "See how high the banks are? In the winter, this stream doubles in size. Didn't the mayor say something about this place flooding?"

Chance nodded. "Yeah, which you would think makes it even more worthless. Being down in this little valley, a whole lot of water must pass through here during the wet season. You can smell how damp the soil is–like a moldy rag. I take it the bridge is washed out?"

"Yup. All that's left are a few rotted pieces of wood. If we want to have a look inside that barn, we'll be going the rest of the way on foot."

Chance turned around and went back to the car. "I'm getting the rifle."

Bennett found the narrowest part of the creek and was about to jump over it when he spotted the outline of a boot print in the mud bank on the other side. It appeared to be no more than a few days old. He looked across the field at the barn that stood like a silent sentinel daring him to approach.

"What is it?" Chance asked.

Bennett pointed to the mark in the mud. "Someone else was here recently. And by the looks of it, he's a big fella."

"My money is on it being our new friend Robert Saul."

Bennett kept staring at the barn. "Think he's here now?"

"Only one way to find out. As far as we know, Noretta hasn't bought the place yet. If he is here, he's trespassing same as us."

Chance kept the rifle aimed at the barn as they both moved cautiously toward its double-door entrance. Bennett knocked. When there was no answer, he grabbed one door handle and told Chance to grab the other.

They rolled the doors open. Chance held the rifle in front of him. The upper windows allowed just enough light to see. Bennett scanned the space looking for any sign of trouble. All was quiet.

"There." Chance pointed to a boot print in the dry dirt floor. It was the same size as the one they found near the creek. Bennett looked around some more.

Chance ran his hand along a lower portion of the barn's framing and found it free of rot. "For its age, it's in good shape. We're a good six or seven feet higher than down at the stream. I don't think it's ever flooded inside here."

Bennett walked slowly along one of the walls. "They used to have pens or dividers or something in here for all the cows. It's all been ripped out. The holes in the walls look recent."

"How long and wide do you think it is?" Chance asked while looking up at the ceiling.

"At least sixty-feet wide and nearly a hundred-feet long– plenty big."

"Yeah, but plenty big for *what*?"

Bennet snapped his fingers. "Storage."

"Maybe, but I feel like we're missing something." He walked further into the barn, stopped, and then called out to Bennett.

"There's a door in the back."

By the time Bennett reached him, Chance had already opened the door and was looking out at acres and acres of grass field.

"What's this?" Bennett said as he reached up and took something down from the wall. It was a scythe. He ran his thumb along the blade's edge. "It's new. A lot newer than anything else around here." He moved outside holding the scythe and looked around. "Notice anything?"

Chance started to say no and then stopped. "The grass has been cut down in a straight line over there–like a road."

Bennett crouched low and looked out at the recently cut path. "It goes back a ways. As much as two hundred yards–maybe more. Whoever did this put in some time."

"Noretta plan on going into the hay business?"

Bennett lit a cigarette. "I don't think so. It's like you said. This is some kind of road."

"That doesn't make any sense. A road to where? It's just field."

"I don't know. We've seen the place. We'll tell Pa about it. Maybe he'll have some idea about what Noretta is up to out here."

The scythe was returned to its place on the wall and the barn doors closed. The brothers walked back to the car.

"Can I drive?" Chance asked. Bennett said yes.

A light rain had started to fall by the time the brothers reached Woods Creek Road. Darkness was fast approaching. Bennett glanced to his right and saw headlights.

"Car's coming."

Chance decided to wait for the other car to pass before pulling onto the road. Bennett sat up straight and rolled down the passenger window to get a better look. "Uh-oh," he muttered.

The other car came to stop in the middle of the road. Both its doors opened. Robert Saul exited from behind the wheel while Noretta stepped out of the passenger side. Robert kept his door open and stood behind it.

"You think they know who we are?" Chance asked.

"Not sure. They're definitely checking us out. Man, look at the stink-eye on that Noretta. Some women turn heads. She turns stomachs."

Bennett frowned. "Time to go, brother."

When Chance gripped the gear shift, Bennett's arm slammed him back in the seat and then yanked him toward the wheel. "Get down!"

The passenger window detonated into a thousand fragments of glass. Bennett reached behind him, pulled up the back seat, and took out the rifle. "Go!"

Chance popped the clutch. The car lurched forward, stumbled, and then stalled.

"What the hell was *that*?" Bennett cried.

Another shotgun blast rang out. The rear window cracked. The car sputtered back to life. Chance glared at his brother. "You gonna use that or what?"

Bennet pointed the rifle out of the broken passenger window. "Don't worry about me. Just get us gone." He fired. Noretta and Robert scrambled for cover behind their vehicle. Chance mashed the gas pedal to the floor and sped off. Once they were safely out of range of the shotgun, Bennett leaned back in his seat, closed his eyes, and whistled. "Those two don't mess around."

Chance eased off the accelerator. He didn't want to break a wheel on one of the road's many deep ruts.

"They meant to kill us back there."

Bennett opened his eyes. "Yup."

Chance swerved to miss a large tree root. The light drizzle was turning into a downpour. He could barely see the road in front of him.

"You hear something?"

Chance cocked his head. "No, I don't hear---"

The back window blew apart. Chance nearly drove off the road. Bennet reached over and grabbed hold of the steering wheel then whirled around in his seat. Noretta and Robert Saul were right behind them. Noretta was driving while Robert leaned out the passenger window with the shotgun.

Chance swerved to miss another pothole and nearly lost control of the car again. "Keep it on the goddamn road!" Bennett bellowed.

"Like you could do any better!"

"Slow down."

Chance looked at his brother like he had just grown two heads. "Slow down? Are you crazy?"

"I can't be bouncing around like this. Slow down and keep it steady so I have a chance to hit what I'm aiming at."

Chance downshifted. Bennett pointed the rifle, fired, then let out a triumphant shout as he watched blood erupt from the top of Robert's shoulder.

Robert Saul didn't drop the shotgun. He didn't cry out. He barely flinched.

What he did do was shoot back.

9.

"You think Pa will go for it?"

Dalton didn't answer. It had been a long and mostly silent drive back from Bellingham. Dylan was behind the wheel while Dalton stared out the passenger window.

"Hey, I said--"

"I heard what you said," Dalton murmured.

The brothers were passing through Monroe. It was nearly dark. Dylan turned the headlights on.

"Well, I hope he does. It could really take our family to the next level."

Dalton rubbed his forehead. "Next level?"

"You know, more business, more money, more everything."

"Yeah, more problems. Just what we need."

"I would think you'd be in a better mood. We went from having guns to our heads to making a potential deal with the biggest bootlegger in Bellingham. We walked off that dock still alive and with the chance to put a whole lot more coin in our pocket. That's better than being shark food."

Dalton pressed the side of his face against the window glass and closed his eyes.

"You tired?" Dylan asked.

"I'm *always* tired."

"You weren't so tired in that shack. You were ready to take a bullet for me. Why is it you care so much for others but so little for yourself?"

Dalton let out a long sigh. Dylan persisted. "I'm serious. After what we just went through, I deserve an answer. This dark cloud that's always hovering over you? It's getting old. I want my brother back, and I know Bennett and Chance feel the same."

"I shared a section of trench for sixteen weeks with thirty-nine other men. Nine died from dysentery. That means they literally shit themselves to death. Seven more were taken by the gas attacks. Four were shot by enemy fire. Two others jammed pistols into their own mouths and pulled the trigger, preferring the certainty of a quick death over the possibility of a slow and agonizing one. That's twenty-two out of thirty-nine men—gone. They were just like me right before landing in France: young, confident, thought they'd live forever. They didn't. As bad as the dysentery was, the worst were those who died from the gas. They lay on the ground with their bodies all clenched up tight, fingers curled in like claws, eyes big and bulging, their mouths opening and closing like fish out of water.

"It liquified the lungs, the gas. Like a searing hot poker being pushed slowly down one's throat. It didn't take them quick. The skin blistered with boils. The eyes watered at first.

Then the whites turned blood red, but later, if the exposure was great enough, they melted into the skull, and the poor bastard went blind. Tongues swelled and darkened. Gums receded. Teeth fell out. I saw lips and noses crack so bad they filled with puss and then broke apart, exposing the cartilage and bone underneath. All day and night, I heard the screams of men begging for someone to kill them. At first, I didn't understand how anyone could hurt so much that it made them want to die. By the end of the war, I knew. By the end of the war... I felt a different version of that same kind of pain."

Dalton stopped talking. Dylan kept driving. Shadows arced across the road, like dark spirits attempting to grab hold of the car as it passed. The sun was setting behind them.

"You know what Ma would say if she were here right now?"

Dalton grunted. "She'd tell me to toughen up."

"That's *exactly* what she'd say. So, listen to her. Toughen up."

"It's not that easy. Besides, you could be standing in front of Ma with an arm hanging by nothing more than a thin piece of gristle, and she'd still tell you to toughen up."

"You're probably right about that."

"I know I'm right. Ma was a hard little bird. In the end, the only thing she couldn't stare down was the goddamn cancer that ate her up from the inside out."

Dylan glanced at Dalton. "You think about her?"

"Sure, most every day. It was often her voice that kept me alive in France. There were times I didn't think I'd make it. Hell, there were plenty of times I shouldn't have. I'd hear Ma's voice in my head yelling for me to never give up, to fight back, and to make sure that if I was going to die it was gonna be on my feet taking as many of those Kraut sons-a-bitches with me as I could. Ma kept on yelling at me... and I kept on living."

"We should visit her grave this week on our way up to Chan's. I don't think we've been out there together since her funeral. She'd like that–to see her two oldest together."

Dalton didn't say anything. His eyes were closed again.

"You're still going with me to Chan's, right?" Dylan asked.

"I don't know."

"What do you mean you don't know? You said you were. Don't tell me you have things to do because I know that's a lie. Are you going back on your word?"

"I told you–I'm tired."

Dylan pulled the car over to the side of the road and pointed at the big steel bridge that crossed over the confluence of both the Sultan and Skykomish Rivers and marked the entrance into the town of Sultan.

"You see the sign at the top of that bridge?"

The sign spelled out SULTAN in big white letters. Dylan reached over and grabbed Dalton by the arm.

"What's it say?"

"Take that hand off me, or you lose it."

"Read the sign."

Dalton's hand clamped down over Dylan's. "Don't play teacher with me."

Dylan ignored the pain around his wrist. "Read it–out loud."

Dalton spit out the word Sultan. Dylan let go of his arm. Dalton didn't let go of Dylan's wrist. He squeezed even harder. Dylan nodded.

"That's right. Now tell me what it means."

The corner of Dalton's mouth twitched. "Fuck you." By then, he was squeezing so hard his hand began to tremble. Dylan winced. Dalton's eyes narrowed.

"Hurts, don't it?"

Dylan made a fist with his left hand. "Tell me what the sign means."

When Dalton ignored the question, Dylan punched him in the nose. Dalton cried out. He let go of Dylan and wiped blood away from his face with the back of his hand while Dylan rubbed life back into his throbbing wrist.

"I didn't want to do that, but I think you needed it."

Dalton started to laugh.

"Something funny?"

"I was just thinking," Dalton said.

"Yeah? About what?"

"About the look on your face after I give it a smack."

By the time Dylan realized what that meant, it was too late. Dalton's fist smashed into his cheek, causing the other side of his head to crack against the inside of the car's door frame.

"There. Now we're even."

Dylan rubbed his face and moved his lower jaw from side to side to make sure it wasn't broken. Dalton pointed at the Sultan sign. "How about *you* tell me what it means?"

Dylan was still massaging his jaw. He glanced at Dalton, looked at the sign, and cleared his throat.

"That sign represents home. Your home. Our home. We're Bowmans. When we cross that bridge, we represent something. We *are* something–something different, something important. There's a legacy on the other side of the bridge that Pa built that we as sons and brothers need to recognize, respect, and carry forward. When we take in pain we always make sure to give some back. Kind of like you just did to me. Then we move on. We move forward. And we never, ever, give up. That's what it means. Do you understand?"

The last remnants of sunlight hit the sign. Dalton mouthed the word Sultan and then nodded. "Yeah, I think I do. How's your face?"

"It's fine. You're getting old. You don't hit as hard as you used to. You ready for home?"

Dalton nodded.

The brothers crossed the bridge.

10.

"Absolutely not." That was Levi Bowman's declaration right before biting off a piece of bacon and then washing it down with a sip of coffee.

Dylan persisted. "Pa, it's a chance for us to expand the business. That means more money. Isn't that why we're doing this? Taking these risks? To make money?"

Everyone else at the table waited to hear Levi's response. It was unusual for any of the brothers to challenge their father's authority so directly as Dylan had just done.

"You want me to go into business with a man who put a gun to you and your brother's head? This Lemkee you met with, the only thing I really know about him is that he threatened two of my sons–*at gunpoint*. You'd have me reward him for that? This part of the discussion is over. Don't bring it up again."

"I promised Mr. Lemkee you'd meet with him. I gave him my word. You always taught us how a man's word is his bond."

Levi tightened his grip on his coffee cup. "That's between you and Lemkee. I didn't promise him anything. You're a part of this family, Dylan, but you don't speak for it. You had no business doing so in Bellingham."

"What? You'd rather me and Dalton get thrown into the bay? I did what I had to do so we'd have a chance to get out of there. I took the initiative. When the girl at the bank said how Lemkee was buying up chunks of Bellingham, when I saw the lumberyard, the boats coming and going, I knew the only way to make as much money as fast as he did was to be in the booze business. You don't rise that fast chopping trees down in the woods. So, I put two and two together and offered Lemkee a business proposition—one that kept Dalton and me alive."

Levi looked at Dalton who hadn't yet said a word that morning. "What do you think about all this?"

Dalton added another dollop of butter to the last bite of his toast, plopped it into his mouth, and then shrugged. "I have no plans on going back to Bellingham, so I don't really care. Dylan talked fast like we all know he can. Lemkee listened, and an agreement was made. I didn't promise him anything, though, and neither did anyone else. As far as I'm concerned, that Bellingham son-of-a-bitch can go to hell."

Dylan massaged his forehead, clearly frustrated by the lack of support for his idea. "Lemkee wants to use this area to expand his distribution range. Once I convinced him our family was the best way for him to go about doing that, he was willing to listen instead of blowing our brains out all over the floor of that stinking dock shed. There also appears to be some tension between him and Noretta, so why not use that to our advantage? Forge a partnership with Lemkee, and then push Noretta out once and for all. She's the real threat to us in Sultan, not Lemkee."

"What about the barn property Noretta is buying? How does that play into all this?" Chance asked. He had earlier spent ten minutes detailing to the rest of the family what had happened to Bennett and him during their trip to Monroe—a trip that ended with Robert Saul taking shots at them from a moving car.

Bennett nodded. "Yeah, that's what I'd like to know. If Noretta's car hadn't hit a pothole and blown a tire yesterday could have ended up a whole lot different. They wanted us dead, and apparently, they're plenty confident in thinking they can get away with trying to make that happen. Whatever plans Noretta has for that barn, it's real important to her, and she doesn't want anyone knowing about it."

Dylan pointed at Bennett. "Which is *exactly* why we need to join forces with Lemkee. He knows Noretta and what she's capable of. And I'm pretty sure he'd like to see her gone just as much as we would."

"Then why didn't he?" Laney had made everyone breakfast and then sat silently listening as they argued their versions of reality. She was silent no more.

"Why didn't Mr. Lemkee take care of Noretta in Bellingham? If he's so rich and powerful, why didn't he eliminate her then? I'm to believe that a man who threatens to feed people to sharks is also a man who gives a woman he claims to despise top dollar for a lumberyard and then sends her on her way to Monroe where she is suddenly challenging this family's authority in our own backyard?"

"Lemkee made a promise to his friend, Noretta's husband, that he wouldn't harm her," Dylan answered.

"And you believe him?" Laney said with a shake of her head. "Just like that? This Lemkee sounds like a thug, a killer, and yet you're so willing to take his word as truth?"

Dylan looked out from underneath heavy lids. "Those are the same words some people use to describe us."

Levi spoke low and slow. It was the sound of soft thunder--a warning that was not to be ignored. "That's enough, Dylan. You won't be taking that tone here. Not at this table eating food Laney prepared for you."

Dylan's cheeks reddened. He was strong-willed but rarely disrespectful to his father or Laney. "I'm sorry.".

Laney reached across the table and patted Dylan's forearm. "I know you didn't really mean to sound the way you did. We're all tense over this situation with Noretta. Your brothers were put in jail in Monroe and then shot at. You and Dalton had your lives threatened in Bellingham, it's all just...."

She stood up and put her dish in the sink while looking through the kitchen window at the tall cherry tree that grew in the side yard. "It's just getting out of hand. This family isn't supposed to live in fear. Not here. Not like this. Yet, I'm scared to death right now that one of you is going to be hurt–or worse."

Bennett lit a cigarette. "We're gonna be fine. I know it."

Laney turned around. "Really? And what makes you so sure of that?"

"We're Bowmans. We survive. It's what we do. It's what we've *always* done."

"You're a little young to be making that claim, don't you think?" Laney said. "Get a few more years on you, experience how bad things can turn out, and then see if you feel so confident."

Bennett started to answer but was cut off by Chance. "Stop it. Look how they got us divided against each other. I may be the youngest here, but I'm plenty old enough to know that with this family breakfast is sacred. It's when we come together but right now? Hell, Noretta has us tearing each other apart. Bennett is right about one thing. We're Bowmans. This is Sultan. Not Bellingham, not Monroe–*Sultan*. That means we're in charge. We decide what does and doesn't happen around here. Am I right?"

When no one answered, Chance slapped the table. "*Right?*"

Dalton stood. "I'll be in my room."

Dylan tugged on the sleeve of Dalton's shirt. "We still on for the Chan run?"

Dalton said sure and then went upstairs while everyone else looked at Dylan.

"He's going with you?" Levi asked.

Dylan said yes. Levi was quiet for a moment and then nodded. "That's a good idea. From here on out, we pair up wherever we go–no exceptions. Also, the back entrance to The

Silo is to be locked at all times. If anyone comes at us there, it'll be through the front door. Laney, tonight make sure we have plenty of shells for the shotgun behind the bar, and keep it close."

Laney gave Levi a hard smile. "I always do."

Bennett took a long drag from his cigarette, tilted his head back, and then blew out a big plume of smoke that drifted up to the ceiling. "What about Noretta's barn property? You want me to do anything more on that?"

"No," Levi said. "I'll look into it myself. Good job finding out about it, though. You did good. You *all* did good."

The brothers put their dishes in the sink and left the kitchen. Laney reached down to squeeze Levi's hand. "I can see the wheels turning inside that head of yours. What are you thinking?"

"I'm thinking you're not going to like my answer."

"Now you *really* have to tell me what you're up to."

Levi leaned back in his chair. "I'm thinking about paying Admiral a visit. Hear what he has to say about all this."

"Do you really need to do that?"

Larson Kohl, called Admiral by all who knew him on account he had spent a year in the Navy before getting kicked out for assaulting an officer, had once been the most feared man in Sultan. Time had taken a toll on Admiral, though, and at seventy-five, he would be the first to admit he was well past his prime. Levi had always looked at Admiral as something of a mentor—a man he first feared and then later came to admire.

Many had challenged Admiral over the years, but none had succeeded. It wasn't until he faded away into a sort of self-imposed retirement that Levi was able to fill the void in Sultan left by Admiral's partial absence.

"He still knows things–more than most," Levi said.

"I've made it no secret how I feel about him. The stories I heard... he isn't a good man."

"Most those stories Admiral spread himself. He wanted people to fear him. You know I do the same thing. I'm not half as bad as some make me out to be. Could Admiral be brutal? Sure, when he had to be. Now he's just an old man."

"Old or not, I still say he's dangerous."

"Admiral would never hurt this family, Laney. He's known me since I was a kid. When I was growing up around here, it was Admiral who protected me, gave me a job, and some self-respect. When it comes to this kind of stuff, he's the smartest man I know."

Laney stroked Levi's cheek. "You're the smartest man I know, and, in this house, that's all that matters."

"I appreciate the vote of confidence."

"You feel it don't you?" Laney said. "Something is coming for us–something bad."

In the Bowman's living room there was an old grandfather clock that had been in the family for three generations. The tick and tock movement of its long, brass pendulum echoed throughout the house as it marked the passage of time. The sound always seemed loudest in the kitchen. Levi tried to give

Laney a reassuring look, but his eyes told her the truth. He was as worried as she was.

"Whatever happens, to my last breath, I'll keep us safe."

Laney leaned over and kissed Levi's forehead and then hugged him tight as she whispered into his ear. "I know."

11.

A light drizzle fell. Levi looked up at the Sultan bridge that loomed over him. Below that bridge, standing on a rock ledge that stuck out over the slow-moving river water, was where Levi found his old friend fishing. Admiral gripped the rod with fingers that were as rough and gnarled as tree roots. His back and shoulders, though partly bent, were still broad. He wore black suspenders over a heavy flannel shirt with blue jeans and boots. It was the same outfit he had worn regardless of the season for as long as Levi had known him. Admiral glanced back and appeared surprised to see someone walking the brush-lined trail toward him.

"What's this? A busy man like Levi Bowman with time to visit a tired has-been mayor like me?" In addition to owning a fortune's worth of properties in and around Sultan, Admiral remained the town's only mayor, a largely ceremonial title created by him for the sole purpose of satisfying the state's municipal charter requirements. Unlike the town fathers of neighboring Monroe, Admiral had always been determined to see less government in Sultan, not more.

"Any bites?"

Admiral shrugged. "Not yet. As long as there's line in the water, though, there's always hope." His was an old man's voice that still hinted of the powerful woodsman he once was.

"That there is, Admiral. How are you doing?"

"Oh, about the same as yesterday and the day before I suppose... waiting to die."

Admiral reeled in a bit of line, paused, then reeled some more. "I first showed you this place when you were barely more than knee-high. Remember that?"

"I do. We took a lot of fish out of here."

"Hmmm, yes we did. You remember where to fish it?"

Levi pointed to an area on the river where the water appeared to swirl in a slow circle right before passing directly below the bridge. "You cast the line about ten yards up from that spot there and let it drift."

"That's right. There's where the big ones hunker down and wait. The smaller fish never see them coming. In that water, where its coldest and darkest, is where the big fish rule– always. Same as life. Of course, you already know that, don't you? You're the big fish now."

"Big fish or not, I could use some advice."

Admiral turned partway around. His blue eyes, though framed by a deeply-lined and age-spotted face, remained clear and bright. "Really?"

"Yeah."

"What's got you so worried? You *are* worried. I can see it on you."

"Have you heard anything about a woman named Noretta Saul living in Monroe by way of Bellingham?"

Admiral gave the fishing rod a few little shakes. "Sure. I might have heard a word or two."

"What do you know about her?"

Admiral reeled in another foot of line. "Oh, not much really. Apparently, she has some money that's she's throwing around. Why do you ask? Since when is someone like you afraid of a little lady like her?"

"I think she might be trying to move in on my territory."

Admiral rolled his head from side to side and winced like he was trying to work out a kink in his neck. "You think so? All the way from Bellingham? Can't say I blame her, though. I envy you there, Levi. All the cash you're making with that little pub of yours. What took me decades slaving in the woods till my bones ached and my back was near broke you've managed to accumulate in just a few years. It don't really seem fair, does it? I've thought about that some. Likely more than I should. I wonder, had this damn Prohibition come twenty years sooner, how much of a fortune I could have made off it. It's not your fault, of course. You were simply here to profit, same as most anyone else with the grit and knowhow to do it. The way you have it all set up, the payoffs to Fenner and that mudhole of a mayor in Monroe, I can't help but be proud of your success. You done it well because you done it right. I just hope them boys of yours appreciate what you've built. Few things sting more than a lingering lack of appreciation."

"They seem to be doing okay. By the way, Laney says hi."

Admiral slapped the side of his thigh. "Bullshit! That woman wouldn't give me the spit from her mouth if I was standing next to her on fire."

Levi chuckled. "You might be right about that. Anyway, back to Noretta Saul."

Admiral held up his hand and nodded. "The old man's mind is drifting. I get it. You want me to focus. No need to ask twice. So, tell me, has she actually threatened you?"

"Yeah. She shot at Chance and Bennett. Well, it was her and a man named Robert Saul who I'm told is a cousin of hers. Before that, she had already filed an assault complaint with Fenner and threatened to take it to Judge Thompson. And last Sunday she declared in front of God and Sultan that me and my family are an evil plague on the town that must be eradicated."

Admiral looked like he was trying not to laugh. "I might have heard something about that. Not that I give a damn what is or isn't said in any church. I bet that stuttering fool of a pastor was fit to be tied. I would have liked to have seen that. She do anything else to you?"

Levi detailed what he knew of Dalton and Dylan's trip to Bellingham and their meeting with Titus Lemkee and Lemkee's association with Noretta. Then he told Admiral about the barn property Chance and Bennett discovered and how Noretta and Robert Saul were shooting at them soon after.

"I recall having to deal with something sort of similar about thirty or forty years ago," Admiral said. "It was before Sultan was officially incorporated. There was this retired railroad fella, a vice president or something. He was a real arrogant son-of-a-bitch. Wore these fine suits, a big top hat, shiny boots. He strutted around here for about a month saying how he was gonna purchase all of Sultan and then build a big hotel and train depot for the new line that was coming in. By then, I was already working hard on buying up as much land as I could for myself. Most everything we call Main Street now, I was busy making my own with money I earned in the woods. Pretty soon, everyone I'm talking to wants more money for their land because that suit-wearing, piece-of-shit carpetbagger was making his own offers. I didn't have enough coin to pay the prices people were suddenly demanding, and it was all that railroad fella's fault. Besides, I didn't want no damn train depot. That would only bring more attention, more rules, more outsiders, and more trouble."

Admiral went quiet as he let out some line. "What did you do?" Levi asked.

"I, uh, I didn't do nothin'. Didn't have to. He died. Fell asleep on the train tracks, tripped and fell, nobody knew for sure. Found bits and pieces of him along the rails for miles. Accidents happen, right? For me, it was more a matter of good fortune. With the money he had been promising for all that property suddenly gone, those sellers were a lot more accommodating to my initial offers. In fact, some of them sold for *less* than what I was originally willing to pay, meaning his coming here actually ended up saving me money. When you take that and add to it the fact he died on the railroad tracks, well, I believe that's what's known as an ironical situation."

"So, your advice is for me to try and convince Noretta Saul to take a walk on the railroad tracks?"

"I see you haven't lost your sense of humor. My point is that I once had to deal with my own version of Noretta Saul. It's up to you to decide what needs to be done about her–find your own way. You willing to consider making her disappear? I'm sure you and I both know a few around here who would do it for cheap."

"That wouldn't be wise. She made her dislike of me very public after the performance at the church. If a hair on her head goes missing, too many eyes will look to me as the cause. That could lead to the county authorities getting involved."

"Hmmm, you're probably right about that. Still, eyes or no eyes, there are times when you must do what needs to be done. Oh!"

Admiral had a bite. He lifted the rod, set the hook, and started to reel in. The fish broke the water's surface about twenty feet from shore.

"Looks like a rainbow trout and a nice one," Levi said. It had been a long time since he had watched Admiral pull a fish from the river.

"It's a fighter all right. Look at that!" The fish twirled out of the water. Admiral continued to reel. His forehead dripped sweat.

"You need some help?"

"No!" Admiral barked. He jerked the pole and flung the trout onto the bank where it spun and twisted as it struggled to return to the river. Admiral let out a loud groan as he leaned over and grabbed hold of the fish. He held its body with one hand, placed his thumb behind its gills with the other, and then turned around with the trout still squirming in his hands. He held the fish in front of him, broke its neck like a dry twig, and dropped it onto the ground.

"I'll have that beauty tonight for dinner. Pan-fried, a bit of butter and garlic–perfection!"

"You're still the king of the river."

Admiral winked. "You're goddamn right, and don't you ever forget it." He shuffled toward Levi and extended his big hand. The two of them shook.

"Thank you for stopping by, young man. Nice to know you still think enough of me to seek my counsel. I was beginning to wonder if you thought of me at all. I'll keep my ears open for you so long as you do me the favor of checking back in soon. Old age can be lonely. I miss the chance to give you a bit of advice, even if you probably don't need it. Maybe next time you can remember to bring your pole, and we can fish side by side like we used to."

When Levi started to step back, Admiral pulled him closer and held him there. "That is, if you're not too busy or too important to make an old friend feel needed."

"I'll do that," Levi said. Admiral let him go. The rain had stopped.

When Levi returned to his car and gripped the steering wheel, he looked down at his hand and noticed it was covered in blood and scales. He slowly rubbed it between his thumb and fingers. The ground beneath him trembled as a train whistle blew.

It started to rain again.

12.

"Are you actually wearing cologne?" Dylan asked.

"Shut up," Dalton answered.

"Hey, I'm not knocking it. Far from it. I fully support any attempt to help you smell less like the business end of an outhouse. You even trimmed up that beard-thing on your face. Nice."

The drive east along the narrow switchback road that led to Chan's was a slow and careful one. The visit to their mother's grave had left the brothers in a contemplative mood. She had been gone for years, but some days, days like this, they felt her presence more strongly than ever.

For a few seconds, the rear tires slid sideways as Dylan took a corner too sharply. He turned the wheel, braked, and then accelerated. Dalton didn't seem to mind the momentary loss of control. He sat in the seat silent and glowering–an immovable mass of indifference. Even though it was the middle of the day, Dylan turned his headlights on. Long branches weighed down with mossy lichen reached across the road and nearly blocked out the sky. It was a dark and wet place where few ventured and fewer lived.

Nobody in Sultan really knew how long Chan had resided deep in the hillside woods across the railroad tracks. The Bowmans didn't care. All that mattered to them was that since The Silo had opened, Chan had been there to provide them regular shipments of reasonably-priced spirits. In exchange for their patronage, Chan agreed to only sell alcohol to them, thus allowing the family to further corner the local drinking market.

Chan's full name was Chan Johansen. His mother had been Chinese, and his father Norwegian. His age was rumored to be somewhere between forty and fifty. He stood six-foot-three with blond hair and blue eyes. If not for the shape of those eyes, his Asian lineage might never be suspected. Rather than hide from his mother's influence, though, Chan chose to embrace it by always wearing an oversized conical straw hat and a long tail of braided hair that hung down his back.

Alcohol wasn't the only thing Chan sold. If someone in the area had a need that couldn't be accommodated by more conventional means, a trip to Chan's often followed where he would somehow find a way to meet it–for a price. Be it weapons, gold, jewels, drugs, or time with a willing woman, almost anything was negotiable.

Dylan slowed down as he approached an especially rough patch of road. The empty bottles in the back of the car clinked together. He elbowed Dalton.

"You're not nervous, are you? Because if you are, you shouldn't be. I hear Chan's girls are always nice. They'll take great care of--"

"Shut up."

"I'm just saying--"

"And I'm telling you to shut up. This isn't my first time with a woman for fuck's sake."

"I know that. It's been a while, though, so I figured you might be a little--"

"Since when are *you* the expert?"

"What?"

"You heard me. You talk like you know all there is to know about women. That's funny because I don't recall you being with anyone recently."

Dylan scowled as he barely avoided hitting a pothole. "I'm doing fine, *believe me*. Besides, I'm a gentleman. I don't kiss and tell."

"Uh-huh."

"Let's just focus on you, okay?"

"No, you focus on driving the damn car and shutting up, *okay*?"

Dylan slowed down and then turned onto a small uphill path that was the entrance to Chan's. "Jeez, I was just trying to help."

The car rocked side to side as Dylan navigated the narrow drive. "I keep telling Chan he's got to fix this road. Pretty soon, nobody will be able to make it up here."

They reached a flat area at the top of the hill with two tin roof cabins. The larger cabin was closest to the parking area. The smaller one sat farther back and was partly hidden behind a row of trees. The front door to the first cabin opened, and Chan walked out wearing his big hat and an even bigger smile.

"I'll unload the old bottles and load up the new ones while you pay the little cabin a visit," Dylan said. "We're in no hurry."

By the time Dylan closed the driver's door, Chan was standing in front of him. "Hello, Dylan. How is Mr. Bowman doing?"

"My father is doing fine Chan. Thanks."

"Is that you, Dalton? It's been a few years."

Dalton nodded. "Yeah."

Dylan cleared his throat. "Uh, my brother would like to visit the back cabin."

Chan's eyes widened. "Ah, of course!" He extended his hand palm-up toward Dalton. "That's two dollars. Just knock on the door and enjoy yourself. My girls will remove that scowl off your face! They see your brothers Bennett and Chance often. It will be their honor to familiarize themselves with the eldest of the Bowman boys."

Dalton slapped the money into Chan's hand and then walked toward the cabin with his head down. Chan watched him go.

"Clearly, he is not the friendliest of you four."

Dylan chuckled. "Dalton? Friendly? No, he'd never be mistaken for that. Is the new shipment ready?"

"Of course! I've been waiting for you. And I won't even raise the price."

Dylan handed Chan five crisp ten-dollar bills. "Per our agreement."

Chan bowed. "Of course. Here, let me get you some help." He stuck two fingers into his mouth and whistled. The front door to the larger cabin opened, and a woman with long raven-black hair stepped out. She wore a gunny-sack style dress that ended at the tops of her cowboy boots.

"Her name is Winona. She was born a Sioux Indian and was just four years old when her tribe was massacred by cavalry soldiers at Wounded Knee. Her parents and grandparents, brothers and sisters–all gone. At fourteen, she fled the Dakota reservation and ended up in Seattle where she spent years living on the streets until a local church took her in. She did odd jobs for them--cleaning, gardening, that sort of thing. She's a mute. Hasn't spoken a word since losing her family. Smart as a whip, though, and understands everything."

"How'd she end up here?"

"Some church members complained. They said she was no longer a child, and they couldn't afford to keep supporting her. I have a contact who helps women find places to live where they don't have to fear abuse. She's a hard worker, honest, capable, so I said yes. She arrived just a few days ago. So far I have no complaints."

Chan turned toward Winona. "This is Dylan Bowman. We do business with his family. There are crates of empty bottles in the back of his vehicle. Please take them inside, and then replace them with the crates of full bottles from the house."

Winona nodded and began to reach into Dylan's car. When Dylan started to help her, Chan put his hand on his shoulder.

"No. Winona prefers to work alone. She refuses charity. Perhaps it's something to do with her tribal traditions. I give her a place to stay, food to eat, and she, in turn, does what I ask without question. When she first arrived, I helped her with something, and she sulked for the rest of the day. Trust me. It's better you step back and allow her to do it herself."

Chan noticed Dylan glancing at the smaller cabin. "No, she doesn't work there, and I haven't asked her to. There isn't a woman here who doesn't want to be. Unlike their lives elsewhere, with me, they are paid well, are safe, and free to leave anytime they wish. I've always found that happy whores make for far more profitable ones."

"No one can say you don't have an interesting perspective on life, Chan."

Chan held up his pointer finger. "Ah! I nearly forgot. I have a line on a case of French wine coming in next week. Said to be an excellent vintage. Is that something that would interest your father?"

"It might. I'll run it by him. Don't move it until you hear back from me."

Chan bowed. "Of course. Mr. Bowman made it very clear to me when we first began our business relationship that if I am caught selling any alcohol to anyone else other than him within ten miles of Sultan, he'll be here the next day burning this place to the ground. I assure you I have an excellent memory. If there is one thing I know about your father, it is that he is a man who keeps his word."

Dylan nodded. "Indeed."

Winona was nearly finished unloading the crates of empty bottles. Her arms were thin but sinewy-strong. Her face, though somewhat long, wasn't unpleasant. Dylan quickly did the math in his head. He knew the Wounded Knee massacre took place in 1890. If Winona had been four years old then, like Chan had said, that would make her thirty-seven--no longer a young woman but far from being an old one.

"You sure I can't help? The crates with the full bottles are a lot heavier. I feel guilty standing here while she does all the work."

Chan shook his head. "You wouldn't be helping. It would only offend her."

"What the hell is going on here? Why are you two making this poor woman do all the work?"

Dalton marched out of the smaller cabin looking thoroughly disgusted by what he saw. He went over to Winona and grabbed the crate she was holding. She refused to let go. He could only see the top of her head as the rest of it was hidden behind the bottles of wine. When Dalton tugged on the crate, Winona tugged back.

"Here, let me take it," Dalton muttered.

Winona held tight. Dalton pulled on the crate some more. Winona kicked him in the shin. Dalton let go while Chan stepped forward waving his hands in front of him.

"I'm so sorry, Dalton! As I explained to your brother she's very stubborn about doing her part. She means well. Please accept my apologies."

Dalton's eyes followed Winona while she placed the crate in the back seat. He continued to stare at her as she went back into the cabin.

"What are you doing out here already?" Dylan asked. "You finish up that quick? I guess it *has* been a long time."

"Nothing happened. I told you I don't want to be with a whore. No offense, Chan. Your women are fine. It's me."

Chan shifted on his feet. "Uh, there are no refunds, Dalton. I'm sorry."

"I don't give a shit about that. Keep it. The rest of the hooch still inside?"

Chan nodded. "Yes."

Dalton walked into the cabin just as Winona was walking out struggling with another crate. They passed each other without saying anything. Dalton soon returned outside holding a crate under each arm.

"What is your brother doing?" Chan whispered out of the side of his mouth.

Dylan grinned. "I'm pretty sure he's showing off."

With Dalton carrying two at a time, it didn't take long to finish loading the remaining crates. Chan bowed to both brothers. Dalton stood next to the car staring at the cabin Winona had disappeared into and then turned toward Dylan.

"I can make the next run out here myself. I don't mind."

"Is that right?"

"Sure. It's no big deal. It'll give me something to do."

"That okay with you, Chan?" Dylan said.

Chan's gaze went from Dalton, to the cabin, and back to Dalton. "Uh, okay. I can have that wine ready if Mr. Bowman decides to purchase. It'll be twenty dollars."

Dylan's brows lifted. "One crate for twenty dollars?"

"It's French!"

Dalton nodded. "That's fine–twenty dollars. I'll be here next week."

The ride down Chan's hill was even slower than the ride up. Dylan had to focus on avoiding getting stuck, going off the side, or breaking any of the full bottles in the back. Only when he reached the bottom was he able to relax and sneak a glance at his brother.

"So, what did you think of that Winona?"

Dalton's answer ended up being the only two words he spoke during the entire trip back to town. "Shut up."

13.

It was an especially busy night at The Silo. With the shelves fully stocked, Levi would often run a two-for-one-until-2:00 special that made the bargain drinkers come running.

Chance stood guard near the entrance with a hunting rifle cradled in his arms ready for any trouble that might show. Laney poured drinks from behind the bar within reach of the loaded shotgun, while Dalton, Bennett, and Dylan sat at the poker table with revolvers hanging off their hips. Levi was in the back office going over the books, something he did religiously at least once a week.

Three other men sat at the poker table. As usual, Dalton was winning. He sat silently counting his chips while his brothers shook their heads.

"How in the hell you knew to call is beyond me," Bennett complained.

Dalton took a sip of whiskey and then shrugged. "Your knee wasn't shaking."

"What?"

"When you have a good hand, you get excited and your knee shakes. That's your tell."

Bennett lit a cigarette. "Bullshit."

The three other men at the table all looked at Bennett's knee. Dylan started to laugh.

"Dalton's right, little brother. That should be your poker nickname--Old Shaky Knee."

Bennett reached across the table and snatched the deck of cards from Dalton. "I'll deal this hand."

"Suit yourself," Dalton said with a smirk.

Dalton won again. Bennett pushed himself away from the table. "I'm gonna get some fresh air. The stink of your damn luck is making it hard to breathe."

Dylan got up as well. He was almost out of chips.

Chance followed his brothers outside. A nearly full moon provided enough light to see most of the cars lined up in the parking lot.

"Man, we should hold a big card tournament here," Bennett said as he puffed furiously on his cigarette. "I'm talking deep-pocket players. Dalton would clean them out. We'd make a killing."

Chance was about to light up his own smoke when he paused to look at Bennett. "That's actually a pretty good idea. You should run it by Pa."

"No guarantee Dalton wins," Dylan said. "Sitting at a table with players like us, sure, he does fine but against some real pros? That might not turn out so well."

Bennett pointed at The Silo's entrance. "It's not just about the poker game. We could charge for people to come in and watch the tournament. We'd get a cut of all poker earnings, there would be side-bet action, and we'd raise the drink prices. Dalton could lose the tournament, but we'd still come out way ahead."

"I was wondering where you boys went off to. Way ahead of what?"

The three brothers all turned to look at Levi. Chance was first to answer. "We were talking about hosting a high roller poker tournament here at The Silo. It was actually Bennett's idea, and I think it's a good one."

Bennett nodded excitedly. "Yeah, we invite some big players, charge for people to watch, raise the drink prices, and have Dalton play against them. If he wins, we win big, but even if he loses, we still make some good money. We're the house, and in the end, the house always wins, right?"

Levi was quiet as he thought it over. His sons were just as quiet as they awaited his decision. "You know what?" he said. "It could work. They have high roller tournaments in places like Seattle and Everett. Why not Sultan? I have some French wine coming in from Chan. Real good stuff. We'll charge by the glass and make ten times what I paid Chan for it."

Bennett's knee started to shake. "So, we gonna do it, Pa?"

"Sure, I don't see why not. You can start getting the word out—create a buzz. Let people know there's a fee to get in the door and limited space available. Dangle the idea of exclusivity in front of them. That always gets folks excited."

Bennett puffed out his chest and grinned at his brothers. He was bursting with pride.

"Any of you know who that is?" Levi was watching a car drive slowly past The Silo. The others shook their heads. Levi's hand went to the gun inside his jacket as he continued to stare at the slow-moving vehicle.

"Whoever they are, they're definitely giving this place a long look," Dylan said.

Levi's eyes narrowed. "Yeah."

Bennett flicked his cigarette away. "You want something?" he shouted at the unknown driver.

The car stopped in the middle of the road. Its windows were rolled up. Clouds blocked out the moonlight, making it too dark to see who was inside. The vehicle had a long, narrow hood and pearl-white paint that had been buffed to a brilliant shine.

It started to move again but even more slowly than before. Levi took his gun out. Bennett and Dylan did the same. The mystery vehicle drove further up the road, turned around, and then drove past them at the same snail's pace as before.

Bennet started to point his gun at the car. Levi pushed his arm back down. "No, let's wait and see. Might just be out-of-towners gathering up the courage to come into an unfamiliar drinking establishment. They sure as hell aren't any kind of law enforcement. Not in a rig like that."

The car stopped. "I don't like this," Chance whispered.

The gravel crunched underneath Levi's boot as he took a step toward the road. They all dropped to the ground when they heard the unmistakable crack-crack sound of gunfire. The car sped off. Levi stood up and whirled around. There were frightened shouts. Dalton's voice. Then a shotgun blast. The shots had come from inside.

Levi ran into The Silo as people were running out. "Move!" he shouted. The first thing he saw was an overturned table. Dalton stood next to it looking down at something.

"What the hell happened in here?" Dalton pointed to something near the table. That's when Levi saw the body. He turned it over to look at the face. Half of it had been blown apart. Blood and bits of flesh oozed down the wall behind it.

"Anyone we know?" Levi asked. Chance, Dylan, and Bennett stood behind him wide-eyed as they stared down at the dead man.

Dalton shook his head. "Nope. Never seen him before. I noticed him earlier sitting here by himself. He just stood up, didn't say a word, and started shooting."

"Did he hit anyone?"

"Yeah."

Levi's throat tightened. "Who?"

Dalton pulled the top of his coat open to reveal a blood-soaked shoulder. "Me."

When Levi tried to look at the wound more closely Dalton brushed him away. "Just a nick. Looks worse than it is. Already poured some whiskey on it. I'm good."

Levi took a deep breath, put his gun back into its shoulder holster, and then ran his fingers through his hair. "Were you the target?"

"Can't be certain but seemed to be."

Levi looked back down at the remnants of the dead man's face. "You definitely got the better of him."

"Wasn't me who killed him."

Levi arched a brow.

"Is the son-of-a-bitch dead?" The shotgun lay across the bar in front of Laney. The cigarette she brought to her mouth was held between two trembling fingers.

Levi nodded. "Yeah, he's definitely dead."

Laney poured herself a shot of whiskey and then swallowed it in a single gulp. Her hands stopped shaking.

"Good."

14.

"Christ, what a damn mess this is, huh?" Fenton Fenner's sleep-deprived eyes were nearly the same color as the blood-soaked wall and floor. He had been awakened by a phone call from Levi thirty minutes earlier but looked like he could fall back asleep at any second. It was nearly 3:00 in the morning. The bar had been cleared out for the last two hours. After Fenner spoke with Laney, Levi had her and the boys go home with instructions they were to keep the doors locked and their weapons close. Fenner knelt to get a better look at the body.

"I'd have cleaned it up myself without bothering to wake you but with all the witnesses...."

Fenner shook his head. "No, you did the right thing, Mr. Bowman. There's no need to try and hide this. Laney isn't in any kind of trouble. I interviewed a couple of your customers outside. It was clearly self-defense. The question I have is if the deceased acted alone or on the orders of someone else. I know there are people around here who don't care for you or your family, but I don't know of anyone who has the guts to actually start shooting up your place of business. You say he aimed for Dalton?"

"Dalton seems to think so. Laney says the same. He sat here alone for a while, stood up staring at Dalton, and then fired off two rounds before Laney took him out."

"And you've never seen this man before?"

"No. We already looked for identification. Didn't find any on him. All he had was a few bucks and the gun."

Fenner stood. "Mind if I get a drink?"

Levi walked behind the bar. "Sure. Take a stool." Levi put two shot glasses on the bar, filled them both, and slid one in front of Fenner while lifting the other to his mouth and emptying it.

"Is his vehicle still here?"

Levi cocked his head. "I'm embarrassed to admit I hadn't thought to check."

Both men walked outside. Except for Fenner's car in the front and Levi's in the back, the parking lot was empty. The two went back into the bar.

"You think he walked here?"

Levi scowled. "Possible but not likely. I'd wager he was dropped off."

"Or he came here with a second person who was sitting somewhere else and who then drove off after the shooting went bad."

"That sounds like a conspiracy."

Fenner sipped from his glass. "Yup. And I bet you and I are thinking the same thing on that."

"Noretta Saul."

Fenner drank the last of his whiskey and pushed the glass toward Levi. "You got something I can wrap the body up in? I'll have to keep it inside my jail cell until I know where to have him buried. Nothing worse than death stinkin' up a fella's workspace."

"You can use the throw rug by that table there. Go ahead and keep it. I won't want it back."

"I imagine you wouldn't. Mind giving me a hand?"

Levi helped Fenner roll the body up into the rug and then drag it out to his rust-covered Ford Model T. "I'm surprised this thing is still running," Levi said.

"It gets me across town and back, and that's about as far as I need to go these days."

The two men struggled to pick the body up and push it into the car and then gave up trying. Fenner apologized for not being able to help more. He leaned against the car door wheezing and wiping the sweat from his brow.

"He's heavier than I thought he'd be. I tell you what. Instead of us both breaking our backs I'm gonna have Double-T come out first thing in the morning and take care of it. To hell with putting it in my office. I won't be able to take my lunch nap knowing a corpse is in there with me."

Twenty-six-year-old Tommy Thompson, who everyone in Sultan called Double-T, loved one thing above all others–

digging holes. At the age of seven, he discovered a shovel inside his grandmother's shed, and from that day on, Double-T was digging. Shortly after his twelfth birthday he was given the job of grave digger and had been digging graves for the town ever since.

"You mean leave the body here in the parking lot?"

Fenner shrugged. "Sure. We have it wrapped up good inside that rug. It won't be no trouble. I promise Double-T will stop by bright and early long before you open. Besides, it'll likely take a few days before folks are gonna want to come back here. After a shooting like the one tonight, they'll be scared. Business will be down for a spell. Can't say I blame them."

Levi lit a cigarette and kicked at the gravel with the heel of his boot. "Which makes it even more likely Noretta is to blame."

"You really think she'd send someone here to shoot your place up? That's a long way from getting a gaggle of teetotalers to give you the stink eye in church."

"There was a car—a fancy one. Drove by here right before the shooting. I figure that's how the shooter got here."

Fenner nodded. "Your boys told me about it, and I'd already considered the same. Problem is the vehicle you saw was white. The only car I've seen Ms. Saul in is black. In fact, I've never seen any white car—ever. Maybe they're more common in a big city like Seattle but not out here."

"I'm sure a woman like her can afford more than one car."

"I won't argue with that. I'm just saying, I don't have anything to go on regarding the description of this mystery vehicle you all saw. If I catch it driving through town, sure, I'll be quick to pull it over. Beyond that, there's not much I can do. I suppose I could ask Chief Moyer in Monroe to keep his eyes out for anything that matches that description."

"Don't bother. We won't get any help from Monroe."

"Really? I thought you and Mayor Brown were tight?"

"Tight? No. We've had an understanding that's similar to the understanding I have with just about every other goddamn government leech I know. Everyone has their hand out. Everyone wants their piece."

"Is that what you think of *me,* Mr. Bowman? Just someone who wants their piece? Because I sure don't see it that way. Say all you want about those assholes in Monroe because I'm right there with you. But *me*? I've been here a long time. Admiral gave me this job, and then you made sure I kept it. I figured we had a history built on mutual respect. Was I wrong?"

Levi flicked his cigarette away. "I didn't say that. If you took it that way, I apologize. It's been a long night. We're both tired. How about one more drink before we flush this day away for good?"

Fenner gave Levi a tight smile. He adjusted his gun belt and then took a deep breath. "Thing is, Mr. Bowman, there's something else I need to ask you about."

Levi folded his arms across his chest. "Yeah? What's that?"

"I was wondering if you'd, uh, seen Roy Coon recently?"

"Can't say I have. Why do you ask?"

"Seems he's gone missing."

"Missing? What do you mean?"

"I mean, he's gone, and nobody knows where he is."

"Who's looking for him?"

"What?"

Levi stared directly into Fenner's eyes. "Roy Coon doesn't have any family. You say he's missing. I'm asking you who's looking for him."

"If you really need to know, it was Admiral who inquired about Coon. Apparently, he was hired to fix a loose porch railing at the Admiral's place but never showed up. Admiral mentioned it to me offhand the other day. I decided I should look into it."

"I assume you've been to Coon's house?"

"Of course. Nobody was there. Some food was left on the counter like he'd left in a hurry or something. It had already gone bad. It was like he was living there all regular-like and then suddenly he wasn't."

"Hmmm. If I hear something, I'll let you know."

Fenner's face tightened. "The thing is, Mr. Bowman, it's my understanding Mr. Coon owed you some money."

"Did Admiral tell you that too?"

"How I heard it isn't important. I'm just asking if it's true."

Levi sighed. "I'm a little confused. It seems pretty clear you think I might have had something to do with Coon's supposed disappearance. What I don't understand is that even if I *did* what the hell do you think you could do about it?"

Fenner stepped back and held up both his hands. "Now hold on there, Mr. Bowman. I wasn't accusing you of anything. I was just making inquiries is all so that if people ask I'd know what to tell them."

"Uh-huh. Okay. How about you do something for me? You're right. Coon owed me money. I understand he let plenty around here know about it. The last thing I want is for him to have snuck out of town never to pay me back what he owes. So, if you hear anything about his whereabouts, anything at all, you be sure to clue me in. Are we clear?"

"Absolutely, Mr. Bowman. Clear as a fucking bell."

"Good. And if Double-T doesn't have this body gone in the morning, the next grave he digs will be his own. Got it?"

"Yup. He'll take care of it. I promise. No worries, Mr. Bowman." Fenner started to turn toward his car but then paused. "Uh, that offer of one more drink still stand?"

Levi lit another cigarette. "No."

Fenner licked his lips and cleared his throat. "That's fine. I understand. Goodnight, Mr. Bowman."

A breeze caused the end of Levi's cigarette to glow bright orange. He drew his jacket tighter around him, turned around, and walked back into The Silo. He locked the front door and went to the back office. The metallic smell of fresh blood and gunpowder still lingered. He sat down at his desk, took out the bottle of whiskey from the drawer, and poured himself another drink. When that drink was gone, he poured another and then another.

Something wasn't quite right—something that went beyond Noretta Saul and that night's shooting, but Levi couldn't put his finger on it. So, he drank some more. He thought some more.

And he waited for morning.

15.

For Levi Bowman, it was that rarest of things–an almost perfect day. It had been nearly a week since the shooting at The Silo. Fenner kept his word. Double-T had taken the body. The blood was washed off the wall and floor. People stayed away for a few days, came back, started drinking again, and life returned to what passed for normal in the town of Sultan.

The morning began as it usually did at the Bowman home. Levi sat at the kitchen table with Laney and the boys eating breakfast. The mood was light, the conversation playful, and the ham and eggs delicious.

Chance was the first to declare his plans to go fishing at the Bowman pond after lunch. Dalton liked the idea, as did Dylan and Bennett. It was decided. They would all fish together that afternoon.

Bennett asked Levi to join them. He said he might be too busy but promised to try and stop by. The boys thanked Laney for breakfast and scattered in opposite directions. Levi sipped his coffee and waited for Laney to say whatever it was that had her staring at him. Eventually, she got around to it.

"You really should join the boys this afternoon. You'll always have time to get back to business, but who knows how much more time you'll have to spend with your sons? It'll likely be sooner than later that they get to making their own families. I'm sure there's more than a few ladies who'd be happy to snag a Bowman boy."

Though he didn't say it then because he didn't like to talk of such things, Levi knew Laney was right. Shortly after the noon hour while sitting behind his desk at The Silo, Levi pushed away the inventory paperwork he had been working on and walked outside to his car.

The sun was perched high in the cloudless, blue sky. The air smelled of spring and the promise of the warmer summer months that would soon follow. Levi passed slowly through town on his way to the Bowman farmhouse. An old friend from his long-ago school days honked as he drove by on the opposite side of the road. Levi honked back. Oscar York, the town butcher, looked up from sweeping the sidewalk in front of his shop and motioned for Levi to stop. Oscar was nearly sixty, bald, with a gray handlebar mustache, bright blue eyes, and a mouth that was almost always smiling.

When Levi parked the car, Oscar held up his pointer finger. "One minute, Mr. Bowman. Please wait there." He walked out carrying a small bag which he then handed to Levi.

"There's some jerky I made from the bear you dropped off. It's been my best seller this week. Can't keep enough of it on the shelf. The rest of the bear I cut up and packaged and delivered at no charge to some of the needier families, just like you asked. They were so grateful!"

Levi thanked Oscar for the jerky and for delivering the bear meat to the ones in town who needed it most. Oscar put his knife and cleaver-nicked hand over his heart. "It was truly my pleasure, Mr. Bowman. Thank you for giving me the chance to help."

The ride home resumed. Levi hung his elbow out of the car's open window. He detected the delicate beginnings of spring flowers. Once home he looked out across the field and saw Chance, Bennett, Dalton, and Dylan sitting shoulder to shoulder while holding their fishing poles. Chance told a joke, and they all laughed. Levi smiled. He had forgotten how much he enjoyed hearing all his boys joking together.

Levi took his time walking to the pond. He enjoyed how the tall field grass made a dry *whoosh* sound as it brushed against his jeans. Dalton was the first to hear his approach. He turned toward Levi, and then the others did the same.

"Have a seat, Pa," Bennett said. "We haven't been here long."

Levi sat and stretched his legs out over the pond bank. "Any luck?"

Chance shook his head. "Nothing yet. It'll happen. Just a matter of time."

Levi lit a cigarette. "Maybe Walter will decide to pay us a visit. Hope you brought the strong line."

Chance slapped his palm against his forehead. "Not that Walter stuff again."

Walter was the legend of the pond Levi had been telling his sons about since they first picked up a fishing pole. Each year he embellished the tale just a little more. It all started with a warning Levi said an old Indian had given to him when he was a boy that he shouldn't step too close to the pond because if he were to fall in, a great fish named Walter might swim up and swallow him whole. Levi's sons used to listen to the stories of Walter with eyes wide and their mouths hanging open. Now those same eyes would roll as they shook their heads.

"Anyone interested in joining me in a bit of libation?" Dylan took a sip of whiskey from a silver flask he had removed from his coat pocket and then passed it to Dalton. The others took turns until the flask made its way back to Dylan. He then withdrew a pipe and tobacco. While his father and brothers all smoked cigarettes, Dylan had always preferred the occasional pipe–especially when fishing. He packed the bowl, struck a match, and puffed until the tobacco was lit. Then he lay back propped up by his elbows with the pipe poking out from the corner of his mouth as a swirling cloud that smelled of leather, ginger, and dark whiskey drifted above him.

Bennett pulled his line in to check the bait. The worm was still secured to the hook. He dropped the weighted line back into the water and watched it sink to the bottom.

Levi looked at each of the poles and then clicked his tongue. "I guess that's why they call this fishing and not catching. You'd think one of you would have something by now."

Dylan dipped his pole toward the water and then lifted it, hoping the bait moving around might attract a fish. Nothing happened. He bit down harder on his pipe and scowled. In the Bowman family, fishing was something to be enjoyed, but it was also serious business, and the longer one went without a bite, the more serious it became.

"You still heading over to Chan's to pick up that wine?" Levi asked.

Dalton nodded. "Yup–later today."

"Hey, Pa, what about the poker tournament?" Bennett said. "We still on for that?"

"Absolutely. I'm a little behind schedule planning-wise because of the shooting, but it'll happen. I was thinking sometime next month."

Bennett grinned. "It's gonna be great. I just know it."

Chance started to reel in his line when the end of his pole bounced up and down. "Hey, got something!" His shoulders slumped. "Ah, it's no bigger than a finger. Won't be worth keeping."

The little trout zigged and zagged underneath the water as it tried to free itself. Bennett pointed at it and laughed. "That's about your size, little brother."

A dark blur broke the water's surface with a loud splash, and Chance's poll suddenly bent nearly in half. The line was pulled out of the reel so fast it hissed. A much bigger fish had come along and taken the smaller one.

Everyone got up and whispered the same thing at the same time.

"Walter."

Bennett reached for Chance's pole. "Here, let me help."

"I got it. Give me some room!"

The pole broke. Chance cursed while reaching out to grab the broken end. His foot slipped on the bank, and the pole fell into the water. Dalton threw his head back and laughed.

"Walter wins again!" he bellowed.

Chance's cheeks burned red. He could see the end of his pole starting to sink.

"Walter wins again, my ass."

Chance jumped in. After that, everyone was laughing. Bennett had tears streaming down his face.

Chance swam to his pole and grabbed hold of it right before it disappeared. He let out a triumphant shout and then made his way back to the shore as the fish tried to escape.

"Not this time, Walter. You're mine!"

Levi offered a hand. Chance took it. He collapsed onto the dry grass, rolled over, and then sat up, gripping the line tightly with both hands. He started to pull. Bennett pointed at the pond.

"There!"

Walter's back broke across the water, creating a wake. Levi shook his head. "That's some fish."

"Don't lose it!" Bennett cried.

"Oh, I hadn't thought of that," Chance answered.

Walter spun and dove. Some line slipped through Chance's fingers. He gritted his teeth and squeezed tighter.

"You're gonna want to let it run a bit," Dalton said. "Go on. Give it some line. Fish that big, it'll snap the line if you don't. It won't ever let you just take it."

Chance loosened his grip. A few feet of line went back into the water, and then a few more. He glanced at Dalton.

"You sure?"

"Yeah, I'm sure."

Chance fought the fish for another ten minutes. He pulled the line in little by little until Walter was finally worn out.

Bennett again offered to help, and again Chance refused. They could all see the fish's green-and-black-speckled body.

Dylan whistled. "Could be twelve pounds, don't you think, Pa?"

Levi's eyes narrowed as he watched Chance reach down and grab hold of the line a foot from the fish's mouth. "That sounds about right."

Chance wore a grin big enough to break his face apart as he started to lift Walter out of the water. "You better grab it by the gills," Levi said. The advice came too late. The fish shook its head violently from side to side and pulled the hook. Chance nearly dove in after it for a second time. He pounded the pond bank's soft earth with his fist.

"Dammit. I had him. You all saw. I had Walter."

Chance stood up still holding the broken line. Bennett clapped him on the back.

"You're right. You almost had him. That was some battle between you two. Best I ever saw."

Chance was about to tell Bennett to shut up but then realized his brother's words were sincere. He looked almost as bad about losing the fish as Chance felt.

Dylan took out his flask. Everyone had a sip and stared out at the pond. A red-tailed hawk circled high overhead. Chance kicked a pebble into the water. "I still can't believe I lost that fish."

Levi squeezed the back of Chance's neck. "I wouldn't worry too much about it. Some things in this world just aren't meant to be caught. It's kinda nice knowing Walter's still down there somewhere swimming free. Besides, now you're part of the Walter legend. You have a story you can tell your own kids someday."

Chance shrugged. "I guess so."

There were more sips from the flask and more tobacco smoked before the five of them turned around and headed back to the house. Levi walked a few paces behind his sons and watched and listened as Bennett retold the tale of Walter and Chance. It was a good first telling, one that made everyone smile. Levi wished they could have walked together like that forever.

They all did.

16.

Dalton drove to Chan's in Dylan's car. Though Pa had told them to go everywhere in pairs, Dalton insisted he make the trip by himself. He wasn't entirely on his own, though. A loaded double-barrel shotgun rode with him in the passenger seat.

It felt good being alone. Each mile Dalton drove was another mile he put between himself and the nightmares of the war. He was home. He was alive. And he was on his way to see a woman.

Dalton hadn't been able to get Winona out of his head since seeing her last week. He knew she likely wasn't what some men would consider attractive. Having experienced so much death in a compressed amount of time had given Dalton an appreciation for things beyond the superficial. Perhaps it was the defiance in her eyes, the proud way her chin jutted slightly upward when she walked, or that, like him, she was also a survivor. Winona was the most stunning thing Dalton had been around in a very long time.

He was white. She was an Indian. That didn't matter. Dalton had seen the skin baked off the bodies of men that revealed how similar everyone was underneath. The outside didn't matter. It was the soul of a person that meant everything, and from what Dalton saw in Winona, her soul remained both beautiful and intact.

The drive to Chan's property seemed even rougher than before. Dalton shifted into low gear to avoid spinning the tires as he climbed the hill. Thick clouds hung low in the afternoon sky. His mind replayed the image of Chance jumping into the pond after the fish earlier that day and everyone's laughter as they watched him struggle to swim back to shore. The memory made Dalton smile. That smile vanished when the smell of smoke and charred wood entered the car.

Something was wrong.

The main cabin was still there, but the smaller one that housed Chan's women, was gone. The only thing left was a smoldering, burnt-out shell.

Dalton parked the car, grabbed the shotgun, and got out. He kept the driver door open and positioned himself behind it with the gun pointed at the cabin. It was quiet. The windows had been shot out and the door hung sideways off a single hinge.

"Anyone here? Chan? It's Dalton Bowman."

Silence. Dalton crouched low as he stepped out from behind the car door and moved carefully toward the cabin while looking through the broken windows for any sign of movement. The boards creaked when he stepped onto the porch.

"Chan?"

Though he spoke the name, Dalton knew Chan wouldn't answer. He could feel it. He could smell it. It was everywhere.

Death.

Dalton went inside and found the place ransacked. He crept toward the back of the cabin holding the shotgun in front of him with his finger on the trigger as glass fragments crunched under his boots.

Chan's naked body hung from the ceiling in a corner. One end of rope was wrapped around a rafter and the other end around his neck. His face had turned a mottled purplish-blue. A knife had been left hilt-deep in Chan's chest with a piece of paper attached to it. Dalton ripped the note free and read words written in blood:

Never again drink the wine for which you have toiled.

He stuffed the note into a pocket, gripped the knife, pulled it out, and used it to cut the rope. The body crashed to the floor. This was followed by a muffled thump. Dalton spun around with the shotgun at the ready. The cabin remained empty. He cocked his head trying to determine where the sound had come from. He took a step and thought he heard a gasp. Breathing. Movement.

Dalton looked down at his feet. His eyes narrowed. He pointed the gun at the floor. His voice was sandpaper over stone.

"Come out of there."

Nothing moved. No one answered.

The heel of Dalton's boot cracked against the floor board. "C'mon. Hurry up, or I'll shoot. Your choice."

He stepped back and watched a piece of the floor shift, pop out, and then get pushed up. Two hands emerged. The top of a head. A tear-streaked face.

Winona.

Dalton took her hand and gently pulled her up through the opening. Her hair and clothes were covered in dirt and cobwebs, and her lower lip trembled. She glanced at Chan's body and then quickly looked away.

"I won't hurt you," Dalton said.

Winona wiped the dirt and tears from her cheeks. Her hands shook. She stared at them until they stopped.

Dalton moved his head lower until he could look into Winona's dark eyes. "Are you okay?"

Her face communicated what Dalton already knew. Death had come, and Winona had once again survived.

"Anyone else left alive?"

Winona shook her head.

"How did you know to hide under the floor?"

Winona pointed at Chan's body.

"Chan told you?"

She nodded.

"The people who did this—you see any of them?"

Winona held up one finger.

Dalton tapped his chest. "Was it a man?"

She nodded.

"Did he take anything?"

Winona pointed to a broken wine bottle on the floor.

"The wine Chan was going to sell to my family."

Again, Winona nodded.

"The other women, did they all die in the fire?"

Winona closed her eyes and put her head down.

"This way." Dalton started to walk toward the open door. Winona didn't move.

"Your safe with me. I promise." He held out his hand and motioned for her to follow. Winona took a step back.

"I know I look like the kind of man who hurts people. Sometimes I *am* that man, but I swear I won't ever hurt you, and I won't ever let anyone else hurt you either. You can't stay here and I'm not leaving without you."

Winona and Dalton walked out of the cabin together. He opened the car's passenger door. She hesitated for a moment then slid onto the seat. Dalton was careful not to slam the door when he closed it. He got behind the wheel. Winona stared straight ahead while Dalton drove away from Chan's without looking back.

17.

"Why'd you decide to take me with you today?" Dylan asked.

A smoldering cigarette extended out of the corner of Levi's mouth. He glanced at the side mirror. Theirs was the only vehicle on the road to Index, a tiny outpost along the Cascade Mountains corridor twenty miles east of Sultan.

"I wanted someone who knows how to watch and listen. That's you."

"What am I supposed to be watching and listening for?"

"Anything that says we need to get the hell out of there if things go sideways. Have you been to the Boarding House before?

"No. I've heard rumors–weird rumors. I assume most are exaggerations."

Levi's mouth tightened. "Maybe. Maybe not."

The Boarding House was a large, twenty-four room structure originally built in the late-1800's to provide sleeping quarters for the gold and silver miners who had descended like locusts upon Index at the turn of the century. Where Monroe marked the westernmost location of what locals called the Sky Valley, Index was the valley's easternmost region. For a few years at the height of the area's prospecting rush, the outpost boasted a population of nearly six hundred. When the gold vanished, so did the people, leaving only a handful of bone-hard homesteaders behind.

One of those homesteaders was a travelling minister named Jacob Piedmont. He had with him a wife and three children–two daughters and a son. The little family moved into the Boarding House which had sat abandoned for six years before Jacob's arrival. It was rumored the wife died sometime during the family's first winter there. Jacob buried her behind the property in an unmarked grave. The next summer, he dug a second grave and put his only son in it.

Jacob never took a new wife, yet he fathered many more children–all of them daughters. Each year that passed, another of those twenty-four rooms was filled. What few neighbors Jacob had would sometimes see him sitting in a rocking chair on the Boarding House's big covered porch holding a rifle over his knees while mumbling to himself. His once thick, dark hair had turned a shocking white and hung well below his shoulders. A beard of the same color covered his entire chest. Few came to the Boarding House uninvited for fear of being shot.

That didn't mean Jacob didn't have the occasional visitor though. He had many mouths to feed. That required money. Jacob sold jugs of rot-gut hooch he made in a bathtub in a shed behind the house. It smelled awful, tasted worse, but for fifty cents a jug could keep a person comfortably numb for several days at a time. People would journey down from the hills that surrounded Index and take a jug back with them, and then in a month's time, repeat the purchase.

"You just be ready if I need you," Levi said.

Dylan nodded. "I will."

After a few minutes of silence, Levi cleared his throat. "You ever wonder where you might be if you'd stuck with college? You would have been an educated man--the first in the family."

"I *am* an educated man, and a I come from a family full of them. I don't need a piece of paper to tell me that."

"This life we live, though, it's not always easy."

"Life rarely is. Even if I'd stayed there and graduated I'm not sure that would have been the life for me. Teaching? That might have been too much irony to handle. Nearly every rule that's been thrown at me, I found a way to break it without it breaking me first. I've always been that way. You know that. Sitting in a classroom day after day closed in by four walls... it wouldn't have taken long for it to start feeling like hard time."

"Still, I worry your potential is being wasted. Who knows what you could have been by now if different choices had been made–by all of us."

"Pa, my choices have been my own. They always are. I'm here in this car right now because you asked me but also because I want to be."

"I suppose that's true. You've always been the most stubborn of your brothers. Maybe even too stubborn to find yourself a woman?"

"I find plenty of women. Finding a good one--that's the challenge."

Levi grinned. "Amen to that." He turned off the main road and crossed the bridge into Index. Massive mountains with snow-packed peaks seemingly high enough to touch the sky provided a spectacular backdrop. It was half-past noon. A chipped-paint picket fence marked the entrance to the Boarding House property.

A circular drive led to the home. Two young women stood on the porch watching Levi and Dylan's arrival. Their dark hair hung limp and unwashed over their shoulders. The taller of the two was pregnant. She abruptly turned and went into the house while the shorter one remained on the porch staring at the car as it came to a stop directly in front of her. Several of the building's windows were broken. Sections of siding had fallen off. The entire home looked to be on the verge of collapse.

"Be ready–for anything," Levi said. They exited the car. Levi smiled at the young woman.

"Hi there. Could you please run and tell Jacob that Levi Bowman is here to see him about some jugs?"

The woman didn't talk or move. She watched.

The front door opened. Three more dark-haired girls walked out. They looked to be between the ages of twelve and sixteen. All of them were with child. The oldest pointed a shotgun at Levi and Dylan.

"No weapons," she said.

The front door opened again. "That's okay, Winifred. Mr. Bowman's reputation precedes him. He's a *genuine* businessman. The real deal. God has brought him to us. Our prayers have been answered."

Jacob Piedmont, dressed in a dark wool suit littered with holes, stepped onto the porch. He had once been a tall man. Now his back and shoulders were badly bent. His head drooped low like a vulture sniffing the ground for its next meal. He shuffled to the end of the porch and looked down at Levi and Dylan. When he smiled, it revealed a mouth of broken teeth and diseased gums. He reeked of dirt, piss, and sweat. One hand cradled a Bible against his thigh. The other gripped a pistol.

"And what brings the great Levi Bowman to my door, hmmm? Ah, I believe I know. You need something I have. Yes, that must be it. News travels quickly–even to this place. I understand your Mr. Chan met an unfortunate end the other day. Now here you are hoping for my help. Yet, all this time, and you never bothered to strike a deal with me before? Never offered me that courtesy? Why is that, Mr. Bowman?"

"I meant no slight Mr. Piedmont. Chan's location was more convenient. That's all. You're correct when you say I'm here for something. I'm here to conduct some business. How many of your jugs do you have available right now for purchase?"

Jacob buried the tip of the pistol into the side of his beard and used it to scratch his face. "Oh, I've some jugs ready to go. Gonna have to add a desperation charge though. A man in need is a man willing to pay top dollar. Am I right?"

"What's your price, Mr. Piedmont?"

The tip of Jacob's dry, red tongue poked out from the bushy mass of whiskers his mouth was buried under. "I have four jugs I can sell you today. The price is five dollars."

Levi knew that was more than double what Jacob normally charged. "I tell you what, Mr. Piedmont. I'll buy those four jugs from you today for four dollars with a guarantee to return next week to buy another four at the same price. You and I both know the best customer is a repeat customer. If that price doesn't suit you, no hard feelings. I have other options."

Jacob's tongue darted out again as his eyes narrowed. "*What* options?"

"Four dollars today and another four dollars next week. What's it going to be?"

Jacob tried to straighten his posture but only partly-succeeded. "This is what I'll offer. Four jugs today and another twenty jugs next week for twenty dollars. That's quite a deal. I'm throwing in the first four jugs for free."

"I don't know, Mr. Piedmont. That's a lot of hooch. I'd have to bring up two cars to transport it all. Can you actually produce that much?"

"Would you call me a liar?"

"No. That's a hell of a lot of jugs is all."

"Those twenty jugs will be ready for you by this time next week. You have my word, Mr. Bowman, and my word is no worse than yours. Do you have the money?"

From somewhere in the big house, a baby started to cry. Jacob's tongue went *flick, flick, flick* as his finger rested against the trigger of his gun. Levi nodded.

"You strike a hard bargain. Okay. We have a deal."

Jacob jammed the pistol into the front of his trousers, spit into his palm, and stuck out his hand. The two men shook. Jacob's hand then turned over until the palm faced up. He motioned with his fingers.

"Twenty dollars, Mr. Bowman."

"You want me to pay you for the other jugs *in advance*?"

"Yes. That was the deal. You shook on it. Is there a problem?"

Dylan's hand inched toward the gun inside his jacket. Levi sighed.

"All due respect, that wasn't my understanding. Normally I wouldn't pay in advance. Especially not on a first deal."

Jacob's head swiveled toward Dylan. "I wouldn't do that, young man. It's bound to make my girls nervous. They get nervous, then they get twitchy, and your blood will be all over my front yard. I've heard your father's quick with a gun, but I doubt he's quick enough."

Dylan looked up and saw four rifles sticking out from four open second-floor windows. Two were aimed at Levi and two at him. His hand dropped to his side. Jacob grinned.

"That's better. Let's stick to our deal, shall we?" His fingers motioned again. "Twenty dollars."

Levi took out his money clip, peeled off a twenty, and handed it to Jacob. "There you are, Mr. Piedmont. I've met my side of the bargain. Now I expect you to meet yours."

The money disappeared into Jacob's pocket. He cupped his hand next to his mouth.

"Delivery!"

Four women carrying a jug each exited the house. Jacob pointed at Levi's car. "Put them in the back."

The young women's arms trembled as they walked down the porch steps. Dylan offered to help. Jacob shook his head.

"No. They'll manage. Leave them be. Hard work is a blessing, and this is a hard place."

Jacob licked his lips and slowly caressed his crotch as he watched his offspring struggling to get the jugs into the back seat without breaking them. After the girls closed the car door and scurried back into the home, Jacob held up his Bible. "Praise Jesus. Let us hope this is just the beginning of a long and profitable relationship between us, Mr. Bowman. See you next week?"

Levi's face was grim. He nodded. "Yeah. Next week."

Dylan sulked in the passenger seat until he could no longer keep quiet. "Now I know why you picked me to come with you today."

"Oh?"

"Dalton would have snapped after seeing what's being done to those girls. There would have been blood spilled. Bennett and Chance would be just as likely to say the wrong thing that might have killed the deal—or worse. So, you chose me, thinking I'd be the one to keep calm. And that's what I did, but it wasn't easy. I'm sitting here now wondering why in the hell we're doing business with that monster."

"Because the situation requires it. If we shut The Silo down now, I don't think we get it open again. We'll be finished. Whoever is responsible for what's been happening to us, whether it's Noretta or someone else, they'll have won. That's not acceptable. Believe me, I have no intention of making this deal with Piedmont long-term. I'm as disgusted as you are by that house of horrors."

Dylan watched the blur of trees through the passenger window. "Never again drink the wine for which you have toiled."

Levi turned his head to look at Dylan. "What?"

"That's what was written on that piece of paper Dalton found stuck with a knife to Chan's chest. I knew it sounded familiar. Then I saw that disgusting shit holding his Bible, and I finally remembered. It's from the Book of Isaiah. Piedmont pretends to be a man of God. What if he killed Chan to force us to buy from him?"

"Did you see any vehicles on his property?"

"No. Why?"

"How does he get all the way to Chan's from Index without a car?"

"Maybe he had help. There's a way to try and find out if he was there. We know somebody who might recognize him as the one who killed Chan."

"Who?"

"Winona."

"What do you have in mind?"

"We'll need two cars to collect those twenty jugs next week. I say we all go up there together and take Winona with us."

"If Winona goes, Dalton will demand he comes too. You know that, right? And you also know what he'll do if she points out Piedmont as the one who killed Chan and his whores. It'll be a mess–a big one."

Dylan nodded. "Yeah."

"You're really willing to risk the possibility of it going that bad?"

Dylan didn't reply. He didn't have to.

Levi already knew the answer.

Dylan remained the stubborn one.

18.

"This smells like something crawled up and died inside of something already dead." Laney pushed the cork back into the jug and set it down next to the three other jugs that were lined up in a row on the kitchen counter.

Levi rubbed his eyes and sighed. "I know. I'm hoping you can work some magic to lessen the stench and help it to taste better. It's strong stuff, so I figure we can water it down some. That'll help the flavor and make it last longer. We're supposed to pick up another twenty jugs next week."

Laney's mouth fell open. "Twenty jugs of *this*? Oh, Levi, tell me you have a better plan than to be buying our alcohol from that *thing* in Index. I won't serve it. I just won't. Not without boiling it first. We can't risk getting people sick."

"You do whatever you think is necessary to make this stuff sellable. We'll need a jug ready by tonight, though."

Laney turned on the stove and put her biggest pot on top of it. "I best get started then. What'll you be doing?"

"I have a meeting with Admiral."

Laney made the same face as when she first smelled the contents of the jug. "I'm not even going to ask. I don't want to know. Though I suppose Admiral is a step up from Jacob Piedmont."

"I would think so. Where's everyone else?"

"Dylan left early–something about a car. The other three went to go take another look at that barn of Noretta Saul's out on Woods Creek Road. They didn't tell you?"

"No, they didn't. Is Winona with them?"

"Of course. Poor thing is still too scared to leave Dalton's side."

Levi gave Laney a peck on the cheek. "Okay, I'm off to see Admiral. I should be back in a couple hours."

"You be careful. Watch yourself around that man. I mean it. Listen to a woman's intuition."

Levi said he'd be fine and then stepped outside. There was still a chill in the late morning air. It had rained heavily the night before. Puddles dotted the gravel driveway. The drive to Admiral's place took just a few minutes. He had lived in the same house for as long as Levi had been alive. It was a narrow single-story enclosed entirely inside of a tall cedar plank fence. Levi parked his car, got out, and pushed the fence gate open.

"An unannounced visit? You must be in some sort of trouble. Come on in, young man. I just put a fresh pot on."

Everything about Admiral's home was exactly as Levi remembered. The dining room was the same. The sitting room was the same. The long hallway leading to the kitchen and bedroom at the back of the house was the same: same colors, same framed photographs, same nicks in the wood floor, same everything. While the world outside might have passed Admiral by, the house embraced him in a never-changing reminder of the past.

"You like a little cream in yours, right?"

Levi took the cup of coffee. "Yeah. Thanks."

Admiral was about to sit but was interrupted by a knock at the door. He put his coffee down. "Be right back." He returned with Fenton Fenner in tow. Fenton removed his police officer cap and nodded at Levi.

"Hey, there, Mr. Bowman. Hope your day is going well."

"Pour you some coffee?" Admiral offered.

"No, thanks," Fenner said. "I won't be long."

Levi started to stand. "You want me to give you two some time to talk?"

"Actually, I'm here to see you, Mr. Bowman. I saw your car out front. Figured I'd save the trip out to your place."

Admiral grunted. "Of course, you're here to see him. Even in my own home I'm playing second fiddle these days. Would you like *me* to leave?"

Levi shook his head. "No need, Admiral." He looked at Fenner. "Go ahead and say what you came here to say."

Fenton shifted on his feet. "Uh, I wanted to give you an update on the Chan situation. I notified the county boys yesterday, being that Chan's place is out of my jurisdiction.

They didn't seem too interested in coming out here for a dead Chinaman and some no-name whores."

"That Chinaman was a friend of mine who was murdered along with the women who worked for him. He's been doing business with the people of this town for years and deserves a hell of a lot better than that kind indifference."

"I'm just the messenger here, Mr. Bowman. The county sheriff's office might get around to looking into it, and they might not. Just thought you should know. Wouldn't want you thinking I didn't reach out to the appropriate agency. I said I would, and that's what I done."

"So, this is your way of covering your ass with me?"

Fenton glanced at Admiral before answering Levi. "It was meant as a courtesy, Mr. Bowman."

Levi nodded. "I apologize, Fenton. Been a rough patch on a lot of fronts lately."

"There's no need for apologies. I understand. If I hear anything more, I'll be sure to let you know. And good day to you as well, Admiral."

After he heard the front door close, Admiral tilted his head, so he could see down the hallway to make certain it was empty. "He seem a little more jumpy than usual?"

"No, not particularly. Why?"

"I don't know. Just seemed different is all. Anyways, what brings you here?"

"I'm thinking of getting into production. Keeping it local. No more being dependent on someone like Chan who had his stuff shipped in from somewhere else. I want more oversight. More control over my own supply. Thought you might know of someone with distillation experience. They'd be well compensated."

Admiral set his cup down and ran a hand over his nearly hairless scalp. "Didn't you say once how much more dangerous it was on the production side of things? Law enforcement goes after manufacturers and importers far more than they do service joints, right?"

"That's my understanding."

"Then why the hell would you want to bring that kind of potential scrutiny down on yourself? Why not just keep running your little bar? Seems you've been pretty much left alone to do your thing. They find out you're not just serving alcohol but also producing, that might get the attention of someone who decides you're worth making an example of."

"I don't want to be depending on someone else to keep The Silo's doors open. And I want to be able to sell more not less. Sooner or later, Washington, D.C., is going to come to its senses and repeal the alcohol ban, and then the big money of the last few years will be gone just as quickly as it arrived. I need to act fast before it does to make all I can while the gettin' is still good."

"Huh. You actually think they're gonna make booze legal again?"

"I do. There'll be a shift in the political winds. Mark my words. It's coming."

"You might be right, but if they do give us booze back, they'll turn right around and take something else away. Government has spent too much on this prohibition mess to see it all just disappear. All those men, the newly formed departments, no way they go back to doing something else. Too much funding involved. Too much power. And either way, The Silo will still be here even if you can't charge quite as much for a sip."

"Not if I'm forced out of business first. Somebody's putting the squeeze on me, Admiral. If I could control production of my own booze and wasn't forced to wait around for a shipment to come in, they wouldn't be able to get at me so easy."

"You really think Chan was killed because he was your supplier? Couldn't it have been a competitor of his? Or someone he owed money to? An unhappy customer? Might not have had anything at all to do with you."

"Fenton didn't tell you about the note?"

Admiral frowned. "What note?"

"A knife was stuck into the middle of Chan's chest with a note on it."

"My goodness. Sounds downright medieval. What did it say?"

"It said enough to make me think it might have been directed at me."

Admiral folded his arms across his wide chest and leaned back in his chair. "Okay, but what's done is done. You taking on more risk isn't going to bring Chan back. You start out making your own booze just for The Silo, then soon you'll find you're not your only customer. No, you're selling it to others because there's even *more* money to be made. That's when the feds start real trouble for you."

"They could do that now."

"Nah, you're still small potatoes. Sure, around here you're the big man, but outside of Sultan you're a nobody—and that's a good thing. That's a *safe* thing."

Levi stared into his coffee cup. Admiral shook his head. "You're hearing my advice, but you're not gonna take it are you?"

"My mind is made up. I want access to my own supply. What I need from you is the name of someone with the know-how to produce a quality product at a fair price."

Admiral looked up at the ceiling. "Hmmm...well, there's that odd fella over in Index. The one with all the daughter-wives. Sells it by the jug I think."

"I know all about him. I said a *quality* product. Not rotgut."

"Well, excuse me, your majesty. I do recall this old moonshiner who lived way out beyond the end of Basin Road. It's about a two-mile hike through woods so thick you felt like you could hardly breathe. His people came from Virginia. Had a great-great grandpappy who fought in the Whiskey Rebellion. Me and a friend used to sneak up there on our horses when we were kids. It was an all-day ride. We'd tie the horses up and walk to his place. Bought my first bottle from him. Drank it. Got sick. Promised myself I'd never drink again.

We went back the next week. He cooked up a mighty fine brew."

"What's his name?"

"Cridert. He has to be dead by now."

"Then why the hell did you tell about him?"

"He had a little boy with him. Always stood a few steps back but never said anything. Rumor is he's still up there. He'd be about ten years older than you are now. I'd also bet he learned moonshining from his pa. And if he did learn it, he might be willing to do business with you–for a price."

"Thanks. I'll look into it." Levi pushed his chair back.

"Hold on," Admiral said. "There's the matter of my finder's fee. I can't be giving this kind of information away for free. Not even for you."

"Finder's fee? Really? You hurting for money?"

Admiral's jaw clenched, and his eyes flashed annoyance. "I provided you a service, Levi. I should be compensated. That's how things work around here. You know that."

Levi reached into his pocket. "How much you want?"

"I'm not interested in a one-time payment. I was thinking more along the lines of a limited partnership."

"I don't have partners and I don't intend to. I have a family, four sons and a fine woman who are all a part of my business, but no partners. Besides, I'm certain I just heard you sit there and try and talk me out of getting into booze production because you think it's too risky. Now you want to be a partner? What gives?"

"Despite the risk I see it the same as you–profit. I want my taste."

Levi stood. "My answer is no."

"Sit the fuck down, you ungrateful little shit."

Levi pulled back his jacket a few inches to reveal the butt of his revolver. "I gave you my answer."

"You and that gun of yours meant something around here--once. Yeah, you used to be fast, but when is the last time you had to pull it when it really counted? When there was a real chance you might just be a little too slow?"

"What the hell has gotten into you?"

"We go way back, Levi, but you didn't build this town–I did. *Me*. It was given to you on a silver platter. Don't ever forget that. You didn't take it. I gave it. Now all I ask of you is a little respect and some goddamn gratitude."

Admiral's big ham fist slammed the table. "Give me mine!"

"I'll ask one more time–how much?"

"Five percent."

"Five percent of *what*?"

"Five percent of the basin liquor profits."

"For how long? A year? Two years? Ten?"

"I'm an old man, Levi. You won't have to pay for long."

"I prefer things to be spelled out clearly."

"This *is* clear–five percent. We have a deal?"

Admiral stuck out his hand. "You said it yourself. You want more control over the supply. This could give you that control, and I would be the one helping you to get it. Five percent is more than fair. Considering all I've given you—it's also the right thing to do. How many times in this life do we get the opportunity to do the right thing?"

"Got to hand it to you, Admiral. You almost make it sound like it's a privilege to have you take money from me."

"This isn't just business, Levi—it's *good* business. The kind I taught you."

"I'll give serious consideration to the five percent, but I don't have partners—limited or otherwise. What's mine is mine."

Admiral's grin made his face look like a content pig. "That's fine. It's nice to be considered."

The two men shook on it.

It was another deal made.

And another hand in Levi's till.

19.

"You stay here with the car. It's okay. We'll be right back."

Winona wasn't having it. She followed Dalton across the road.

"She's loyal like a dog," Chance joked. Dalton wasn't laughing. He whirled around and grabbed his brother by the throat.

"Don't talk about her like that. She understands everything."

Chance started to choke. "Hey," Bennett said. "It was a stupid thing to say but he didn't mean nothing by it."

Dalton let go. Chance rubbed his neck. "One of these days, Dalton."

"One of these days, *what*?"

Bennett rolled his eyes. "C'mon you two. We don't have time for this shit." He motioned toward the other side of the road. "Shall we?"

Chance and Bennett led the way. Dalton and Winona followed. They had parked well back from the road behind a big cedar tree after deciding it would be better to walk to Noretta's barn this time instead of announcing their arrival by driving to it. It took nearly thirty minutes up and down side hills and through tall grass and damp ground before they stood at the barn's back entrance.

"They're treating this place like Fort Knox," Bennett said while moving toward the front of the barn. "Makes you wonder what they have in there. If it's booze how the hell are they getting it here? With the bridge washed out they'd have to walk it in by hand all the way from the road. That'd take forever."

Chance pushed against the back door with his shoulder. "I could break it down."

"Then they'd know someone was here," Dalton replied. "I thought we were trying to keep that a secret."

Chance still looked like he was pissed at Dalton. "Yeah, well, we also want to know what's going on inside the barn, right? They won't know who it was who broke in. We've come all the way out here. I say we do it."

Bennett walked around the corner. "Do what?"

"Chance wants to break the door in," Dalton said.

"But then they'd know someone was here."

"That's what I told him."

Chance pointed at the door as the big vein in the middle of his forehead popped out. "I'm not leaving here until I have a look at what's going on in there. And I'm sure as hell not going back to Pa and telling him we were stumped because

Noretta didn't leave us a welcome back sign and a plate of cookies." He pointed at Dalton and then pointed at Bennett. "So, fuck you, and fuck you, and let's figure this out."

Bennett rubbed his stomach. "Plate of cookies sounds really good about now."

Dalton felt something tug his sleeve. He looked down. It was Winona. She pointed up at a small window about six feet above the top of the locked back door.

"She really thinks you're gonna climb up there Dalton?" Bennett said while squinting at the window. "That's a small space. We might have fit through there when we were kids, but no way any of us pulls that off now."

Winona tugged harder on Dalton's sleeve. "You think you can get inside?" he asked her. She nodded.

Chance stepped aside. "It's worth a try."

Winona pulled Dalton's hands lower and then placed her foot into them. She kept her leg straight as Dalton lifted her up high enough until she was able to step onto his shoulders. He shuffled back toward the barn while holding tight to her lower legs. Winona's balance was perfect. She pushed the window open, grabbed hold of the sill with both hands, and pulled herself through. Dalton looked up just in time to see her feet disappear into the barn. They all heard a soft thump, the click of the lock, and then the door opened. A smiling Winona motioned for them to follow her inside.

Bennett touched one of several newly-constructed ten-foot-high shelves that nearly ran the entire length of the barn.

One of the shelves had several kerosene lamps on it. The rest were empty. The barn smelled clean and dry.

"None of this was here when Chance and I first saw it," Bennett said. "They've been busy."

"But why?" Chance asked.

From somewhere deeper in the barn, Dalton called out. "For storage. Come here."

Three crates that had been stacked in a corner. Dalton rapped the middle crate. "Each one is stamped."

"Where?" Bennett said.

Dalton pointed. "Right here."

"What's S&L Transport?" asked Bennett. "Never heard of it."

Dalton shrugged. "Me neither."

Chance ran his hand along the side of the top crate. "We need to have a look. Pull the top off. Nail it back in. Nobody will be the wiser."

Dalton grabbed hold of the top crate and set it on the ground. "Each of you get a side." He counted off. "One... two... three."

The brothers all lifted at the same time. The nails screeched as they were pulled out of the wood. Dalton set the crate lid aside. Chance carefully pushed back the straw and then gripped something cold and hard. He pulled it out and held it up.

It was a bottle. Chance uncorked it, smelled its contents, then tipped it back and had a drink.

"It's whiskey–*good* whiskey."

Bennet took a sip. "You're right. That's top-shelf." He turned the bottle over. "It's Canadian. What are crates of Canadian whiskey doing in a barn outside of Monroe?"

Chance counted eleven more bottles inside the crate. "Noretta's going to fill this place up with it–bottles and bottles. It's a distribution center. I say we burn it down. Use the kerosene in those lamps back there."

Dalton shook his head. "No."

"Why not?" Chance asked. "We take the whiskey with us and burn the barn. Let Noretta chew on that for a spell."

"Because she'll know we did it, that's why."

"So?"

"I'm with Dalton," Bennett said. "We want her thinking she's safe. Let her keep on planning whatever this is. We wait, and we watch. Then, when the moment is right, we take care of it. We take care of her."

Chance sighed. "Fine, we'll do it your way. Can we at least bring the bottle with us?"

Dalton took the bottle from Bennett, uncorked it, and had a long swig. He wiped his mouth with the back of his hand and smacked his lips together. "Mmmm... we're definitely taking it."

The straw was pushed back into place and the crate lid secured. The brothers went out the back door. Winona stayed inside. Dalton motioned for her to follow.

"C'mon, we got to go."

Winona shook her head. She pointed at the window.

"Shit," Bennett mumbled.

"What is it?" Chance asked.

"The door locks from the inside. They're gonna know somebody was here."

Winona shook her head again. Bennett glanced at Dalton. "Any idea what she's trying to tell us?"

Dalton looked up at the window. "She's gonna take care of it." He nodded to Winona. "Go ahead. I'll wait for you out here."

Winona shut the door. They heard it lock and then listened as Winona climbed up the exposed wood of the barn's interior wall. Her head poked out of the window. She inched herself forward, clung to the sill, and let her feet dangle while she pulled the window closed behind her.

"Now that's someone who knows the meaning of a job well done," Bennett said. "She's better than a circus act. You say you picked her up at Chan's?"

Dalton nodded.

Chance lit a cigarette as he continued to watch Winona hang from the window sill. "She's got to be the best thing we ever took from there, that's for sure."

Dalton held his arms out in front of him. "Go ahead. I got you."

Winona didn't even bother to look down. She let go. Dalton caught her. Their eyes locked for a moment. He pulled her closer. She didn't pull away.

Chance flicked cigarette ash onto the ground. "Hey, Bennett, check these two out. Ain't they sweet?"

Bennett rubbed his cheek. "Too sweet. I think I feel a cavity coming on."

Dalton set Winona down, shot his two brothers a hard look, and then started walking. "C'mon. Let's get back and tell Pa what we found."

After taking just a few steps Dalton stopped. He turned toward Bennett and Chance.

"When you two were here last, you noticed that part of the field where the grass has been cut down, right?"

Bennett nodded. "Yeah, like a road."

Dalton stared up at the sky. "It's not a road. It's a runway."

Chance's cigarette stopped halfway to his mouth. "Runway? You mean like for a plane?"

Dalton looked back at the barn. "Uh-huh. They're flying the stuff in. I saw it in France. Planes landing and taking off day after day using fields just like this. That down there is a runway. I'm sure of it."

"It's genius," Bennett said. "No roadblocks, no checking cargo at the shipyard or the train station. They just have it all flown right across the border to here. Credit where credit is due. If this was Noretta's idea, the woman is smart—real smart."

"Yeah, but then what?" Chance asked. "Where does it go from here?"

Bennett shrugged. "Wherever they want. If they were to fill a barn this size, they'd have enough booze to supply half the state. Bring the big loads in by plane, and then distribute it out from here in smaller amounts to make it easier to hide. It's like Bennett said—genius."

Chance looked like he was having a hard time envisioning such a vast operation. "Out here a plane is like an honest politician—rarely seen. One coming and going over Monroe all the time is bound to attract attention."

"Not if they fly at night," Dalton said. "Look around. Nobody else is out here. Remember those lamps in the barn? You light them up and put them down in a row along the runway. That guides the pilot in. He lands. They unload. He takes off."

Bennett had another sip of whiskey. "Then that's what we'll do. We come back here when it's dark to confirm they're using a plane. You in?"

Chance grabbed the bottle and drank. "Yeah." He passed it to Dalton.

"Me too," Dalton said after a long swig. He was about to give the bottle back to Chance when Winona reached out and snatched it from him. She brought it to her lips and tilted it back until half of what was left was gone. After lowering the bottle, she poked herself in the chest while looking at the others.

"You got your work cut out for you with this one big brother," Bennett said with a laugh. He kept on laughing as he continued the long walk back to the car.

Dalton hoped Bennett was right.

He had never wanted to work so hard before in his life.

20.

Twelve miles from Noretta Saul's barn, deep in the woods high atop the Sultan Basin, Levi Bowman was muttering a long litany of curses to himself. He lost count of how many branches had whipped his face, or the number of mosquito bites that now covered every inch of his exposed skin. The further into the forest he went, the more difficult it was to continue as the trees and brush grew thicker and thicker.

"Please don't move. I'd rather not have to kill you."

Levi went for his gun.

The world went dark.

Levi's head hurt, his eyes stung, and his mouth was dry as desert sand. He tried to move but couldn't. His hands were tied behind him. He looked down and saw his feet were bound as well.

"There you are. I'm real sorry for whacking you like that. You didn't give me much choice. I saw you going for the shooter. You mind telling me what you're doing out here?"

"Damn," Levi said. "You really did a number on me. Feels like I got a herd of elephants running through my skull."

"I said I'm sorry. I warned you not to move." Levi's vision cleared enough he could make out his captor's features: bald, lean-faced, gray whiskers, unusually large ears. Levi guessed him to be pushing up on sixty.

"Is your last name Cridert?"

"Who wants to know?"

Levi sat up. "I do."

"And who are you?"

"Name's Bowman–Levi Bowman."

"Never heard of you."

"Larson Kohl sent me. Everyone calls him Admiral. He told me he knew your pa."

The man didn't say anything to that. Levi looked around. They were inside a tool shed. Axes and saws hung from the walls.

"I came here to try and do some business with you, Mr. Cridert–cash money."

"Never said my name was Cridert."

"You never said it wasn't. Look, I won't hold a grudge about the thump to my head. I showed up here unannounced. You have every right to protect what's yours. I just thought you might be interested in getting paid. You know the name Larson Kohl?"

Cridert sat down on the floor cross-legged. "I might."

"Yeah, that's what he said. He also said your father was a hell of a moonshiner. That true?"

"He was. Died three years ago. He was eighty-seven. I miss him terribly."

Levi whistled. "That's a good long life. We should all be so lucky. Did he teach it to you?"

"Moonshining?"

"Yeah."

Cridert got up. He was tallish, all elbows, knees, and awkward angles. "Maybe. Can I trust that you won't try and hurt me if I untie you?"

"I didn't come here to hurt anyone."

"Say it. Say you won't hurt me."

Levi shut his eyes as another wave of pain enveloped his skull. "I won't hurt you."

"Just so you know, I already took your gun." Cridert pulled the rope loose from around Levi's hands and feet.

When Levi stood, he nearly fell over. Cridert caught him. "You okay?"

Levi took a few deep breaths and then nodded. "I'll get there."

"C'mon, let me show you around." Cridert opened the shed door.

Levi shuffled outside, bent over, and vomited. He spit the last of it out and wiped his mouth. Cridert looked like he was about to cry. "I shouldn't have hit you so hard."

"Well, you did."

"I'm gonna get you something that'll make you feel a whole lot better. Be right back."

With Cridert gone, Levi had his first real chance to look the place over. The branches that extended across the clearing were so dense hardly any daylight could get through. The area beneath the trees had been cleared out. There were no stickers, no stinging nettles, no thorny brush--just hard-packed dirt. The shed was the only structure Levi could see. He heard a sound above him. His eyes widened when he realized it was a door swinging shut.

Cridert lived in a tree.

There was a front porch, four walls, a door, and even a pair of windows all covered by a wood shake roof. Cridert opened the door and asked Levi if he felt good enough to come up. "Stairs are on the other side," he said with a smile.

Levi found the stairs. They were wood steps nailed into the side of the tree trunk that went around the tree to a small porch that was suspended forty feet off the ground. Levi carefully stepped onto the porch and looked up.

"My goodness."

The valley and the town of Sultan were spread out below him. Levi could see the bridge, both rivers, the top of the church, and his home.

It was beautiful.

"Not bad huh?" Cridert said. "You should see the sunsets in the summer. Every color you can imagine. It's the best show on earth."

"You built this?"

"I did–about five years ago. I grew up in the shed with my pa. That was the original home. Now I just keep the tools and whatnot in there. I remember climbing this tree as a kid, looking out at that view, and telling myself that one day I'd build a home up here."

"It's remarkable."

"Thank you. It was all done one nail, board, and shake at a time."

Cridert pointed to a clearing several hundred yards away that could be seen through a gap in the trees. "There's a little stream over that way. It provides all the fresh water I need. I built a garden shed over there as well. Insulated it with loads of lichen I picked off the rocks and tree branches. I grow potatoes most the year except during the very coldest months. Here, come on inside."

Levi stepped through the front door. The treehouse was just big enough for a narrow cot, a chest, a circular table with a chair, a bookshelf, and a little pot belly stove. The view through the windows was just as spectacular as from the front porch. It was a clean, bright, and cheerful place that smelled of dry pine and mountain air.

Cridert pulled out the chair. "Have a seat. I'm sorry if it's a little cold. I usually only use the stove when I'm cooking something or if its freezing outside. It warms it up in here nicely. I heat with tree bark mostly. It burns the hottest. I find trees that have already fallen over and then strip the bark from them. With as much wind as we get up here during the winter months, there's never a shortage."

Levi sat stunned by the little world Cridert had created. The bookshelf was stuffed with books on science, history, and engineering. Most the spines appeared to be badly worn.

"You do a lot of reading?"

Cridert nodded as he rummaged through the chest at the foot of the cot. "My pa collected them. He taught me the beginnings of how to read and write. Those books taught me the rest. I've likely read every one of them a hundred times. Ah, here it is!" He held up a dark bottle and a small glass and then placed them both in the middle of the table.

"What's this?"

"That," Cridert said, "is a bottle of my blackberry wine. I make some at the end of every summer. I only have a few bottles to work with. Used to have more, but I've broken the others and never bothered to replace them. You see, I don't much care for the world outside these woods. Pa was the same way. He used to trade with others–Indians mostly. They exchanged all kinds of things, but that wine was a favorite of theirs. He also made potato whiskey. We sold that to the white men–like your Mr. Kohl."

Cridert's words kept coming faster and faster, like a dam that was breaking apart. "When the Indians went away from here, Pa decided he'd had enough of people. He said we'd already collected everything we needed. I still have boxes of nails, tools, bags of seed, candles, lamp oil. I go through it all sometimes. Every piece of something comes with a story. Helps me to remember him."

Cridert uncorked the bottle. "Please, you have to try this. It'll help the hurt in your head. I promise."

"It's been my experience alcohol delivers a hurting *to* one's head, not the other way around," Levi said.

Cridert poured. The wine was the darkest Levi had ever seen--nearly black. He lifted the glass to his nose and breathed deeply. The smell reminded him of rich jam.

Cridert stood grinning as he waited for Levi to take a drink. "Go ahead."

Levi handed the glass to Cridert. "You first."

The grin fell from Cridert's face. "I don't understand."

"We just met. You live out in the woods alone--*in a tree.* You knocked me out, tied me up, and now you want me to have a drink? Fine—but you first."

Cridert's mouth formed a nearly perfect circle as his eyes got big. "Oh!" He shook his head. "You think I'd poison you? Now why in the world would I go and do that? We just met. I *did* untie you. That has to count for something."

Levi shrugged. "Maybe and maybe not. When's the last time you had someone other than yourself sitting at this table?"

"My pa is the only other one who has ever sat there, and that was just one time. He preferred the shed. Didn't like all the stairs it took to get up here."

"Which means I'm the first person you've talked to in three years?"

"Yes."

"Jesus."

Cridert stiffened. "Don't do that."

"What?"

"Say the Lord's name in vain. It's not proper."

"I'm sorry. I didn't mean to offend."

Cridert stared at Levi for a few long seconds and then drank the wine in a single gulp. He put the glass on the table. "That's okay. I forgive you because I believe you. You're just ignorant is all."

"Normally, I'd take offense at being called ignorant. Given I'm unarmed and forty feet up in a hermit's tree house, I guess I won't complain–this time."

Cridert refilled the glass. "Your turn."

Levi brought the glass to his mouth as Cridert watched. "Go ahead. Drink it down. You'll feel better. You really will."

Levi drank. "Hey, that's not bad." He pushed the glass toward Cridert who then happily poured more wine into it. "You hardly taste the alcohol. It's sweet but not too sweet."

"See? I knew you'd like it."

Levi took another drink. "You said you have just a few bottles of this?"

"That's right."

"If I brought you more bottles to fill, could you make more?"

"How much more?"

"Ten or twelve bottles a week? I'd pay you well."

Cridert put the bottle on the table. "I'm sorry, but I could never make that much. It takes weeks just to pick the berries, and you can only do that at certain times of the year. And besides, I'm not interested in money. I already have everything I need."

Levi leaned forward. "*Everybody's* interested in money."

"I'm not. I'd be happy to give you a bottle for free. Would you like that? And then you could come back after the summer, and I'd refill it for you with a fresh batch. And it wouldn't cost you anything then either, because... because we'd be friends."

"I should be going. I have family to get back to."

Cridert blocked the door. "You don't need to go just yet. I can boil up some potatoes for supper. You like potatoes, right?"

Levi stood. "I said I need to go. Thank you for the wine. It really was good–good enough that people would pay top dollar to drink it. Shame we couldn't make a deal."

"Wait. My father, he made a lot of whiskey for a very long time. Bottles and bottles of it. Even when people stopped coming here, he kept on making it. I don't know where he got all the bottles to put it in. He had the still going all the time. I cut so much wood to keep the fire going, I thought we'd run out of trees. He was obsessed. It's why these days I try not to cut down any trees. I feel obligated to let the woods grow back what we took from it. Funny thing about that. Pa hardly drank. A few sips here and there, but he mostly just finished one bottle, put it away, and started on the next."

"What happened to it?"

"It's in the cave right where he left it. All stacked and dry."

"What cave?"

"Where the still is."

"And where's that?"

Cridert smiled. "That's right. I didn't tell you. See? You don't want to leave yet. There's still more I can show you. It's over by the creek." He opened the door. "C'mon."

Levi followed Cridert down the stairs and then to a narrow path that dissected the thick undergrowth that surrounded the treehouse clearing and led into another clearing. A small stream was to the left. Cridert pointed to the right.

"This way." He walked up and then into the hillside. Levi had to stoop low to get through the opening in the rock but was then able to stand up. He could hear Cridert shuffling around somewhere deeper in the cave but couldn't see him. He was surprised by how dry and warm it was. When he moved his boots made little dust clouds where he stepped.

Cridert struck a match, lit a lamp, and held it up in front of him. The light made his grinning face look like an overly excited jack-o-lantern. "There's my father's still."

A greenish-gold copper tub sat in a corner of the cave next to two wood barrels. Next to that was a neatly-stacked pile of old firewood.

Cridert put the lantern on the ground and then grabbed hold of something. Levi realized it was a piece of burlap that was nearly the same color as the cave stone. "Seems the older

I get, the heavier this gets," Cridert said. "It goes all the way to the top."

Levi looked up and saw a length of rope stretching from one side of the cave to the other from which the tarp hung down from. With a grunt Cridert pulled the tarp back. It was too dark to see what was behind it. Levi picked up the lantern and held it high. Light reflected back at him like a thousand gleaming eyes.

He gasped.

"Jesus."

21.

"Check out at all those stars. You ever think there could be someone up there looking back at us?"

Bennett didn't wait for an answer. He kept on staring at the night sky while smiling, smoking and talking–three of his favorite things. "I mean, that's a lot of stars, and it seems real possible there could be life somewhere else. Maybe even another version of me. Imagine that!"

"God help us," Chance said.

The brothers had been sitting in the dark for nearly three hours watching and waiting for something to happen at Noretta's barn. Winona had wanted to come, too, but Dalton had firmly, but gently, told her to stay at the house. There might be danger, and he didn't want her getting hurt. The look on Winona's face as he got into Bennett's car made clear she wasn't a bit happy about being left behind. Dalton felt guilty about making her mad, but he knew it was best even as he didn't hide wanting to be back with her as soon as possible.

"How much longer we gonna give this?" Bennett asked.

Chance hadn't taken his eyes off the barn since they had settled in behind a hillside thicket nearly a hundred yards away. "A little longer, okay?"

Bennett lit another cigarette and pulled his coat tighter. "It's a cold one. Did we bring anything to drink?"

Chance reached into his jacket and brought out a flask. Bennett rubbed his hands together. "Ah, that's better!" He took a sip and promptly spit it out. "What the hell is this?"

"The stuff Pa brought back from Index. Laney said she was going to try and improve it."

Bennett kept spitting. "Good luck with that. Tastes like cat piss filtered through a dog's ass."

Dalton's gaze drifted sideways at Bennet. "You've tasted cat piss?"

"It's an expression. Stop being a smart ass."

Dalton put his hand out. "Let me try."

Chance gave him the flask. Dalton drank. He licked his lips, drank again, and then handed the flask back.

"I've had worse."

"Cat piss?" Bennett said with a wink.

"Maybe."

Chance pointed into the darkness. "Someone's coming."

A pair of headlights moved toward the barn. There was just enough moonlight to allow the brothers to make out the outline of a car. The vehicle stopped and a large man got out.

"Pretty sure that's Robert Saul," Chance said.

Dalton nodded. "Yup." He turned toward Bennett. "Put out your smoke."

Bennett paused with his cigarette a few inches from his mouth. "Oh, right. Don't want him to be able to see us up here."

Robert walked into the barn. Another hour passed. Bennett heard chewing, looked over, and then watched Chance take a bite of a cookie. "Where'd you get that?" he asked.

"Brought it with me. Laney baked up a batch the other day."

"You've been holding out on us? C'mon, give me one. I'm starving. Dalton, you want a cookie?"

Dalton didn't answer.

Chance plopped the last of the cookie into his mouth. "Sorry, that's it. You should have brought your own."

"How many did you bring?"

"A few."

"And you didn't bother to ask if we might want one? What the hell?"

"Since when am I responsible for keeping you fed? By the looks of it, you're doing just fine in that department."

Bennett poked Chance in the chest. "Now you're calling me fat?"

"Hey, if the cookie fits."

Bennett poked him again. Chance's tone let his brother know he was no longer joking.

"I'm gonna take that finger and pull it back until it breaks."

Bennett held his pointer finger in front of Chance's face. "I'd like to see you try."

Dalton pushed the two away from each other. "I didn't come here to babysit."

Chance shoved Dalton back. Bennett made an uh-oh look and moved to the side. "This isn't like before you left for the war Dalton," Chance said. "I'm not a kid. Stop treating me like one."

"I'm not treating you like a kid," Dalton growled. "I'm treating you like the annoying little shit you are who I'm gonna knock into the dirt if he doesn't focus on the real reason why we're here. Keep your mouth shut and your eyes and ears open. Got it?"

Chance's lower lip stuck out. It was a sure sign he was angry and about to say something that would get him into even more trouble.

"Put your lip away," Dalton said. "I'm in no mood for even one more word of your nonsense."

Chance clenched his fists. Dalton cocked his head. "You really want to try me Chance? *Really*?"

"Anyone else hear that?" Bennett asked.

Chance nodded. "Yeah, I hear something. What is it?"

Dalton turned around and looked up. "That's the reason we're here. See? That Robert fella is lighting the runway."

Nearly all the lanterns from inside the barn had been lit and set out over the field in two parallel lines. The noise above the brothers grew louder.

"Sounds like something with a bad cough," Chance said.

Bennett pointed. Of the four Bowman boys, his eyes had always been the sharpest. "There."

The plane lurched dangerously to one side before the stacked wings straightened. It appeared to hover for a few seconds before dropping down onto the grassy runway where it skidded, took out one of the lamps, and then came to a complete stop. The door opened, and the pilot hopped out just as Robert Saul reached the plane. The pilot was the shorter of the two and had narrow shoulders and hips. The brothers were too far away to see his face.

Robert opened a door in the belly of the plane, removed a crate, and took it into the barn. The pilot didn't help. He stood by himself several paces away from the plane in the darkness smoking a cigarette.

"From the looks of it, I'd say the flyboy is the one in charge," Bennett remarked.

"I'd agree," Dalton said. "That was a difficult landing. He managed it well. I'm guessing he flew in the war."

Chance crept down the hill trying to get a closer look. His brothers followed.

The pilot took off his leather flying cap, releasing a mass of long blonde hair. Chance and Bennett looked at each other wide-eyed as Dalton chuckled. "Now I've seen everything," he said.

Chance stared in wonder at the pilot smoking her cigarette. "That's a woman."

Bennett put an arm over Chance's shoulders. "Not that you would know much about it, but yeah, that down there is *definitely* a woman."

When Robert returned from the barn on his way to grabbing another crate, the pilot ordered him to hurry up. "She sounds tough," Bennett said.

"Tough, crazy, or likely both if she's willing to fly one of those contraptions." Chance whispered. "I still don't understand how they don't just drop out of the sky."

Bennett popped another cigarette into his mouth and prepared to light it. "I bet she's pretty."

Dalton grabbed the cigarette and threw it away. "No lighting up, remember?" Bennett barely acknowledged him. He had a faint smile on his face as he continued to watch the pilot.

"I sure would like to meet her," Chance said.

Dalton muttered to himself and shook his head. His brothers had once again managed to find something else to argue over.

"Meeting someone like that is man's work," Bennet replied. "You're not qualified. Best leave it to me."

After Robert carried four crates into the barn, the pilot closed the cargo door and climbed into the cockpit. Robert grabbed hold of the prop, rotated it a few times, and then backed away. The pilot's voice rang out. "Contact!"

The plane shook like a wet dog as its motor fired. The pilot drove it slowly to the end of the runway, turned around, and then sped back. She was nearly to the barn by the time the plane lifted off the ground. With its nose pointed almost straight up, the engine cut out. The plane drifted backward. The motor coughed, growled, and then roared as the aircraft righted itself. It climbed higher and higher until it disappeared completely into darkness.

Chance shook his head. "In all my life I've never seen anything like that. I mean that was *something!*"

Bennett noticed Dalton staring at the barn. "What now?" he asked him. "We know they're using the barn to store booze and how the booze is getting here. What we don't know is what they plan to do with it. Are they going to sell it in Monroe or somewhere else?"

"Doesn't matter," Dalton answered. "We give it a few more days. Let them fill the barn up. Then we come back here, and we take it. We take all of it."

Chance turned around. "That's gonna be a lot of alcohol to move. We'll need to bring more vehicles. A lot more."

Dalton was already heading back to the car. "Then we bring more. Let's go."

Chance lingered on the hillside staring up at the spot in the night sky where the plane had disappeared into. He took out a cookie and bit into it, smiling as he chewed.

22.

"I tried. It's just too vile. It can't be made any better than that."

Levi took another sip. "It's really not so bad. Much better than before. The mint was a nice touch. We can sell this."

Laney frowned. "Not at regular prices. It wouldn't be right. We do have a reputation for serving a quality product, and this is far from quality."

"We'll offer it at a discount. Even then we'll still make a decent profit."

"Are you really going back to Index and pick up another twenty jugs?"

"Yes. I gave my word and shook on it. After that, my business with Piedmont will be done."

"Good. That's a promise you're making to *me*, Levi Bowman. Don't you dare break it."

Levi lit a cigarette. His head dropped a little to the side as he looked at Laney and smiled. "I know better."

Laney poured them both a drink from one of the bottles Levi had brought back from Cridert. "Now *this* on the other hand, is going to sell out about as fast as we can stock it. It's liquid gold."

They clinked their shot glasses together and then drank it down. "Mmmm, you're right about that," Levi said. "About the smoothest whiskey I've ever had."

"And this Cridert you met up there is just giving it to you? All of it?"

"Yeah. I told him I couldn't take it all at once. That it would have to be done over several trips. I think that's really all he cares about–having someone to talk to from time to time."

"And you like him?"

Levi drew from his cigarette and shrugged. "He's okay. A bit eccentric."

"Is he trustworthy?"

"As much as I can tell. Even though he doesn't care about the money I don't feel right not giving him anything for all that whiskey. I'll figure out a way to pay him something back. I didn't count it, but I'd guess there's a thousand bottles or more stacked inside that cave."

Laney glanced up at the ceiling. Levi could see her mouth moving. "You're doing the math aren't you?"

"We get about twenty shots per bottle at fifty cents per shot. That's a value to us of ten dollars per bottle for basic whiskey. Cridert's stuff is a lot better than just basic. We could charge more. A *lot* more. Maybe as much as a dollar a shot.

That would make every bottle worth twenty dollars. If he's sitting on a stash of at least a thousand bottles that's twenty thousand dollars value to us that we would be getting *for free*."

"I know. It's good money."

"That's more than good money, Levi. Around here, it's a fortune. What about Admiral? Didn't you say he wanted a piece of whatever your brought back from Cridert?"

"Admiral will get his five percent."

"I doubt he'll be expecting five percent of twenty thousand dollars."

"I imagine he won't."

Laney scowled. "Unless he is."

The two were interrupted by the arrival of a man they'd never seen before. He looked to be at least ten years older than Levi. He was tall, lean, and walked a bit slanted like one leg was longer than the other. His gray hair was combed back from a deeply-lined forehead. Even deeper lines framed a downturned mouth that sat beneath a hooked nose and small, deep-set green eyes. He was clean-shaven, and his clothes fit him snug like they were tailored just for him: dark wool jacket and matching trousers, crisp white dress shirt, and a pair of rattlesnake cowboy boots.

An ivory-handled revolver hung off his hip. He glanced at Levi and Laney as he moved past them. His boot heels thumped hard against the wood floor. He sat down at the very end of the bar.

"Get you something?" Laney asked.

"Whiskey," the stranger answered.

Laney poured him a shot from one of the Index jugs. He emptied his glass and then grimaced. "People actually pay you for this shit?" His spoke with the hint of a southern drawl.

Laney locked eyes with him. "They better. That'll be twenty cents."

The man pursed his lips in a little half-smile way that made it clear Laney's acting tough amused him. He dropped two dimes on the counter. "What happens if they don't?" He looked sideways at Levi. "They have to deal with him?"

"That's if they're lucky," Laney said. "The not so lucky ones have to deal with me."

The stranger chuckled. "A place like this, out here amongst all these trees, I was expecting something rougher. This is a pleasant surprise."

"What brings you here?" Levi asked.

The man swiveled on the stool, so he could look at Levi straight on. "For now, I'm just wanting to rest a bit and have a drink."

"And later?"

"Who knows? Guess we'll all wait and see."

Laney reached down with one hand to make sure the shotgun was still under the bar where she had last left it. "What's your name?"

The stranger looked her up and down and smiled. "It's Calwin Quick. Perhaps you've heard of me?"

"No. Why would I?"

The man slid his shot glass toward Laney. She refilled it. "Oh, you might say I've led something of a colorful life. Born in southern Kentucky. Spent several years in what used to be the Dakota Territory. I was barely older than a boy at the time. Could handle myself, though. Knew Seth Bullock from Deadwood. That name mean anything to you?"

"Nope," Laney replied.

Calwin put his hand around the shot glass but didn't drink. "Huh. And here I thought I was among educated folk. Seth Bullock was friends with Teddy Roosevelt. You've heard of *him*, right?"

Laney stuck her chin out. "Sounds familiar."

"Well, old Seth passed on a few years back. We'd lost touch before then. I read about it in the papers. Anyways, I left Dakota and worked for the Pinkerton office in Coeur d'Alene under the leadership of Charles Siringo during that nasty labor dispute with the Gem Mining Company. Any of that ring a bell?"

"Is there a point to you telling me your history, Mr. Quick?"

Levi cleared his throat. "He wants us to think he's someone important because he once knew people who actually *were* important."

Calwin wagged a finger at Levi but kept his eyes on Laney. "Mr. Bowman, you're coming dangerously close to outright rudeness."

Levi put his cigarette out, stood, and inched open the shoulder holster side of his jacket. "You know my name."

Calwin kept looking at Laney. "That I do."

Levi's hand drifted toward his gun. "Why are you here?"

Calwin turned. He was still grinning. "I wouldn't do that if I were you, Mr. Bowman. I've been told you were pretty fast at one time. If you're thinking of drawing on *me*, well, pretty fast isn't nearly fast enough. I'll shoot you dead sure as the sun rises in the east and sets in the west. You see, I kill people, Mr. Bowman. Those in my line of work don't live to be my age if they aren't good at that sort of thing, and I assure you I'm very good. I don't mean to come off as arrogant, but there really is no other way to say it. When it comes to killing, I might just be the best there ever was."

Levi kept his hand close to his gun. "Who do you work for? Is it Noretta?"

Calwin slid off the stool, rolled his head from side to side, and then let out a long sigh. "I'm sorry to say this isn't yet our time, Mr. Bowman. It will come, and I'm certain it'll come soon. Maybe not soon enough for me, but likely much too soon for you. You best get your things in order. Until then, the both of you have a lovely afternoon."

Calwin moved toward the exit. Levi stepped in front of him. "I asked who sent you."

Calwin stood a few inches taller than Levi. He looked down and shook his head. "That's not important, Mr. Bowman. What *is* important is that I'm here. Even more important to you is that I'll be back. When I am, you best be ready."

Laney pointed the shotgun at Calwin's back. "We'll be ready all right."

Calwin scratched his nose and snickered. "You're pointing that blaster you kept reaching for behind the bar aren't you, Ms. Lorne? I know all about how you recently used it to splatter a man's brains against a wall in here. I admire that kind of initiative. I truly do. But you know that if you pull that trigger, you're just as bound to hit me *and* Mr. Bowman. You don't strike me as a fool, so I'm confident in calling your bluff. Take care now."

Calwin stepped around Levi and walked out. Laney lowered the shotgun. Levi hadn't realized he'd been holding his breath. He exhaled loudly.

"Was that Noretta Saul's doing?" Laney asked.

Levi went back to the bar and sat down. "That would be my guess."

"So, what are we gonna do about it?"

"Don't know."

"You think he's as big a threat as he makes himself out to be?"

"It's been my experience that a man who talks himself up that much is trying to hide weakness."

Laney lit a cigarette. "And this time?"

Levi was quiet as he turned his hand over and stared at it. He looked up. "His pistol grip was worn. It's seen a lot of use."

Laney slowly traced the inside of Levi's palm. She felt the callus on the bottom of his trigger finger. Levi slowly closed his hand around hers. "Can you handle him?" she asked.

Levi didn't answer.

THE BOWMAN BOYS

23.

The Bowman boys were bored. For the rest of Sultan, that usually meant trouble.

"No way you can make that turn."

Dylan's impish grin as he gripped the wheel said different. "Wanna bet?"

Bennett glanced at the back seat where Chance, Winona, and Dalton sat. Chance shook his head. "You dumbass. You're gonna total your new car the day after you bought it."

Dylan revved the engine. "You know what that sound is? That's a flathead V-8. Seventy horsepower. She'll do sixty in a pinch."

Dalton grimaced. "Sure, but how fast can it stop?"

Dylan kept revving the new Cadillac's motor. "No brakes all the way down. I'll make the turn at the bottom and then coast to The Silo. If I make it, you all pay up–five dollars each."

"Yeah, and if you *don't* make it we're the ones who'll have to scrape what's left of you off the road," Bennett said.

Dylan put the car in gear. "What? I figured we'd all do this together. You chickening out? How about you Winona? You in?"

Winona sat between Dalton and Chance. She glanced at them both and then nodded. Dylan clapped his hands together.

"Hah! Apparently, the young lady has more courage than the big, strong, and *cowardly* brothers sitting beside her."

"And just as likely more brains than the one behind the wheel," Chance said. "At least you're already dressed for your funeral. Is that *another* new tie?"

Dylan adjusted the knot around his neck. "It matches the Cadillac—wine red. Each one compliments the other. It's basic color coordination."

Bennett placed his hand against the side of his face and shook his head. "I have to wonder if Ma was sneaking around because for the life of me sometimes I don't know where you came from. Matching the color of your tie to the color of your car? Who the hell does that?"

Dylan put his hands back on the wheel and stared straight ahead. "I do."

"He'll chicken out," Chance said. "He knows he can't make that turn without putting on the brakes first."

Dylan gripped the shifter. "You ready to find out, little brother?"

Dalton reached up and flicked the back of Dylan's head like he was testing a melon for ripeness. "Go ahead. Chance is right. You'll slow down before the turn. And when you do, you'll owe each of *us* five dollars–including Winona."

Dylan adjusted the rearview mirror, so he could see Dalton's face. "You covering her share?"

"Yeah," Dalton answered.

"What about you, Bennett?" Dylan asked. "You in? If not, you'll have to get out here and watch. Then I'll come back for the money you owe me."

Bennett lit a cigarette and shrugged. "Sure, why not? I'm just sitting in the front seat. That means if this goes bad I most likely get to take a ride through the windshield. That'll be great. Just great. I can't collect my five dollars if I'm dead."

Dylan put the car in gear and stomped on the accelerator. The rear tires spit gravel. He had to shout so he could be heard over the roar of the engine.

"It's about a thousand-foot drop from the top of the Basin hill to the bottom. We'll coast all the way down–no brakes."

Chance leaned forward and pointed at Dylan's feet. "I'm watching. No cheating."

Dylan grinned. "Here we go."

The Cadillac moved at just over twenty miles an hour. Dylan put the car in neutral. Winona hid her face in her hands and peeked out between the spaces of her fingers.

Bennett puffed furiously on his cigarette while Chance bit down on his lower lip and Dalton looked like he was about to fall asleep. The Cadillac's plush interior was filled with the sound of the tires moving over the uneven gravel. Dylan had to keep correcting the steering to prevent the car from drifting off the road.

"Thirty miles an hour!" he yelled.

Bennett finished his cigarette and quickly lit another one. "I don't know about this," Chance said from the back seat.

Dalton closed his eyes. "It'll be fine."

By then, Dylan's confidence appeared to be wavering. His knuckles were white where he gripped the wheel. The Cadillac slid to the left.

Bennett winced. "Keep it straight!"

Dylan turned the wheel hard to the right. The Cadillac's steel frame groaned as the back wheels started to spin sideways. "Fuck me," Chance said. Dalton opened his eyes, yawned, and then closed them again.

The car straightened out. The speedometer showed forty miles an hour. Dylan's forehead was covered in sweat. They struck a pothole. The top of Bennett's head bounced against the roof causing his cigarette to drop from his mouth and fall into his lap.

"Don't you dare burn my seat," Dylan told him.

Bennett slapped at his lap until he found his cigarette. He promptly stuck it between his teeth and laughed. "Crotch burn."

"Fifty miles an hour," Dylan called out. "We're halfway there."

Everyone stopped talking. The only sound was the whoosh of the wind and the crunch of the tires. The tobacco smoke coming out of Bennett's nose made him look like a nervous steam train.

The speedometer hit sixty. Every time the Cadillac rushed past one of the big trees that grew alongside the road, it made a paper ripping noise that shook the car's windows.

"We hit something going this fast, there'll be nothing left of us," Chance said.

Dylan gripped and re-gripped the wheel. "That won't happen."

They were nearly to the bottom of the hill. The sharp turn onto U.S. 2 was straight ahead.

"Slow down," Bennett whispered.

Dylan didn't touch the brake.

Bennett repeated his warning. "Dylan, there could be traffic. You have to slow down."

Chance joined the plea. "C'mon Dylan. The bet is off. Hit the brakes. You won't make the turn."

The road flattened out. The car slowed to fifty. U.S. 2 was just two hundred feet further.

"Brakes!" Bennett yelled.

Dylan ignored him. He was focused on timing the turn. Everyone went quiet again.

Fifty feet. Thirty feet. Ten.

Dylan spun the wheel hard to the right. The Cadillac's nose lurched while the back end screeched and drifted. Dylan hissed as he turned the wheel back to the left. A horn. A truck.

A second horn blast. The smell of burnt rubber. Bennett screamed.

The Cadillac rocked from side to side. Dylan's head struck hard enough against the side window he worried the glass would crack. It didn't. The truck missed them by inches. Dylan straightened the wheel. Sweat-drenched strands of hair stuck to his forehead. The car kept coasting.

"Thirty miles an hour," he said.

Bennett lit another cigarette with shaking hands. His breath escaped from between his lips in short little bursts. He looked at Dylan.

"You could have killed us."

Chance leaned over the front seat. "Hold on. You're supposed to make it all the way to The Silo. There's another two hundred yards to go."

"Shit," Dylan said. "You're right."

Chance pointed at the speedometer. "Twenty miles an hour. We're slowing down. Looks like you'll be paying us."

Bennett started to rock from side to side. Dylan shoved him. "Knock it off. Don't interrupt the forward momentum."

Chance laughed. "You hear that, Bennett? The professor asks that we not interrupt his forward momentum."

"That's what she said," Bennett teased. Though she didn't make a sound, Winona put her hands over her mouth like she was stifling laughter. The car kept moving.

"We're gonna make it," Dylan said. "Almost there. All I need is to have one tire in the parking lot."

Bennett shook his head. "No, no, no. It has to be the *entire* car. Otherwise, you pay up."

Chance nodded. "I'll second that."

Dylan rolled his eyes. "I see how it is. I make the turn just like I promised, and now you two are acting like you weren't shitting yourselves before. I'm pretty sure Bennett was the one screaming."

"Oh, I'll admit I was concerned, but I wasn't even close to shitting myself. And I sure as hell didn't scream."

Dylan gave Bennett a quick sideways glance. "Uh-huh."

The Cadillac coasted at just over ten miles an hour. The Silo was straight ahead.

Chance pointed to the back of The Silo. "Double or nothing you can't park it behind Pa's car."

"Deal," Dylan said as he aimed for the indentation in the parking lot he had driven over countless times before.

"It won't be enough," Bennett chuckled.

The Cadillac slowed. "Hah!" Chance shouted. The front wheels crept over the hard-packed little hill. Dylan leaned over the steering wheel. "C'mon," he whispered.

The car inched ahead and then stopped ten feet behind Levi's car. Dylan leaned back in the seat grinning. "We made it."

Bennett's face tightened. "Hmmm, I don't know..."

"Pay him," Dalton said.

Seconds later Dylan leaned against the hood of his car and collected his winnings. Chance and Bennett looked grief-stricken as they handed over the money. Dalton had them take Winona inside. He waited until the door closed and then turned to face Dylan. He didn't seem angry, but something was clearly bothering him.

"What's up?" Dylan asked.

Dalton stuck his hands into the pockets of his jacket and looked down." You push it too far, Dylan."

"Too far? What do you mean?"

"I mean, that stunt going down the hill. Why? Why do it? There were all kinds of ways for that to go wrong and only one way for it to go right. There's something inside of you that makes you take risks that shouldn't be taken. If it keeps happening, sooner or later your luck's gonna run out."

"Dalton, that wasn't luck that got us down the Basin. It was skill. I knew I could do it."

Sadness flickered across Dalton's eyes. "I was around guys like you in France. They were convinced they were bullet proof. Young and dumb and in the end all dead--every single one."

"And you think I'm like them?"

"Not think, I *know* you are. You believe you're just out of reach of everything and everyone. That the normal rules don't really apply to you, but they do. Dead is dead, and if you're stupid enough death won't care. It'll get you. I don't want to see that happen."

"Dalton, I don't mean to offend, but it wasn't that long ago you spent every hour of every day hiding from the world behind the door in your room. Now you think you're qualified to dispense life lessons to *me*?"

"This isn't about me being qualified or not. It's about me being your brother. Pull the arrogance out of your goddamn ears and listen for once. I suppose nobody would confuse me for being the smart one, but on this, I know what I'm talking about. The life we live, our family, it's plenty risky on its own, especially now. Why add to it? Why push it further? There's no need."

Dylan held out his hand. "Pay up."

"That's all you have to say? *Pay up*?"

Dylan shrugged. "A bet's a bet and fair is fair. And don't forget how you said you'd cover Winona's share."

Dalton slapped the money into Dylan's hand hard enough it made Dylan wince. "Straighten up. This family needs everyone to be ready and prepared for what's coming. This isn't a game or a bet. It's real life with real consequences. We all need you."

"Even you?"

Dalton blinked several times like he'd been slapped in the face. His shoulders slumped. "Yeah, especially me."

The Silo's back door opened, and Levi's head poked out. "Everything okay out here?"

Dylan hooked an arm around Dalton's wide shoulders. "Yeah, everything's fine, Pa."

"Good. Then come on in. We have some things we need to go over."

Dylan extended his other hand toward the door. "Age before beauty."

Dalton shrugged Dylan's arm off. "Idiot."

"Love you too big brother."

Dalton glared at Dylan. Then his features softened. He was trying not to smile. "Get your ass inside. Pa's waiting."

24.

L evi sat down with his four sons and told them about Calwin Quick while Winona helped Laney clean the bar.

Bennett smacked the table hard enough it made the whiskey glasses rattle. "I say we go find the son-of-a-bitch and end him."

Levi put out his cigarette and shook his head. "No."

"We can't just sit and wait for him to come for you."

"If and when Quick comes back, I'll know about it. He wants an audience—a show. The man is an attention whore. That much I'm sure of."

Chance scowled. "So, we just let him get away with threatening us?"

"For now, it'll be business as usual. We move forward with the poker tournament. We keep an eye on Noretta's barn. Bennett and Chance, you're the ones I want taking a trip to Bellingham this time. Find the lumberyard that used to belong to Noretta's husband—the one Titus Lemkee bought from her. I want to know if it's connected to the plane you saw bringing the crates of alcohol into Monroe. If it is that means Lemkee and Noretta are working together."

Dylan looked up from his whiskey glass. "And what do we do if they are?"

"I'm not sure," Levi answered. "It'll be better to know what we're up against, though. That brings me to you and Dalton. The both of you go to Index and pick up the last of the Piedmont jugs. Tell him we won't be needing any more. That might piss him off. Be ready for possible trouble."

"Be *careful*," Laney added.

Levi nodded. "Yes, all of you watch yourselves out there."

There was a loud knock from outside. Laney went to see who it was. Levi told Chance to go with her. They came back with Admiral. His face was flushed and covered in sweat.

"Thought I'd stop in to say hello. Haven't been inside your place for some time. Business must be pretty good if you can afford to lock the front door in the middle of the day."

Levi stood. "We were having a family meeting."

"Oh, I'm sorry. I didn't mean to interrupt."

If Laney's eyes were knives, they would have already been cutting into Admiral's flesh. "Yet here you are doing exactly that."

Admiral ignored the remark and kept shuffling toward Levi.

"Can you all give me a moment with Admiral?" Levi said. The brothers and Winona left. Laney stayed.

Admiral licked his lips. "Boy, I'm parched. How about a glass of your best?"

Laney rolled her eyes and walked behind the bar as Admiral plopped down in a chair across from Levi. Levi lit a cigarette and peered at Admiral through a curtain of smoke. "Did you walk all the way here?"

Admiral nodded. "I did. Been walking more and more lately. Lost a bit of weight. Hell, I might come out of retirement and see if I can still run this town like I used to." He smiled. "With your permission of course."

Laney dropped one of the Index jugs in front of Admiral along with a full shot glass. "We can all hope," she said.

Admiral took a sip and then flinched. "Eeewww, this is your finest?"

"That," Levi said, "is the shit that comes out of Index."

"You're actually able to sell it?"

"We manage. Laney cleans it up a bit so it's not quite so offensive."

"And what version did she just give me?"

Levi pulled the jug toward him and sniffed the top. "I'd say you were given the original in all its natural glory."

Admiral pushed the glass away. "I can see why you told me you needed a supply other than Index. How'd the Basin shake out for you? Any luck?"

"Maybe."

"Is there really still a Cridert living up there?" Levi didn't answer. "Well I'll be damned," Admiral said. "How much?"

"How much what?"

"Don't play dumb with me. How many bottles can he produce for you? Will it be enough to keep the doors open?"

"He doesn't brew like his father did, so he's not a long-term solution to my inventory problem. Rest assured I'll make good on your share of the profits."

Admiral rested both his meaty forearms on the table. "How much profit are we talking?"

"I don't know yet."

"What if I told you I might have a way to keep the booze flowing for The Silo?"

"I'm listening."

"Noretta Saul," Admiral whispered.

Levi casually puffed on his cigarette. "You're gonna have to explain that one. I'm pretty sure she's doing her best to stamp me out permanently."

"Maybe so. That's where I come in."

Levi stared at Admiral and waited. Admiral sat up straight, folded his hands, and cleared his throat. "I know you two haven't been playing nice. And we both know that's not good for business. I think I can mediate something between you and her. An agreement, an understanding, whatever the hell you want to call it."

Levi's eyes narrowed. "A partnership?"

"No, nothing like that. Just an arrangement to keep the peace is all."

"And you're going to do this out of the kindness of your heart?"

"Of course not," Admiral said. "Same as before–I get five percent."

"Five percent of *what*? I don't do business with Noretta Saul. That means you're getting five percent of nothing."

Admiral propped his elbows onto the table and pointed at Levi. "There you go. You two *will* do business. A lot of business. A lot of money. Nobody gets hurt. Everybody stays alive. Everyone wins."

"Cut to the chase Admiral. What business are you talking about?"

"It's simple. Noretta can be the long-term supply you need."

"You think she has that kind of access to alcohol?"

Admiral poured himself another drink from the Index jug and then held the glass up in front of him. "That's the rumor, one you're likely already aware of, and it's a far better product than this sewage. If she's bringing alcohol in, she'll need buyers. Why not you? Why not The Silo? You benefit. She benefits. We all benefit."

"Noretta Saul has attacked my family and my reputation. She's made it clear she wants to destroy my business. If she's somehow bringing alcohol into the area, I assume it's to open her own drinking establishment. Working with me would be working with the competition. Why would she do that?"

Admiral put the shot glass down. "You let me worry about the how and why. I'm willing to bet she doesn't want you and your boys coming after her any more than you want her and her goons coming after you."

"Goons?"

"Goons, her cousin or nephew, whoever the other one is whose ear Dylan nearly cut off."

"Do you know of anyone else working for her?"

Admiral frowned, "No, why would I?"

Levi put out his cigarette. "You talk like you would know."

"I'm here to try and help. That's all."

"And your five percent."

"Why do you keep mentioning the fucking five percent? It's like anything else I say you don't hear."

"The five percent was *your* idea. That means it's important to you. I just want you to know I won't forget."

Admiral picked up the shot glass, threw his head back, and emptied it. He slammed the glass upside down onto the table. "I really don't care for your tone, Levi. You want my help or not?"

"How do you figure on making this meeting happen?"

"I already reached out to Mayor Brown. I've known his family for years. You know that. The sit down will take place at his office–a neutral location where both you and Noretta Saul can feel safe. Just you and her–nobody else."

"You actually think she'll go for it?"

"Sure. Why not? At the end of the day, it's about money, right? It's *always* about money. She wants it. You want it. So, let's all make some goddamn money."

Levi leaned back in his chair. "No, it's not always just about money. There are principles involved–namely to the people of this town."

"Yeah, right, Levi Bowman the saint of Sultan. Give me a break. The people of this town fear you and your little private army of four sons. Don't think it's anything more than that. Noretta already has some of them turning against you. Besides, don't you feel preventing a war between you two is the right thing for the town?"

"I don't know, Admiral. Even if you managed to bring us together to talk, and then somehow, we agreed to terms, that agreement is only as good as Noretta's word. Why should I trust her not to stab me in the back the first chance she gets?"

"If you don't do something, there'll be an all-out war. Are you willing to risk one of your boys getting killed in the crossfire because you were too scared to have a sit down with a woman?"

Levi shook his head. "Stop it."

"What?"

"Stop baiting me. This isn't about my being afraid or her being a woman. I had a visit from somebody today. A fella named Calwin Quick. Sound familiar?"

"No. Should it?"

"He seemed to think his name meant something. Anyway, he showed up here dragging all kinds of threats with him. Gun hanging off his hip. He's a bit older. Had that look about him."

Admiral's brows lifted. "Look?"

"Yeah, the look a man gets when he's seen plenty, and killed plenty, and stopped feeling anything about it a long time ago. It's reflected in the eyes, like a vacancy sign for the soul."

"What did he want?"

"To scare me."

"That's no simple thing. You don't scare easy."

"No, I don't. He said he's coming back. Told me to be ready."

"For what?"

"To die."

Admiral shifted in his chair.

"Christ, Levi, let me help to make a deal between Noretta and you, so we can put an end to all this shit. I assume this Quick was someone she hired?"

"Probably."

"Then we don't have any time to waste. I can do this for you. For all of us. We don't need blood in the streets. Men like you and me, we already have enough blood on our hands, and it don't ever wash away. Not completely."

Levi fired up another cigarette. "How soon can you make it happen?"

"Oh, uh, with the mayor's help, I figure very soon. A day or two, three at the most. Just say the word."

"You almost sound desperate. That's an odd thing coming from you. Like a suit that don't quite fit."

Admiral's head dropped, and his voice lowered. "I *am* desperate. This is a chance for me to have some purpose again. To do some good before whatever time I have left is gone. Is that so wrong? You're like a son to me, Levi. I don't have a family. You're the closest I got to that. Let me help you before it's too late."

Levi blew a couple of smoke rings, flicked his cigarette, and then nodded. "Okay."

Admiral leaned forward. "If I make the meeting happen, you'll go to the mayor's office in Monroe? I have your word?"

"Yeah, you have my word."

Admiral's big meat hook of a hand reached across the table. The two men shook. Admiral pushed himself out of the chair. "You're doing the right thing. Hopefully, it'll keep the people you care about most from getting hurt. I'll be in touch." He turned and lumbered toward the exit. The weight of his steps made the floorboards creak. He glanced at Laney. She glared at him. He nodded. She didn't nod back but watched him go until he was gone.

Laney's head swiveled toward Levi. "I know you're no fool, Levi Bowman. Tell me you aren't seriously going to let that man coral you into going to Monroe for some bullshit sit down with Noretta Saul."

Levi got up. "Laney, honey, let's just see how this plays out."

"*Plays out*? No--nothing good will come from this. I don't know how or why, but I can feel it. He's manipulating you. Do you actually trust him?"

"Not entirely."

"Then why go along with his idea for a meeting?"

"Because it might actually help to keep you and the boys safe. That's it. And that's enough. Any time, every time, that will *always* be enough to get me to do something."

"You ever consider how Admiral might be using your need to keep us safe as leverage to get you to do what he wants?"

Levi bit down on his cigarette. "If there's a meeting, I'm going to it. End of discussion. You serve the drinks. I take care of everything else. That's our deal."

Laney's eyes flared. *"That's our deal*? What does that mean?"

"It means I'm gonna do what I'm gonna do, and I don't need an earful from you when I do it."

"Oh. I see. So, I pour the drinks, make the meals, clean the bar, clean the house, open the bar, close the bar, and then make sure that while doing all that I also keep my mouth shut. Do I have that about right?"

"I don't want to argue."

"I'm afraid that train has already left the station. I also see that since there are no customers here for me to pour drinks for, *per your orders*, I'll just leave so you can go on with doing what you're gonna do."

Levi strode toward the office door. "No, you stay. I'll go."

A glass shattered against the wall a foot from Levi's head. "Stop telling me what to do!"

Levi paused but didn't turn around. Laney threw another glass. "Go on," she said. "Get out!"

Levi slammed the door behind him. He sat down at his desk, stood, sat, then stood again. A minute passed. He could hear Laney cleaning up. He walked out of the office and found Laney bent over sweeping bits of glass into a dustpan. She looked up revealing cheeks wet with tears.

"I know I can't stop you from going to that meeting. I also know you're doing it because you think you have no choice, and that's what scares me the most. Everything I feel tells me it's a trap, but it's a trap you think you can't refuse. And you know what? You might be right."

Levi crouched down and pushed the last few bits of glass onto the dustpan with his fingers. "I know neither one of us is really mad at the other," he said. "We're scared is all. There's no shame in that. We should be. You're right to doubt Admiral. You're right to worry. Come to think of it, you're right about most things. This meeting, though, if it actually happens, it's about the only move I can see to make."

Laney stood with the broom in one hand and the dustpan in the other. "You need to find a way to change that because that being your only choice isn't acceptable. Not to you. Not to me. Not to this family." She turned around and went back to the bar.

"I'm working on it," Levi said.

"Work harder," Laney answered.

25.

Bennett and Chance's trip to Bellingham took longer than expected due to two blowouts along the way. Having to change out tires twice had put them both in a foul mood. Chance's knuckles were bruised and bloodied where they had scraped against the ground while jacking up the car.

"How many times have I told you to get new tires?"

The car's interior was thick with the smoke from Bennett's cigarette. He glanced at Chance and shrugged. "At least I'm smart enough to carry two spares."

"Or dumb enough to need them both. What are we supposed do if there's another blowout?"

Bennett rolled his window down a few inches and dropped his spent cigarette outside. "Stop worrying. We'll be fine. Hey, there's the mill sign. See? We found it. This trip isn't going so bad."

Chance sulked as he rubbed his knuckles. "Yeah, it's been a real peach. Park it over there behind that row of shrubs, and we'll walk the rest of the way. It's probably best we not announce ourselves."

Bennett shut off the car and double-checked that the gun in his shoulder holster was loaded. "You ready?"

Chance nodded. The brothers walked through the woods toward the lumber mill and then stopped.

"You hear that?" Bennett said.

"No. What?"

"Exactly. It's too quiet. No equipment. No trucks. That sound like a lumber mill to you? What time is it?"

Chance checked his pocket watch. "Two-thirty."

"Okay, let's get a closer look and try and find out why a supposed lumber mill is so quiet in the middle of the workday."

They came to a wood fence with a sign that warned trespassers to stay out. Bennett ripped the sign off, flung it onto the ground, and hopped over the fence. Chance followed close behind.

Bennett crouched behind a shrub and pointed at the dirt field that stretched out in front of a warehouse-sized building. "That look familiar?"

"It's a runway–just like Monroe. What now?"

"Now? We wait."

Chance took out a flask and had a sip and then handed it to Bennett. "Seems we do a lot of that lately."

"I figured you'd be excited about this trip. You might get to see that pretty pilot we watched fly into Monroe the other night."

"If she's working for Noretta, I doubt we'd hit it off."

After having a drink, Bennett handed the flask back. "Why let a little dispute between the old folks come between true love?"

Chance slid the flask back into his jacket. "Don't start. I'm not in the mood."

"Pa should have sent you here with Dalton. You two would have made quite the grumpy team."

"Actually, Dalton's been a lot better lately. I wouldn't go so far as to call him cheerful, but he's definitely improved."

"You're right. See? It's all that time he's spending with Winona–true love. It changes everything–even Dalton."

Chance held out his hand. "Got a smoke?"

"You didn't bring your own?"

"C'mon, I just gave you a nip of my whiskey, and you didn't even have to ask. Stop being so damn stingy."

"Stingy? You must be confusing me with Dylan."

Chance grinned. "You got that right. I guess it's all those fancy ties he wears. Doesn't have anything left to share."

"If Dylan's not buying for himself, he's as tight as a frog's ass in a flood. That said, he might be running things eventually. Pa seems to be pushing him in that direction."

"You think?" Chance said.

Bennett shrugged. "Could be. Dylan's got the brains for it."

"But he doesn't like to get his hands dirty."

"Not so sure about that," Bennett replied. "He does it different. Kind of a roundabout way like Pa does these days."

"What do you mean?"

"Well, Pa, he don't hardly deal with things face to face anymore. He doesn't have to."

"Yeah, because he has us."

"That's right," Bennett said while handing Chance a cigarette. "Now there was a time, back when Pa was working for Admiral, where he was always out front. Pa has us, and Admiral had Pa. You ever see his gun from those days?"

"No. What gun?"

"I saw it once when I was real little. You might not have even been born yet. Anyways, I was nosing around Ma and Pa's bedroom. Ended up in Pa's closet, and there it was hanging next to his shirts. A big old beautiful piece of dark steel and this leather gun belt with all these pretty gold bullets wrapped around it. I could just reach up and touch the bottom of the belt and pull it down so that's what I did. Not thinking of course how I was going to put it back."

"Dumbass."

Bennett grunted. "Yeah, dumbass. It almost came down on top of me. I sat inside the bottom of the closet tracing every bit of that gun with my fingers. I was hypnotized bit it, how heavy it felt in my hands, the smell of the leather belt, everything about it fascinated me. I lost all track of time. Ma found me first and scolded me something fierce. Then Pa arrived, and I got about the worst ass whooping I'd ever had. He was *real* pissed. I was sent to my room for what felt like weeks. It was some years later when I brought up the subject of the gun to Admiral, and it was Admiral who explained to me how that gun had been Pa's calling card. He went around with it hanging off his hip, and people stood at attention.

"This is when Pa was young. Not much older than we are now. Every so often, someone would challenge him. Bets were made. And each and every time, it was Pa who was the one left standing."

Chance's eyes got big. "Are you telling me Pa was a gunfighter? C'mon..."

"It's true. At least that was Admiral's version of it, and I don't see a reason why he would have lied to me. He even told me the story of Pa's last gunfight. The one right before he hung up his belt. Admiral can really talk a tale when he's in the mood to. You wanna hear it?"

Chance looked up at the darkening clouds. A storm was moving in. "Sure."

"There was this kid, younger even than Pa, who came into town talking all kinds of tough. Said he was the fastest gun in the whole state and he'd heard about how fast Pa was. He was there to prove Pa was slower than him. This went on for a few days. Him showing up and talking, and then leaving, and then coming back and talking some more. Admiral said he was just like a carnival barker how he went about getting the crowd all worked up. People kept asking Pa when he was gonna meet the kid in the street to settle who was really the fastest, but Pa kept quiet about it. It was a hot summer in July. Folks were showing up from all over wanting to see a gunfight. Admiral asked Pa if he wanted him to set it up. Pa said no. Admiral asked him why. Pa said he was done with that sort of thing.

Admiral told him he was too young to retire, and the answer Pa gave him for that was that he was also too young to die.

"So, Admiral backed off. The kid kept showing up in town saying how Pa had turned coward. Pretty soon, other people were saying the same to Pa's face."

Chance's mouth fell open. "Really? To his face?"

Bennett nodded. "Yup, and more of them every day that went by. Then it happened."

"What?"

"The kid finally got what he wanted. He confronted Pa on the street and called him out. Pa stepped by him and kept on walking. The kid ran up in front of him and then slapped Pa right across the mouth. Didn't hit him–*slapped him*. Cut his lip. There were about ten people who actually saw it happen, but soon everybody in town was saying they witnessed the slap. That settled it. Pa had no choice. He agreed to the gunfight. It was scheduled for the following day at noon in the middle of Main Street.

"Hundreds came to watch. They lined both sides of the road from one end of town to the other. People were selling souvenirs; there was food, and drink, and music. The whole thing had turned into this blood sport shindig. Admiral said the betting was off the charts. It was more money than he'd ever seen wagered at one time in his life–thousands of dollars.

"And that's when Pa struck a deal with Admiral–*after* all that money was already out there waiting on the outcome of the draw."

"What was the deal?" Chance asked.

"The deal was for the property that became The Silo. Pa wanted to open his own business–to be his own boss. Admiral owned the property like he owned most the places in town. If Pa won, Admiral was to sign over the property to him– effective immediately. I can still hear Admiral chuckling about that when he told me the story. He said Pa had the balls of a Brahman bull to come at him with that kind of demand an hour before Pa was to be staring down the barrel of a gun.

"Admiral agreed to the deal, not that he could have refused. There was too much money on the line, much of it his own. So, noon had almost arrived, and Pa stood in the street looking at that kid who was staring back at him. It was already hot. There was no breeze. Everything went quiet. The kid looked confident. He was all smirks, and smiles, and winks to the girls in the crowd. Admiral said Pa's face wasn't indicating anything. No fear. No emotion. No nothing. He was just waiting to pull out that shooter so that a building on a little city lot at the end of town would be all his.

"Back then, Sultan had a clock tower at the west end of Main Street. It's not there anymore. Got washed out in the flood of 1915. The clock gave off a noontime chime, and that's the sound everyone was waiting on. The way Admiral described, it felt like it took forever and a day for the chime to sound. When it finally did, you couldn't even see Pa's hand reach for his gun. It happened that fast. His face never changed. He didn't even blink when he fired.

"The kid's gun was still in its holster when Pa's bullet struck him in the neck and he went down. Then he got back up crying and begging for help. He could hardly talk. His mouth kept filling with blood. He'd spit it out and try to say something then have to spit again. He was bawling by then, saying how he didn't want to die. He collapsed into the dirt on the side of the road. Women were screaming and children crying. Apparently, it was quite the spectacle. The sound was the worst. The kid was gurgling and choking on all that blood while clawing at the hole in his throat. A woman demanded someone to do something. More shouted the same. Everyone turned to look at Pa. He hadn't moved. The gun was still in his hand with smoke drifting out of the end of the barrel.

"Admiral said Pa stared back at every set of eyes on that street. Every stinking one. He didn't say anything right away as he walked up to where the kid lay dying. He looked around and then pointed his gun at the kid and asked if that's what everyone wanted. When nobody answered, he yelled the same question. The kid was still gurgling but getting weaker. He'd a been dead soon regardless. Pa hurried it along, though. Put a bullet in the dumb bastard's head. Then he holstered his gun, turned around, and walked all the way to the other end of town and waited for Admiral to show up with the deed to the property.

"He didn't have to wait long. Admiral gave him the deed and the keys to the front door. He also tried to give Pa a hundred dollars as his remaining share for the gunfight, but Pa refused the money. He was done working for Admiral. He was done working for anyone but himself. He didn't go respectable, of course, not all the way, but a lot more respectable than he'd been as Admiral's muscle. The gun and belt were put away. He's never worn them since."

Chance took out the flask and had another drink. "Damn. I had no idea. So that's why Pa's so good with a gun."

"I guess so."

"You think he's still that fast?"

Bennett scratched the stubble on his chin. "Hard to say. That was a long time ago."

The brothers heard a vehicle coming and moved deeper into the bushes. Chance pushed a branch to the side to get a better look.

The car stopped in front of the warehouse. A tall, powerfully-built man wearing a dark suit and tie exited the driver side. The passenger door opened and a serious-faced, middle-aged man with a handlebar mustache stepped out.

"From how Dalton and Dylan described him, that's got to be Titus Lemkee," Chance said.

Bennett grunted. "Mr. Mud Shark himself."

It started to rain, but that's not why Chance looked up. "You hear that?"

Bennett cocked his head. "Airplane."

It was the plane they had seen do the nighttime landing at Noretta's barn outside of Monroe. Bennett nudged Chance. "Now we get to see if it's the same pretty lady who was flying it before."

It was. She removed her cap and the same blonde hair cascaded over her shoulders. Chance was close enough he could make out her high cheekbones, full lips, and proud chin. Bennett tugged on his sleeve.

"Get down," he hissed.

Chance pushed Bennett's hand away and kept staring at the pilot. She looked to be no more than a few years older than him.

"Hey dumbass," Bennett said, "you want them to see us?"

"We'll be fine if you keep quiet."

Bennett pulled on the back of Chance's collar. "I said get down."

Chance shoved him away. "Knock it off."

The driver of the car turned and looked toward the woods. His hand slipped into his jacket and came out holding a pistol. The brothers froze. The man they believed to be Titus Lemkee pointed in their direction.

"Goddammit Chance," Bennett whispered between clenched teeth as he took out his gun.

Chance crouched down with his pistol already in his hand. "Relax."

The man stopped no more than twenty paces from the bush holding his gun in front of him. He took another step, stopped, then turned around. "Don't know, Mr. Lemkee. I don't see anything."

"Fine," Lemkee said, "then get your ass back here and help load up the plane. She needs to be in the air before the winds pick up. Isn't that right, my love?"

The brothers watched three crates get put into the aircraft. Lemkee and the pilot embraced. Chance shook his head while looking like he had just smelled the greasiest fart in all of human history. Bennett patted him on the shoulder.

"Tough break, little brother. Maybe you're meant for the next one."

Lemkee and the other man got back into the car and drove off. The pilot walked into the warehouse.

"Well, that confirms it," Bennett said. "Noretta's definitely working with that piece of shit Lemkee."

Bennett turned around to leave. After a few steps he realized he was alone and glanced behind him. Chance was walking toward the plane.

Bennett looked up at the sound of distant thunder. A gust of wind pushed the beginnings of a hard rain into his face.

"Goddammit, Chance."

26.

The transaction ended with someone dead.

"Shut your damn mouth," Dalton said while pointing his gun at Piedmont's face.

Dylan put a hand on Dalton's shoulder. "Hold on. No need for anyone to get hurt. Mr. Piedmont, you need to understand something. We're just here to collect twenty jugs per the agreement you made with my father and then we'll be on our way. After that our business will have been concluded."

Piedmont pointed at Dylan. "You got the devil's tongue in you. Uh-huh. I can hear the slither between the words. Talking of agreements and conclusions. You're gonna pay me what I'm owed and not a penny less for the other ten jugs I've already brewed up for your father who's apparently too important of a man to afford me a second visit."

"Mr. Piedmont," Dylan said while shaking his head, "there'll be no talk of more jugs. We paid for twenty. That's it."

"So, deliver the twenty jugs and not another fucking word," Dalton growled. "And tell the girl upstairs to stop pointing that shotgun at me."

Piedmont spit out a frothy ball of green goo that splattered near Dalton's feet. "Or what?"

Dalton tilted his head back, snorted loudly, and spit back. It struck Piedmont right below his nose. He cried out like he'd been shot, and then wiped it off with the grimy sleeve of his jacket. "I'm not afraid of you," he said.

"You should be."

Dylan cleared his throat. "The twenty jugs Mr. Piedmont."

Piedmont straightened himself as much as his bent spine would allow, snapped his fingers, and ordered his daughter-wives to fetch the jugs. "Put them next to the vehicles," he barked.

Dylan and Dalton watched a procession of women and girls march outside. Each carried a jug. Some of the older and stronger ones carried two. They lined the jugs up next to the cars. Most were with child. All appeared to be starving. Scabs covered their sticklike arms. Piedmont's eyes narrowed.

"You brought someone else. I see them sitting in one of your vehicles. It's a girl. Who is she?"

Dalton stepped toward the porch. "None of your business."

Piedmont grinned, licked his lips, and clutched his Bible to his chest. "Her skin is dusky, but that's fine. I love *all* God's little creatures–even the red and brown ones."

The heat coming from Dalton's eyes was volcanic. "You don't look at her. Don't talk about her. Don't think about her."

The smallest of the girls broke a jug on the bottom porch step, spilling its contents. She appeared to be no older than twelve. Her narrow chest was flat, but the bump on her belly indicated she was also pregnant. Piedmont roared, grabbed her by the hair, and flung her behind him.

"Clumsy wretch!" he bellowed. "What you just wasted represents my work to put food in your always hungry mouths."

When the girl tried to get up, Piedmont smashed the Bible across her face, knocking out one of her teeth.

"That's enough," Dalton said.

Piedmont turned his head and sneered. "This doesn't concern you. She'll fetch another." He pointed to the girl. "Go!"

With a whimper, the girl scrambled back into the house. She returned holding a second jug. Her arms trembled as she struggled to carry it. Piedmont leaned down until his rotting mouth was just inches from her face.

"Place it with the others," he hissed. "Drop this one, and it'll be the lash for you."

Dalton stepped aside to allow the girl the shortest path to the closest of the two cars. It was the same one Winona sat in. Piedmont extended his hand toward Dylan. His fingers were curled inward like claws.

"Now we'll discuss the ten other jugs you owe me for. Well, nine since this stupid child broke one of them. I won't charge you for that misfortune. I'm an honest businessman." He glanced at the girl who stood a few feet from him on the porch. "That payment will come from her."

Another of Piedmont's daughter-wives came outside. She appeared to be the oldest and tallest of them, and despite her gaunt frame, likely the strongest. Her dark hair was cut short. She had a wide mouth, sunken cheeks, and eyes that hinted at an awareness of the monster that ruled over her. She began to gently pull the younger girl inside. Piedmont scowled.

"What do you think you're doing? Leave us."

The woman retreated into the home. Piedmont rolled his eyes. "The lesser sex are such simple creatures. My work is never done."

"We'll load up the jugs and be on our way." Dylan said. "Thank you."

Dalton walked backward keeping his eyes and his gun on Piedmont. "Not another goddamn word."

Piedmont's cracked lips drew back into a silent snarl as he watched Dylan place the jugs into the cars. Dalton motioned for Winona to roll down the window. "You recognize that man on the porch?" he whispered to her. "Was he there when Chan was killed?"

Winona shook her head.

"You sure?"

Winona nodded.

Dylan stood next to Dalton. "Well?"

"She says it wasn't him."

"What are you two talking about?" Piedmont yelled from the porch. "Are you reconsidering my offer of more jugs? Nine jugs for just five dollars. Surely you can't pass up such a deal as that."

Dylan waved. "You take care, Mr. Piedmont."

The brothers started their cars while Piedmont stood statue-still glaring at them. Dalton was the first to drive away. Dylan put his car into gear. He heard shouting coming from the porch. The girl who had broken the jug was on her back as Piedmont stood over her aiming his gun at her belly while holding his Bible high over his head.

"But Jesus said, suffer little children, and forbid them not, to come unto me; for such is the kingdom of heaven."

The girl's hands covered her stomach. She pleaded with Piedmont for forgiveness. "You are not worthy of God's grace!" he screeched. Spit flew from his mouth. His eyes were wide. "You cost me a deal. Your clumsiness took money from me and vengeance will be mine!"

Piedmont rammed the heel of his boot into the girl's crotch like he was killing a spider. She screamed. He pummeled her with the Bible again and again until he looked up and saw Dylan walking toward the porch. "I told you both this isn't your concern." He pointed his gun at Dylan. "Now get off my---"

Dylan fired. Piedmont's head snapped back. Both gun and Bible dropped from his hands. He lurched to the side, took a half-step, and then collapsed.

The girl pushed herself up and stood with her back against the house. She stared at Piedmont's body. Her lips trembled, and tears streamed down her face. She still covered her belly with her hands, clearly wanting to protect the life inside.

Dylan put his gun away. "It's okay. He can't hurt you anymore."

The front door opened. The oldest of the daughters walked out. She looked at Dylan and then down at her father's body.

"I'm sorry," Dylan said. "He might have killed her. I couldn't let that happen."

The woman guided the girl into the house and then called out for someone to clean her up. Her voice was strong. She closed the door and turned around to face Dylan. Her eyes showed no fear or sadness–only determination. She cocked her head to look at something behind Dylan. It was Dalton driving back to the house.

"Go," she said.

"What?" Dylan asked.

"Go."

Dalton got out of the car with his gun drawn. Dylan put a hand up. "That's not necessary."

Dalton saw Piedmont's body. "Jesus. What the hell happened?"

The woman stepped to the end of the porch. "Go. Now."

"We can help," Dylan offered.

The woman shook her head. "We'll take care of it. Finally, this is our home–not his." She reached down, took the money out of Piedmont's pocket, and placed it into the front of her dirt-encrusted dress.

"Are you sure?"

The woman nodded.

Dalton pulled Dylan toward him. "You heard her. Let's go."

Dylan returned to his car. He watched as several more women came out of the house to help drag Piedmont's body inside. One of the girls stayed with a bucket and brush and started to clean the blood off the porch.

An hour later the two brothers stood outside The Silo's back entrance. Dalton was finishing a cigarette. "Pretty sure Pa sent you up there to be the sensible one. Surprise, surprise if it wasn't you who finally put a bullet into that shit stain. Good on you. I mean that."

Dylan shook his head. "I still don't feel right leaving all those girls up there to fend for themselves."

"You kidding me? They survived living with that thing all this time. Believe me, they're a whole lot better off on their own. You gave them a chance to finally be free. In their eyes, you're a goddamn saint. I'm a little embarrassed I didn't take care of him myself."

"I can't help but wonder why they hadn't run away or attacked Piedmont by now. There didn't appear to be any shortage of weapons."

Dalton blew smoke out through his nose while kicking a stone with the toe of his boot. "During the war, I heard stories of guys who had been taken prisoner by the Germans, and after just a few months, they had been so traumatized, they never even thought to escape. After the war was over, they had to be convinced they weren't prisoners anymore. I imagine those girls were dealing with something similar. I'll say this. You did them a favor today. A big one."

"I suppose, but that still leaves us not knowing who killed Chan. I guess we're back to pointing the finger at Noretta Saul for that too."

Dalton shrugged. "Seems so."

"You tell Pa about Piedmont?"

"Yeah."

"What did he say?"

"Not much. Just asked if you had no choice. I told him the truth. You didn't."

"And that's it?"

"Yup. That's one of the best parts about being a Bowman. When things like that go down, we have a father who understands. He's lived it. He knows it. He's done it. Shit happens."

Dalton unlocked the back door and pulled it open. "C'mon, I'll buy you a drink."

"We drink for free."

Dalton grinned. "Yeah, I know."

27.

"Jeez, look at you," Bennett said while driving. "Just a big lump of lovesick sitting there."

Chance didn't deny it. Now that he knew more about her, he was even more obsessed with the pilot.

Her name was Scarlet Lange. She was twenty-nine and born in Bonn, Germany. Her parents immigrated to America shortly before her first birthday. Her father had been a wood smith by trade and found ample opportunity logging the hills surrounding Bellingham. He was killed by a fallen tree when Scarlet was ten. He had been working for Titus Lemkee at the time of his death. Lemkee personally delivered the news to Scarlet's mother along with an envelope containing $100 as compensation. That is how her family came to know him.

Lemkee took an interest in Scarlett's formal education. She saw her first aircraft at an air show in Vancouver, B.C., when she was twenty-two. She asked Lemkee if he knew of anyone who could teach her to fly. He said yes, paid for lessons from the only pilot then available in Bellingham at the time, and three years later, bought her a plane. Scarlet had been spending as much time as possible in the sky ever since.

The Canada to Bellingham to Monroe route she now flew multiple times each week earned her a reasonable salary from Lemkee as well as paid for the fuel and maintenance of the aircraft. Scarlet had already rebuilt the motor entirely herself. The engine didn't need it. She just wanted to know how.

Lemkee and her weren't a couple. He often acted in a way that would suggest otherwise, including long embraces and quick kisses on the lips, but Scarlet remained her own woman free from the encumbrances that came with a man claiming her as his.

She told all this to Chance like they were the oldest of friends while she fueled the plane. He caught her repeatedly glancing up at the sky as if she couldn't wait to get off the ground.

Scarlett shrugged when Chance asked about Lemkee's business with Noretta Saul. "Not sure. Obviously, it involves a bunch of booze that Titus has me bringing in from Canada, but beyond that I don't know, and I don't really care. I get paid to fly. That's it."

"But you're doing something illegal," Chance said. "You could go to jail."

Scarlett laughed. "They'd have to catch me first!" She kept talking while she walked into the building as the brothers followed her. "Besides, this whole Prohibition thing is a joke. Half the country is already ignoring it, and the other half is soon to follow. It's a stupid law, made up by stupid politicians, who should be focusing on more important things. And let's not forget how it's made men like Titus Lemkee very rich in a very short amount of time, and I'll assume the same can be said for your family. This country wouldn't have nearly so many criminals if the government would just stop making things illegal, am I right?"

It was then that Bennett joined the conversation. "Your friend Mr. Lemkee threatened some of my family. He wanted to feed them to the mud sharks."

Scarlett rolled her eyes. "Oh, he's always doing that kind of nonsense. Fact is, he's in way over his head with all of this. He'll never admit that, though. He really is still just a logger at heart. That's what he loves most. It's why he still spends so much time at his old mill getting sawdust in his hair. He can't stay away from it. It can be tough making all that money. I know that sounds sort of crazy, but it's true. He has this big target on him now. That's why he's willing to pay me so well to fly these crates to Monroe. Titus has people watching him, watching the boats going into and out of the harbor. They don't know about this plane. Not yet anyway. I just fly over all their silly roadblocks and port inspections. I land, the stuff is unloaded, and I take off."

"But why Monroe?" Bennett asked.

"I don't know. I suppose because it's far enough out in the middle of nowhere that Titus thinks the authorities won't bother him. The plan is for him to distribute the alcohol from there to Everett, Seattle, maybe as far south as Tacoma. With all the backroads in your neck of the woods he figures it's a lot safer than trying to drive it all the way down from

Bellingham. A person keeps doing that, and eventually they'll get caught."

Scarlet pointed to a wrench lying on a table. "Can you hand me that?"

Chance grabbed the wrench and gave it to her. She said thank you, jogged out to the plane, hopped onto one of the wheels, flipped open the hood, and then stuck her upper body inside the engine compartment.

Bennett lit a cigarette. "Has Lemkee mentioned anything about our father, Levi Bowman?"

Scarlet looked out from underneath the hood and shook her head. "No, sorry, not a word. Maybe you should ask Titus about that yourself. Also, no smoking around my plane."

After Bennett put out his cigarette, Scarlet gave him big smile. "Thanks."

"Don't you think Lemkee will mind you talking to us like this?" Bennet asked.

"Maybe, but I do what I want, including talking to the people I want. My mother is the same way—just talk, talk, talk. It makes life so much more interesting when you find interesting people to talk to. You seem to think Titus is some dark force overseeing a vast criminal enterprise. It's not like that. Not really."

Chance stared at Scarlet's long-legged backside. "You need a hand?" he offered.

Scarlett said no, closed the hood, hopped down, and walked quickly back into the warehouse where she dropped the wrench on the table, zipped up her leather jacket, and then rubbed her hands together. "Okay, that should do it. I'm ready to go."

"Back to Monroe?" Chance asked.

Scarlett scowled like she wasn't sure Chance's elevator went all the way to the top floor. "Uh, yeah, back to Monroe."

"We're on our way to Sultan," Chance said while grinning like a nervous halfwit. "That's close to Monroe. We'll be going right by you."

"Except I'll be in Bellingham by then–because I'm flying."

Chance nodded. "Right, of course. We'll be driving and that's... slower."

"Uh-huh. I really do need to get going. I'm sorry I didn't know more about whatever business Titus has going with Noretta Saul, but it's like I said--my focus is on the flying. They load the plane, I fly it, they unload it. That's as far as my involvement goes."

Bennett stepped in front of Chance. "Just one more thing, if you don't mind?"

"What?"

"My family is going to be hosting a big poker tournament at The Silo. That's our drinking joint in Sultan. Lemkee might already know about it. I'd like to invite him to the tournament. Could you tell him? The buy-in is a $1000."

"How'd you know?"

"Know what?" Bennett asked.

"How much Titus enjoys poker. He loves it. Some think he loves it too much. A $1000 is a lot of money which means he'll *have* to be there. He can't refuse that kind of game."

"So, you'll tell him he's invited?"

"Sure."

Chance stepped in front of Bennett. "And you're invited too."

"Oh, I don't play poker."

"You don't have to play. You can just watch. I like to watch. Do you like to watch?"

"Depends on what I'm watching."

Bennett nudged Chance to the side. "Excuse my brother. He was dropped on his head as a child—a lot."

Scarlet smiled. "Yeah, but he *is* awful cute."

"Oh, no," Bennett said. "Wish you hadn't told him that. Now I'll have to hear him repeating it all the way back to Sultan."

"Can I get one of you strong men to give me a hand starting her up?"

Both brothers offered. Chance was first to the front of the plane. Scarlet positioned the prop so that each blade extended out sideways like a steel mustache.

"Normally, I do this myself, but it's much easier when there's someone to help. Stay here, and I'll climb into the cockpit." Scarlett dropped behind the wheel, tucked her hair into her leather cap, and adjusted her flying glasses over her eyes. "When I say contact, you're going to pull down on the prop and then jump back. That last part is important because if you don't, and the engine fires, the prop will cut off anything in its way."

Chance looked at his hands. Scarlett nodded. "Yup, it'll definitely slice through those–along with anything else of yours that happens to be sticking out."

Bennett chuckled. "Well, go ahead. You were so anxious to help her out, so help her out."

Chance took a deep breath and then grabbed onto the prop blade. "That's it," Scarlett said. "When I say contact you pull it down as hard as you can and step away."

Scarlett yelled contact. Chance pulled. The motor spit once and then went silent. Scarlett tilted her head and smiled. "We'll try it again."

Chance gripped the prop, waited to hear Scarlett say contact, and then pulled down so hard he nearly fell forward. The engine fired. The prop buzzed like an angry hornet's nest. A whoosh of air struck Chance in the face. Bennett grabbed him by the collar and pulled him back.

Scarlett stuck her arm out and gave Chance a thumbs up. "Nice job! Next time we see each other, I'll owe you a ride."

"I'd like that," Chance said as he watched Scarlett drive the aircraft onto the runway. She revved the motor and then sped off toward the other side. Right before reaching the tree line, the plane lifted off the ground. She pointed the nose toward a gap in the trees, went through it, and then continued to climb until she was a barely visible speck in the sky.

Chance heard someone saying his name. He turned his head and realized it was Bennett. They were in the car on the road back to Sultan.

"Hey, snap out of it. I'm talking to you."

"Sorry," Chance said. "Guess I'm a little tired."

"More like you were daydreaming about Lemkee's pilot."

"She's not Lemkee's pilot. They're not together. She made that clear."

"Or you heard it the way you wanted to."

"What's that supposed to mean?"

Bennett swerved to miss a pothole. "It means Lemkee paid for her flying lessons. He paid for the plane. Now he's paying her to transport his alcohol. She might not want to admit it, but I'm pretty sure Lemkee sees her as his. Besides, she's too old for you."

"No, she's not."

Bennett lit a cigarette and shrugged. "Whatever. We have more important things to deal with."

"Yeah, like explaining to Pa why you invited Lemkee to the poker tournament."

"I invited him because it makes sense."

"How so?"

"Your new girlfriend said Lemkee isn't a bad guy, right? Either that's true, or she's lying."

"Or Lemkee has her fooled."

Bennett nodded. "That's possible, but she doesn't strike me as someone who gets fooled easily. I think she might be right. Think about it. Dylan wanted to arrange a sit down with Pa and Lemkee. I'm seeing the wisdom of that now. He thought we could use Lemkee to isolate Noretta."

"But that was before we knew Lemkee was working *with* Noretta. Besides, Pa shot that idea down."

"Yeah but things have changed since then. Everything we've learned confirms that it's Noretta who's the threat to us in Sultan–not Lemkee."

"I still say Pa won't go for it."

"We're not talking about a business arrangement. This time it's a poker game. Since when does Pa turn down a chance to take someone's money? Lemkee's pilot told us how he loves to gamble. He's a high roller. That's exactly the kind of player we want at the tournament."

"Her name is Scarlett."

"What?"

"The pilot's name is Scarlett."

"Man, she's got her hooks deep into you, little brother. Okay, Scarlet it is. I admit she's an interesting looker, but I'd urge you to proceed with caution because as long as she's taking money from him, she has to answer to him."

"If a woman like Scarlett invited you to be with her, would you be willing to risk it?"

Bennett was quiet as he puffed on his cigarette. They were nearing Monroe. "You know," he said, "if I'm being honest, I'd have to admit I probably would chase a sweet thing like that. To hell with who she's working for."

Chance nodded. "Exactly."

28.

Levi sat behind his desk looking up at his four sons. Bennett and Chance had just finished telling him about their trip to Bellingham. Things were getting loud on the other side of the office door. It was a busy night at The Silo. A boisterous group of loggers had come in an hour earlier with money to spend. They had emptied one Index jug and were well into a second.

"Now we know for sure that Lemkee is working with Noretta," Levi said.

Bennett scratched his chin. "It's probably more accurate to say she's working *for* Lemkee. He's definitely the one in charge. It's his alcohol coming in from Canada. His runway in Bellingham. His pilot. His operation."

Levi struck a match and lit a cigarette. "Which makes what he told Dalton and Dylan a lie, right? Why seem so open to working with us and against Noretta when he already has Noretta in his pocket?"

"Not necessarily," Dylan said. "Maybe he wants us to be a regular customer. We buy his product from Noretta, and he gets his cut."

"Then why would Noretta be coming after us like she is?" Chance asked. "Wouldn't that piss off Lemkee?"

Dylan shrugged. "She's greedy. She wants our share and whatever Lemkee is paying her. She owns her own joint, has Lemkee providing all the hooch she needs, and helps to distribute more of it to places like Everett and Seattle."

Levi nodded. "She'd make a fortune."

"Yeah," Dylan said. "She would."

Chance took a sip from his flask. "You gonna cancel the sit-down in Monroe with Noretta tomorrow?"

"No," Levi answered. "I'm still going. She doesn't know what we know. I want to get a better feel for what she's planning."

Dalton scowled. "It could be a trap."

"I'm with Dalton," Chance remarked. "Noretta's turned Monroe into enemy territory for us. We should go with you just in case they try something."

Bennett's eyes narrowed. "What if that's what they want?"

"Exactly," Levi said. "Why give them the opportunity to get all of us at once? No, tomorrow I go alone. That way, if they do pull something, I have you four free to deal with it. And regardless of what might happen in Monroe, the poker tournament goes forward as planned understood?"

All four Bowman boys nodded their heads. Seconds later a loud crash shook the floorboards. Laney was yelling at someone.

Levi got up. "What the hell?" Dalton was first to open the door. Laney asked for some help. One of the loggers had jumped on top of the bar and wanted to dance a jig for a free jug of whiskey.

Levi pushed past Dalton. "Get off there!" he bellowed.

The logger turned and looked down. "Who the fuck are you?"

"This is his place," Laney answered. Her hand reached for the shotgun as The Silo's regular customers made for the exit.

"You heard her," Levi said. "This is my place. Now get off that bar and sit your ass down."

The logger was a short, wiry, thirty-something man with scarred hands, and a full beard. His eyes glimmered from too much alcohol and adrenaline. "Think you can make me?"

Levi pulled his jacket open to show his gun. "Yeah, I do."

The other loggers stood. Three were of similar age and size to the one on top of the bar. The fourth was a giant who stood well over six feet. His thighs were tree trunks, his shoulders nearly as wide as a doorframe. They were all drunk and seemingly unimpressed by Levi's threat of gunplay.

The logger on the bar started to dance. The heels of his boots dug into the oiled wood finish. His four friends began to clap. Dalton stepped forward.

"You were told not to do that."

The logger kept dancing as his friends laughed and pointed. Dalton grabbed one of his ankles and pulled. The man's legs flew out from underneath him. His shoulders struck the bar with a heavy thud, and then he fell face first onto the floor.

The loggers moved toward Dalton. "You could have killed him," one of them said.

"Ah, ah, ah." Dylan had slipped in behind the fallen logger. He pressed his blade against the man's throat. "You all stay put, or things are going to get real bloody real fast."

The four loggers froze. "Who do you work for?" Levi asked.

The biggest of them stepped forward. "His name is Admiral. He's got us clearing twenty acres off the side of Haystack Mountain. He's the one who told us about this place. Said we'd be welcome here."

Levi arched a brow. "Admiral? What the hell is he doing hiring on a logging crew? And outsiders no less. Where you from?"

"Everywhere," the big logger answered. "We go where the work is. You mind telling him to back the knife off?"

Levi nodded. Dylan withdrew his blade. The logger stood up and whirled around. "Let's see how tough you are without the knives and guns."

Dylan held his knife in one hand and his gun in the other. "Decisions, decisions," he said.

Laney grabbed hold of the shotgun and pointed it at the big logger. "I think it's time you all leave–and don't come back. I should have known it would be Admiral who was responsible for bringing your kind of trash in here."

The logger Dylan had held his knife to grunted. "What kind of place is this? Even the old cunt behind the bar has a scatter gun on her."

Levi punched him in the mouth. When the logger went to say something more Levi hit him again. "Turn around and look at the wall behind you," he said.

The logger, with one hand over his mouth, turned around. "You see that spot where the wood is little darker? That's where the brains of the last man who crossed the woman behind the bar ended up. Now if you don't apologize, I'm going to take a big step to the side and let her fire away."

"Bullshit." The logger wiped the blood from his lips. "She didn't shoot nobody."

"Fine. Have it your way." Levi started to step to the side.

"Wait," the big logger said. "Tell her you're sorry, West."

"I'll do no such thing, and fuck you, Riley, for thinking I would. These hicks ain't so tough."

Levi smiled, but his eyes were ice. "Last chance to tell the lady you're sorry."

"Suck my ass," West sneered. "No, better yet, get the old cunt to do it."

Levi's hand was a blur as he drew his gun and pointed it at West. "Tell you what. I'm not going to kill you because you're drunk and maybe, just maybe, not of sound mind. I *am* going to shoot you in the foot though."

"What?" West cried right before Levi pulled the trigger.

West gasped as he looked down. "Sonofabitch, you shot my toe off!"

"You had it coming," Riley said. "Now shut up so we can get you out of here."

Levi waved his gun. "Not yet. He hasn't apologized."

One of the other loggers stepped forward. "Let's get 'em. They can't stop all of us."

Bennett and Chance drew their guns. Bennett laughed. "I know plenty of loggers, but I've never met any as dumb as you. Let me give you some advice. I hope you take it otherwise I'll be helping to clean up the blood in this place again. I really don't want to have to do that. I'd much rather sit, have a smoke, and enjoy a drink. Sounds reasonable enough, right? So, listen carefully. The advice comes in three parts. Part one is getting that one there to say he's sorry. Part two is shutting the hell up after he does. And part three is you all getting the fuck out."

Riley clamped his hand around the back of West's neck. "Apologize to the lady."

West resisted. Riley squeezed harder. West nodded. "Okay." He glanced at Laney. "Sorry you're an old cunt."

Riley grimaced. "Jesus, West, you're a dumb bastard."

Levi fired a second bullet into West's foot. The logger screamed and collapsed onto the floor. "Get him out of here," Levi told Riley. "Next one is in the head, and if I kill him that means I have to kill all of you. Understood?"

Riley nodded. "Yeah." He ordered the others to drag West outside. Before Riley left, Levi called out to him.

"You want a break from working in the woods?"

When Riley didn't answer Levi continued. "I have a big poker tournament coming up. Could use another hand to make sure everyone stays in line. All you have to do is stand there looking pissed just like you're doing now. Pays twenty

THE BOWMAN BOYS

dollars for a night's work. That's about what you'd make for a whole week of cutting down trees. What do you say?"

Riley shrugged. "Sure."

"Good. You come by here in a couple days, *just you,* and speak with Laney. She's the one behind the bar. The one your friend insulted."

"West ain't my friend. We just work on the same crew is all."

Levi slipped his gun into his jacket and lit a cigarette. "Whatever, you just make sure to do exactly what she tells you. Oh, and if you think your friend is in need of some medical attention there's a little shack on the right just past the bridge on your way out of town. Bang on the door. Might take some time but eventually you'll wake Finnicus, and he'll take a look as long as you have a few coins to pay him for his trouble."

"Who's Finnicus?"

"He's the town vet. Closest thing we have to a doctor around here. He's patched his share of gunshot wounds."

"You want me to take West to someone who works on animals?"

"Sure. A bullet doesn't discriminate between an animal and a human being, and neither do stitches. Finnicus knows what he's doing. He's also the town drunk. Well, one of them. Actually, hold on a second."

Levi grabbed an Index jug from the bar and handed it to Riley. "Here, you can pay Finnicus with this. It should brighten his mood some. He'll likely do better work. Just don't let him start drinking it before he cuts into your friend. Unless his hands are shaking bad. Then a few nips should sort him out."

263

"This just gets better and better," Riley said.

Levi clapped him on the shoulder. "We might do things a little different here in Sultan. I like to think we do them the right way. We're not a violent family. We just find it necessary from time to time to act violently. You understand?"

Riley looked back at Bennett and Chance who were still pointing their guns at him. "Do I have a choice?"

"No. I suppose you don't. Remember, stop by in two days and speak with Laney."

After Riley left, Laney lined up a row of shot glasses on the bar and filled them with whiskey. Levi took one and lifted it high.

"To another interesting night at The Silo."

Everyone drank. Laney refilled the glasses. "Pa," Chance said, "why'd you hire the logger? You don't think we can handle security during the poker tournament ourselves?"

"I'm sure you boys would do fine, but Dalton will be playing cards. Laney's pouring drinks. That leaves you, Dylan, and Bennett to watch the place if I happen not to make it back as soon as I hope to from Monroe. The tournament happens with or without me. A big fella like Riley can go a long way toward keeping folks in line without anyone having to resort to guns."

"He seems all right," Dalton said. "Didn't care for that other one, though. He made a mess of the bar."

Bennett ran his hand along the fresh gouges in the wood. "Ah, just a bit more character is all–another story to tell when we're old and gray."

"You plan on being old and gray?" Dalton asked.

"Sure. You don't?"

Dalton stared at the shot glass he held between his fingers. "I don't think old and gray are in the cards for some of us."

Laney tilted her head toward the floor. "I know that before *I* get old and gray one of you boys is going to clean the blood off the floor that jig-dancing moron leaked out after your father shot him. Don't make me have to ask twice."

Chance sighed. "I'll do it." He slid off the bar stool. Laney handed him a bucket and sponge. Bennett raised his glass.

"To the youngest among us who cleans up the mess!"

Everyone laughed–except Chance.

He was too busy cleaning up blood.

29.

"What the hell is *this*?" Levi said as he turned onto Main Street in Sultan on his way to the sit down with Noretta Saul in Monroe. A line of nine women marched down the middle of the street holding painted signs that read GAMBLING IS THE DEVIL–SAY NO TO THE SILO.

One of the women noticed Levi's car. Her face twisted into itself like a fractured jigsaw puzzle. Soon they were all pointing and chanting.

"Shame on you!" they cried. "Shame on you!"

Levi honked his horn and waved. The women kept chanting. He kept driving.

He had left the house with Laney and the boys telling him to be careful. Laney seemed especially worried. The drive to Monroe was uneventful with few other vehicles on the road. Levi parked in front of City Hall, took out his pistol, and placed it under the seat.

The town streets and sidewalks bustled with early afternoon activity. Levi walked inside and took the stairs two at a time. He was greeted in the hallway by a smiling Mayor Brown.

"Good to see you again, Mr. Bowman, and thank you for accepting my invitation to meet with Ms. Saul."

Levi nodded. "Sure."

Mayor Brown motioned toward a door at the end of the hallway. "Right this way is our conference room." The mayor rapped on the door. It opened, and Chief Moyer stepped out.

Levi glared at the mayor. "What's he doing here?"

"Now, now, Mr. Bowman, we just need to ensure there'll be no trouble. The chief is going to pat you down. It'll only take a second."

"I don't have any weapons."

"I believe you. Think of it as a formality. I wasn't sure if you'd show up here alone or with some of your boys armed to the teeth. Please don't be offended."

"I am."

Moyer stood in front of Levi. "Arms out."

Levi lifted his arms. "Don't you dare double-cross me, Mayor. You check Noretta for guns too?"

The mayor's smile widened. "Of course, we will. My job is to ensure a level playing field."

"What? She's not even here yet?"

"She'll be here soon. She gave me her word."

Levi flinched as Moyer's hands thumped him in the side. "I'd be careful about putting so much faith in the word of a snake."

Moyer stepped away from Levi and nodded. "He's clean."

Mayor Brown opened the door. "Have a seat wherever you like, Mr. Bowman."

It was a narrow room with a long table surrounded by chairs. Levi sat down at the far end, so he could face the door. The mayor cocked his head.

"I believe I hear Ms. Saul coming now. I'll be right back."

Levi sat and waited. He could hear voices coming from the hall outside. Those voices lowered to whispered murmurs. A minute passed. The door opened. The mayor stepped into the conference room, opened the door further, and then moved aside to allow Noretta to walk by. She took a seat without looking at Levi.

"Leave us," she said. The mayor appeared confused. He opened his mouth to speak, but Noretta cut him off. "I said leave us. Stand outside. If I need anything, I'll call for you. Go. Now."

The door was closed.

"You treat the mayor like a broken dog," Levi said.

"I really don't think you care how I treat him, Mr. Bowman. We're here to talk business. To put our cards on the table and stop with this nonsense that admittedly began with my own involvement in your town. I'll just put my apology for that out there right now, so we can get it out of the way. I'm sorry."

"You want to apologize for threatening my business? My family? I just left Sultan. You know what I saw on my way out?"

"I have no idea, but I'm sure you're about to tell me."

"Lady, you're really something, you know that? There was a line of your church friends marching down Main Street with signs condemning my establishment. Now you're gonna sit there and try and tell me you don't know anything about it? Fact is you won't be satisfied until you have *everyone* in my own town marching against me."

Levi started to stand. "Please sit down, Mr. Bowman. I give you my word. I have no idea what you're talking about. I assure you I haven't been in contact with anyone from the church in Sultan for several days. Their zealousness for stamping out all sin is a bit much."

"You mean you started a fire that you're now having a hard time controlling. Am I right?"

"Yes, you could say that. We're both in the alcohol business, Mr. Bowman. As you well know, business is booming. I've come to realize some in that church would be just as willing to turn on me as they were to go after you. I now have plans for Sultan that don't involve them."

Levi arched a brow. "Who do those plans involve?"

"You. We don't need to play coy. Your sons have been out to my barn property. Your other sons were in Bellingham and spoke with Mr. Lemkee. I give your family credit. They move quickly. You've kept me on my toes. I didn't expect to find such capable opposition out here."

Levi lit a cigarette and leaned back in the chair. "How about you go ahead and tell me what you think I know?"

"I think you know I'm in business with a man who has access to a great deal of quality Canadian alcohol. Mr. Lemkee needs to move some of his business outside of Bellingham. Increased scrutiny is making things more difficult for those in our line of work. Prohibition doesn't appear to be going away anytime soon. The larger cities are being targeted. The rural areas? Not so much. I admit my first inclination was to remove your business and replace it with one of my own. That has proven more difficult and dangerous than I anticipated. Mr. Lemkee suggested instead that you become our client–one of many we plan to establish in this area."

"What's the catch?"

Noretta's head tilted upward. "Our only requirement is that you purchase from us and us alone–no secondary sources. All previous agreements you have with other suppliers are to be null and void effective immediately."

"That's putting all my eggs in just one basket–yours. And if I refuse?"

Noretta gave Levi a tight smile. "Then this war we've been waging will continue. I'm warning you. Mr. Lemkee will not take a refusal sitting down. He'll see you and your family as a threat and be required to do what he must to move his own business forward."

Tobacco smoke hung thick over the table. Levi took another long drag and then flicked the ashes onto the floor. "I won't refuse Lemkee outright. That said, I need some assurances."

"Go ahead. I assumed you would."

"You don't sell to anybody else within a thirty-mile radius of Sultan. If I'm to go exclusive with you as my supplier, then you need to extend me the same courtesy. Monroe remains a dry town. I don't want to have to worry about your booze creating more local competition for me."

"Agreed. Anything else?"

"You deliver directly to The Silo. We won't be responsible for transporting the alcohol from your barn. That's on you."

Noretta's face tightened. "That's more risk, manpower, expense."

"Sure, and that's the deal."

"Did you require your other suppliers to deliver to you?"

"No, but this is different. If things go well, it'll be higher volume, which as you said, is more risk. I can assure your safety inside of Sultan, but not outside the town limits. Will you be providing direct delivery to your Seattle clients?"

"Possibly—for a surcharge."

Levi shrugged. "There you go. We want the same delivery service you're offering to others but without the surcharge because the travel time doesn't justify that. We pay for the alcohol. That's it."

"So, you want something for nothing?"

Levi's cigarette hung down from the corner of his mouth. He didn't reply as Noretta stared at him. She nodded. "Fine. We have a deal."

They both turned at the sound of yelling from the other side of the door. Mayor Brown was telling someone to leave. There was a brief knock and then the door opened. The mayor entered the room. His face was red and his eyes wide. He cleared his throat.

"There's someone here to see you, Mr. Bowman."

"Who is it?" Noretta asked.

The mayor looked at her, glanced at Levi, and then looked away. "Uh, it's the county sheriff–a Mr. Blight."

Levi stood. "What's he want?"

The door opened further. Blight had been the Snohomish County sheriff for nearly forty years. His back was bent, his eyes cloudy, and his thin-fingered hands trembled at his sides. His gun hung off hips that looked to be too thin to hold the belt up. He pointed at Levi.

"That him?"

The mayor said yes. "Mr. Bowman I'm placing you under arrest for the murder of Roy Coon." Blight's voice was a whispery squeak.

Noretta got up and turned around. "What's this all about, Mr. Mayor?"

"Like you don't know," Levi growled. "You set me up."

Noretta leaned across the table. "I have nothing to do with this."

The sheriff rested his shaking hand on the butt of his gun. "I don't want no trouble, Mr. Bowman. Just come with me."

Levi lit another cigarette and sat back down. "No. This is Monroe. You're county. This isn't your jurisdiction. I've no idea what you're talking about, and I'm sure as hell not going anywhere with you."

The sheriff puffed out his bony chest. "Now hold on. You're right. I am county and this here town is in my county. I damn well *do* have jurisdiction, and I don't believe for a second you don't know what happened to Roy Coon."

"What's your evidence?"

Blight gritted his teeth. "I don't need to tell you that. Now c'mon. Enough of this. Let's go."

"I said no. You go on and leave, so I can get back to my business."

Blight took out his pistol and pointed it at Levi. "You sonofabitch. I'm the goddamn sheriff. I know what you are, Mr. Bowman. I know what you do. I know all about it. Now move your ass."

Noretta stepped in front of the sheriff and glanced down at the gun. "Put that thing away."

"Ma'am, you need to step aside. This is law enforcement business."

"Are you going to shoot an innocent woman?"

"No, but I'll arrest you for obstructing an officer of the law."

"Who sent you here?" Levi asked.

"Again, that's not your concern, Mr. Bowman."

"You just said you intend to arrest me. If that isn't my concern, I don't know what is."

Blight tried to gently push Noretta away. She swatted his hand down. "I can have my deputies come here if necessary. A whole slew of them."

Levi's eyes narrowed. "Then why don't you? If I'm the terror you say I am, then why did you show up here alone? That don't add up, Sheriff."

The mayor clapped his hands together. "I have a proposal. How about we hold Mr. Bowman in our jail until this can all be sorted out? I'm happy to make a call to Judge Thompson and ask him what he thinks regarding jurisdictional disputes."

Blight's eyes darted side to side like a cornered rat looking for escape. He jammed his pistol back into its holster. "Fine. Lock him up. There's no need to be bothering the judge with this. I'll review the situation and get back to you, but Mr. Bowman don't leave that cell until I say so, understand?" The sheriff poked the mayor's chest. "You fail to do that, and I'll be happy to arrest you as an accomplice. Don't test me. I want your word he stays behind bars until I say different."

Mayor Brown agreed. Blight nodded. "Okay, then get to it. Cuff him and march him straight to your jail. I don't leave until I hear the click of the lock on the cell door."

The mayor called out for Chief Moyer who then quickly entered the room. Mayor Brown motioned to Levi. "Mr. Bowman will be staying as a guest at the jail for a short while. Please escort him there."

Moyer's eyes lit up as he grinned. "With pleasure."

"Chief Moyer," the mayor said, "you're to treat Mr. Bowman with the upmost respect."

Moyer shrugged. "Sure, whatever. Right this way, Mr. Bowman."

Levi remained seated and smoking his cigarette. "Swapping out the sheriff for Moyer doesn't change my mind any. Me sitting inside *any* jail cell is bullshit. It's not gonna happen." He stood and walked toward the door. Blight again took out his gun and aimed it at him.

"I don't give a damn what you think. You're going with Chief Moyer, or I swear on your children's graves I'll shoot you dead right here and now."

Levi's eyes were dark ice. "My sons are alive and well, Sheriff Blight."

Blight grinned and grunted. "Is that right? I was sure you'd lost one or two by now. Guess I was mistaken. I'm glad to know you've been spared that kind of pain. I hear it's a terrible, terrible thing to lose a child. Now how about you go with Chief Moyer like everyone else in this room thinks you should?"

Levi looked at Noretta. "Is that what *you* want?"

Noretta avoided Levi's hard stare. "I think it's best. We can get this sorted out very soon. I can have my attorney expedite your release. Again, please know I had nothing to do with any of this."

"After everything you've done and tried to do to me and my family already, why should I believe you?"

"All I can do is prove it. Our agreement does me no good if you're sitting in jail. I'll be in touch."

Blight hitched a thumb into his belt while keeping his pistol pointed at Levi. "What agreement would that be?"

"None of your business, little man," Noretta replied. "Now get out of my way."

"Hold on," Levi said.

Noretta turned around. "Yes?"

"A man named Calwin Quick came to see me."

Noretta's face was unreadable. "And?"

"And I was wondering if you knew anything about it."

"No. Should I?"

Not long after Noretta gave that answer Laney picked up the phone at The Silo while all four of Levi's sons sat at the bar waiting for their father to return from his meeting in Monroe. They watched her nod her head once and then hang up.

"Who was it?" Chance asked.

"That was Mayor Brown," Laney answered. "I knew that meeting was a bad idea. Your father's sitting in the Monroe jail."

Bennett slammed his fist against the bar. "That fucking Noretta set him up. Fine. We're just gonna break him out. Let's go."

"Wait," Laney said. "The mayor promised me he'd have him out by tomorrow."

Chance shook his head. "That mayor is a piece of shit. He can't be trusted."

Bennett nodded. "He's right. We should go get Pa out of there."

Laney looked at Dalton and Dylan. "What do you two think?"

Dylan finished the last of his whiskey. "Me? I say we wait until dark and turn the place upside down until we have Pa back. We don't go in half-cocked, though. We plan it out. We do it right."

Laney waited for Dalton to say something. He looked up and grinned. "Lock and load. Looks like the Bowman boys ride again. We go break him out and woe to any poor bastard who tries to stop us. People need to be reminded why they should fear this family. You don't fuck with a Bowman."

Chance clapped Dalton on the back. "That's my big brother. Let's do this."

The brothers got up and walked out together. Right before the door closed Laney called out to them. "Be careful. Any of you boys get hurt, I'll kill you!"

30.

"It shouldn't be long now, Mr. Bowman. There were no formal charges. No evidence. Nothing. Clearly the sheriff is stretching the limits of his authority. I've already been in contact with Judge Thompson. You shouldn't be too concerned."

Joseph Broadmoor was an older man of average height and build. His full head of thick gray hair was slicked back from a prominent brow. He wore horn-rimmed glasses, a custom tailored dark suit, and white tie. He asked Levi if he wanted a cup of coffee. Levi said no.

"How did you come to know Noretta?" Levi asked.

Broadmoor sat in a chair next to the cell. He crossed one leg over the other and shrugged. "I was suggested to her by Mr. Lemkee in Bellingham. I've some experience in dealing with matters relating to the sale of certain products currently banned by the federal government."

Levi chuckled. "That's a fancy way of saying you defend people like me."

Broadmoor smiled. "Yes, Mr. Bowman, I defend people like you. I'll assume we share a common indifference toward the abuses of power currently being practiced by our government and its views on the production, sale, and enjoyment of alcohol."

"If you think it's bullshit, I imagine we do. Someone told me recently that you were threatening to turn me into the feds."

"Ah, yes, that was during my conversation with Officer Fenner after the altercation your sons had with Robert Saul. As you know, Mr. Saul nearly had his ear cut off, but I assure you it was merely a positional threat. We, Ms. Saul and I, were attempting a bit of intimidation. I'm pleased to see it appears her relationship with you has since improved."

"Why go to all this trouble to get me out of here?"

"Because that's what Mr. Lemkee wants. I'm to do everything in my power to expedite your release. He also mentioned something about a poker tournament."

"Yeah, later this week. Apparently, he wants to play in it."

"Oh, I don't doubt that. Mr. Lemkee is nothing if not a man attracted to risk and reward."

"Is that what he considers working with me? A risk?"

"Likely a calculated one, yes. He's managed to become very successful very quickly. This ridiculous policy of Prohibition has created a thousand Mr. Lemkees all across the country. And don't for a second think a good deal of the profit they make isn't finding its way back into the pockets of the very politicians who outlawed alcohol in the first place. The entire thing is disgusting. And when alcohol is made legal again, and it will be, the government will then find something else to take from us to replace it so that this cycle of corruption can continue in one form or another."

Levi got up from the cot and rubbed the back of his neck. "Can't say I don't think the same, but until then, I plan on squeezing every cent I can out of Prohibition. Financially, it's the best thing that's ever happened to me."

"But that doesn't come without a certain degree of danger, does it, Mr. Bowman? Danger to you, your family, your reputation among friends and neighbors?"

Levi shrugged. "The family part is all I worry about. Nobody lives forever. I just want to live free to do whatever I want when I want. Today is today. Tomorrow? Who the hell knows?"

Broadmoor lit a cigarette and passed it through the bars to Levi and then lit a second one for himself. "You're an interesting man, Mr. Bowman. I hope we can continue to do business. It would be my privilege to represent and protect your interests going forward."

"I've always looked at lawyers the same as I do doctors and cops–things best to be avoided."

Broadmoor laughed. "There's certainly wisdom in that. Still, your future with Mr. Lemkee will likely prove a very profitable one. That kind of money often generates even more scrutiny. The kind of scrutiny a good lawyer can help you to better navigate."

"Get me out of here first, and then I'll think about it."

"Fair enough," Broadmoor said as he stood. "I'm going to make another call to the judge. Be right back."

Levi returned to the cot, leaned back against the cold concrete wall of the cell and closed his eyes.

"Pa?"

Levi sat up and looked around.

"Hey, Pa, you in there?"

"Bennett?"

"Yeah. I'm on the other side of the wall. We're all here. Brought some dynamite with us. We're gonna blow you out. You should probably move to the other side of the cell."

Levi flicked his cigarette away. "Did you say dynamite?" Bennett didn't answer. "Bennett, did you say *dynamite*?"

"Sorry, thought we heard someone coming. Yeah, we had three sticks left in that box in the barn at home from the time we blew those tree stumps in the field. Remember?"

"Christ, Bennett, that was six summers ago! It could've become unstable by now."

"Dalton looked it over real careful. He thinks it's fine. You ready for us to light it up?"

"No, put it away. I'll be out of here soon. Until then, just hang back and stay out of sight."

"You sure? We're ready to blast away out here."

"Sorry to disappoint you boys, but yes I'm sure. The last thing we need right now is to be blowing shit up. Noretta's lawyer seems to be competent enough. It's like I told you. I'll be out soon."

"Pa?"

"Yeah, Chance?"

"I want you to know we're not going anywhere until you're free. We'll be right here waiting with the dynamite ready just in case, okay?"

"Thanks, boys. I appreciate it, but please be careful with that stuff."

The jail room door opened. "Were you talking to someone?" Broadmoor asked.

"Mumbling to myself is all," Levi said.

"I have some good news. The judge called the mayor directly and ordered your release." Broadmoor looked back. "Ah, I think I hear someone coming now."

Chief Moyer walked in looking like he had just stepped in dog shit. "I guess you already know then? The judge just ordered him released."

Broadmoor nodded. "Yes. I'm sure Mr. Bowman is more than ready to get out of here. Thank you, Chief."

When Moyer went to put his key into the cell door's lock an explosion rocked the building. Bits of dust floated down from the ceiling. Moyer's eyes were as big as saucers. "What the hell was *that*?"

Broadmoor glanced at Levi. "I have no idea, but before you go find out you need to free Mr. Bowman first."

Moyer glared at Levi. "Not if those damn sons of his have something to do with that racket."

"That's not actually true. Mr. Bowman was locked up in here. Whoever or whatever was the cause of the explosion, it isn't Mr. Bowman's fault. You need to let him out–now. That is, unless you want me to get Judge Thompson on the line and inform him you've refused his direct order for Mr. Bowman's release."

Moyer mumbled a profanity under his breath and then opened the cell door. "Get out of here."

"Right this way, Mr. Bowman," Broadmoor said. A small crowd had gathered outside.

"Anyone know where the explosion came from?" Moyer asked. A woman pointed to the side of the police station. "Came from over there," she said. Moyer drew his gun and went to the back of the building.

"Probably a good time to get going, Mr. Bowman," Broadmoor whispered.

Levi shook his hand. "What do I owe you?"

"This one was on Ms. Saul. Just promise me you'll be in touch regarding retaining my services in the future."

Levi told Broadmoor he would. He looked up and down the street for any sign of his sons while silently praying none of them were hurt. He spied the top of Dylan's car parked a block away and then saw Bennett standing next to it waving at him.

"Everyone okay?" Levi asked when he reached the car.

Dalton nodded but looked annoyed. "Yeah, we're all fine. Bennett decided he'd chuck the dynamite into the river. One of the sticks blew up when he did. We're lucky none of us were killed. Drove all the way here with those things bouncing around in the back."

"I thought you checked them out and said the dynamite was safe?" Levi said.

Dalton shrugged. "Guess I was wrong."

Bennett was all smiles. "Nice to have you back, Pa."

Dylan got out from behind the wheel. "I imagine the explosion didn't go over too well with the cops."

Levi looked back at the police station. "No, it didn't. We best get going."

"None of you move." Moyer stood forty paces away with his gun out. "I knew you Bowmans had something to do with that blast. I'm taking you in on endangerment and disturbing the peace. If the judge don't like that he can kiss my ass."

Levi opened the passenger door. "You think this new car of yours can outrun him?"

"Oh yeah," Dylan said with a grin.

The Bowmans piled into the car. A bullet ricocheted off the roof. Chance glanced through the back window.

"That crazy son of a bitch is shooting at us."

Levi lit a cigarette and nodded at Dylan. "Let's go."

Dylan put the car into gear and mashed down on the accelerator. The car lurched and then stalled.

"Goddammit Dylan!" Chance yelled. "What the hell?"

Another bullet sent sparks flying off one of the back bumpers.

"Moyer's got another cop with him now," Bennett said. "I can hear him yelling for us to stop."

Dylan restarted the car. Levi leaned back in his seat and closed his eyes. "Dylan, you really don't need to make this any more exciting than it already is. I'd rather we just tear on out of here. What do you say?"

The car's tires squealed as it leaped onto the road and sped off. Dylan glanced at Chance in the rearview mirror.

"That better?"

Chance grunted. "It couldn't have been much worse. Where'd you learn to drive? A funeral home?"

Dylan gripped the wheel tight enough it made his knuckles white. "You're the last person to be judging anyone's driving. I'm happy to pull this car over and kick your ass. Don't think I won't."

"That'll have to wait," Dalton said. "We have company."

Levi sat up and turned around. Moyer and another officer were driving after them.

"He's a tenacious prick," Levi said. "I'll give him that."

Dylan dropped the car into another gear and accelerated. Bennett leaned forward. "You really think Fenner will show like he promised?"

Levi cocked his head. "Fenner?"

"A contingency plan," Dylan answered. "And a good thing, too. We might just need it. Moyer's not gaining on us, but he's managing to keep up. This car is loaded up with the five of us. His only has two."

"We're past the Monroe city limits," Chance said. "Why's he still following us?"

Bennett took out his gun while looking out the back window. "Because he's just another small dick with a badge. Let him follow us. We get to Sultan, he won't like how this'll end. Not if I can help it."

Levi pointed at Bennett's pistol. "*That* is a last resort."

Bennett looked like a scolded puppy. "I know."

"You better."

It started to rain. Dylan rotated the manual windshield wiper. "I think I see the bridge up ahead."

Levi's eyes narrowed. "Yup, that's it. We're almost home. Moyer still behind us?"

"Yeah," Dalton answered.

Dylan turned his headlights on and off. Seconds later a pair of headlights further up the road did the same.

"I'll be damned," Dylan said. "He actually came through for us."

They crossed the bridge. As soon as they passed him, Fenner parked in the middle of the road, blocking the way into Sultan. Dylan pulled off to the side just as Fenner was getting out of his car. He tipped his cap at the Bowmans.

Moyer's vehicle came to a screeching halt. He honked the horn and yelled at Fenner to clear the way. Fenner refused and ordered Moyer to drive back to Monroe where he belonged.

"I'm in pursuit of a crime, you crooked son of a bitch," Moyer said. "Now move that piece of shit, or I will."

Fenner drew his weapon. "This is my jurisdiction, Chief. I'm gonna tell you one more time--turn around and go."

The rain had turned into a downpour. Puddles of water collected on the road. The Bowmans stood a few paces behind Fenner. Moyer pointed at them.

"I know you were the ones who caused the explosion."

Levi stepped forward. Rain dripped off the end of his nose. "That's nothing more than an accusation. You really should listen to Officer Fenner. I don't want to see anyone get hurt. This here rain isn't the only thing that could come down on your head right now."

"Fuck you, Bowman. Fuck your family. And fuck this river-mud town. You're no goddamn king. You're nothing but a backwoods thug."

"And you're the dumb bastard who drove all the way out here to tell me something I already know."

"It was worth it. Some things just need to be said."

"And some people just need to know when it's time to shut up and go."

"You threatening me?"

The Bowman boys all took out their guns at the same time and pointed them at Moyer. "Looks like you're outgunned, Chief," Levi said. "That's no threat--just basic math. The next move is yours. I'm done talking, and my boys are ready to start shooting. You wanna dance? Let's dance."

After one more 'fuck you' Moyer returned to his car, backed it up, and then sped off toward Monroe. Fenner's shoulders slumped.

"Jeez, for a second there I thought he might actually draw down on us."

"Nah," Levi said. "Fella like that? He's a coward. As soon as he saw he was outgunned, he was done. It was just hot air from there. Hey, how'd you know to be here on the bridge when we came in?"

Fenner pointed to Dylan. "Your boy let me know what was going on. Said you might need me. So here I am."

"It's appreciated. I won't forget what you did. Maybe it's time we look into getting you a raise?"

"I won't argue with that. Is there anything else I can do for you, Mr. Bowman?"

"Actually, there is. My car is still in Monroe."

Fenner tipped his cap. "Say no more. I can leave it at your house or The Silo if you like."

"The Silo would be fine. I'll be there all night. We all will. Have a poker tournament to get ready for."

Fenner snapped his fingers. "That's right. I almost forgot. Admiral said if I saw you first to make sure I ask you to save him a place at the table. He seems pretty excited about it."

"Is that right?"

"Yeah. He's ready to play."

"Sure. Let him know we'll have a spot for him. His money spends just as well as anyone else's."

A horn honked. A line of cars waited to cross the bridge. Fenner left while the Bowmans stood to the side and watched the vehicles go by. The last one was driven by Pastor Jim. He stopped and rolled down his window. His stutter made it hard for him to get the words out.

"What on earth are you all doing out in this rain?"

"That's a long story, Pastor," Levi answered. "Since you're here, I do have a question for you though."

"What is it?"

"Earlier today there was a gaggle of your congregation marching down Main Street condemning my business. They had signs and everything. You know anything about that?"

"Uh, well, it was probably Ms. Saul's doing."

Levi frowned. "Really? It's my understanding she hasn't been in contact with anyone in your church for a while."

"How would you know that, Mr. Bowman?"

"Just something I heard. No worries, Pastor. Thought I'd ask. Looks like another car is coming this way. You should get going."

The pastor smiled. It took him four tries before he was finally able to spit the words out. "Perhaps I'll see you in church again?"

Levi glanced up at the rain-soaked sky. "That might take a miracle, Pastor. You never know though."

Levi watched the pastor drive away. A cool, early evening breeze hit him in the face. He pulled his jacket tighter. The rain started to let up.

"Pa? Everything okay?" Chance asked.

"Sure. C'mon, let's get out of this cold. I can't be the only one dying for a drink."

The Bowmans left. The bridge was clear. Day gave way to night.

31.

It was the morning of the poker tournament. Dalton sat with Winona on the top of the Bowman family's barn loft with their legs hanging out over the opening. The place smelled of old hay and dry wood. Winona's arm was around Dalton's waist. His was around her shoulders. Both their faces wore faraway smiles.

"I used to come here as a kid with my brother Dylan. After Ma passed, we spent hours up here looking out at the pond, the field, and the hill behind our property. Being the two oldest, I think we felt the pain of her loss more deeply than Bennett and Chance. Dylan was actually the quiet one back then. I would try to convince him everything would be okay. I don't know if I succeeded. Dylan never said. He put up this invisible wall around himself. That wall is still there. The others might not notice, but I do. I promised him I'd always be there if he needed me. Then I went off to war and came back... different. I wonder sometimes if he thinks I broke that promise I made to him all those years ago. I suppose I can't blame him if he does. The thing Dylan hates more than anything is when the people he loves the most let him down."

Winona shook her head.

"Gosh, you're pretty. About the prettiest thing I've ever seen." Dalton blushed. "I'm sorry. I'm babbling. Fact is, I'm nervous about tonight. I've never played for so much money. If I win, you want to know what I plan to do with all that cash?"

Winona nodded. Dalton pointed at the field beyond the pond. "Gonna build a house right over there. It'll have a porch and everything." He looked at Winona. "And plenty of room to start a family."

A raven landed on a branch in a tree near the barn. Its head bobbed as it watched the two of them. Dalton cleared his throat. "I said it'd have plenty of room to start a family."

Winona looked up. Her brows lifted. She pointed at her chest. Dalton nodded.

"Yeah, if you'll have me."

Winona tilted her head. Her eyes were nearly as dark as the raven's. Dalton bit down on his lip.

"I mean, you don't have to decide now. We're still getting to know each other. I understand that. I might look it, but I'm not stupid. I get it. A woman should have some time to think about a decision like that, and you can have all the time in the world. The last thing I'd ever want to do is make you feel uncomfortable or rushed into doing something you're not sure about."

Winona half-turned, put her hands around Dalton's face, and pulled him down toward her. Their lips touched. Her tongue flicked against his. He pulled away. She scowled.

Dalton grabbed her under her arms, lifted her up, and then plopped her down on his lap. She wrapped her legs around his waist. "That's better," he said. "Now we don't have to keep twisting around to look at each other."

Winona glanced behind her at the twelve-foot drop below. "I got you," Dalton whispered. "I'd never let you fall."

They hugged. Winona nuzzled Dalton's neck.

"Hello? You two up there?" It was Dylan.

Dalton got up with Winona still clinging to him. He set her down. "Yeah, what do you want?"

"Sorry for interrupting. We're having a meeting in the kitchen with Pa. He wants to go over some things before the tournament tonight. Speaking of which, are you ready to win some big money?"

Dalton walked across the hay loft and looked down. Dylan stood in the middle of the barn. He was wearing another new tie.

"Yeah, I'm ready."

"Good. Hey there, Winona. Nice to see you. Dalton showing you the hay loft, huh? We sure spent a lot of time in this place as kids. Especially after Ma passed."

"I told her about it," Dalton said. "You remember all the tunnels you'd build after the hay was delivered?"

Dylan grinned. "That's right. They'd stack it twelve rows high, and I'd squeeze in between the gaps and crawl toward the middle and push the bales out bit by bit to make more room. I created my own little world inside there."

"And the time you found the litter of kittens?"

"Uh-huh. Four little fur balls crying away. Something happened to their mother. She wasn't there to take care of them. Just like us."

"You brought them a saucer of cream every day."

"I had to. I couldn't just let the poor things starve. One of them didn't make it. It was kind of strange because it was the biggest and strongest of the four, but then it got sick or something. I tried and tried, but it stopped taking the cream. Like it just gave up."

Dylan leaned down, picked up a bit of hay from off the floor, and rubbed it between his fingers. "It wasted away and died. I learned that no matter how many bales of hay I put between myself and the real world, pain and loss would still find me."

"You saved the other three, though."

Dylan watched the hay fall from his hand. "Yeah, I guess so." He looked up. "Anyways, you on your way?"

Dalton nodded. "Sure." He climbed down from the loft first, waited for Winona, and then walked with her and Dylan back to the house.

Levi looked up from his seat at the kitchen table. "Well, there you are."

Winona went upstairs while Dalton and Dylan sat down. Laney poured them all cups of fresh-brewed coffee. She paused next to Dalton.

"You hear that?"

Dalton looked up. "Hear what?"

"Sounds like wedding bells."

Dalton's head dropped. "C'mon, it's a bit early for that kind of talk, don't you think?"

Laney shrugged. "Maybe, maybe not. What I do know is you boys aren't getting any younger. I was just a little older than Chance when I married my first husband–God rest his soul."

"That's different," Bennett said.

Laney looked at him over the brim of her coffee cup. "How so?"

"You're a woman."

Laney arched a brow. "And?"

"Women marry younger. I mean, how much older was your husband when you two hooked up?"

"Hooked up?"

Bennett nodded. "Yeah–got married?"

"He was fourteen years older."

"See? There you go. So, if we use you as an example, then I have at least another ten years before I should start thinking about settling down."

"I love you dearly Bennet, but ten more years of you living in this house? I'm not sure I could take it."

"Sure," Chance said with a chuckle. "And when Bennett somehow manages to find a girl who'll have him, they'll both live here together, and I'll bring my wife, and Dylan can bring his and look at Dalton. Seems he's already on his way to doing the same. It'll be one *really* big, happy family."

Laney's mouth fell open. She shot Levi a hard look. He shook his head. "Keep me out of this."

"I will *not* spend the rest of my days playing mother to four grown men and their wives. No. I won't do it."

Bennett shrugged. "I guess I could live under the bridge. I'll have to change my name to Troll or something, but that's okay. You do what you have to do."

Laney gave Bennett a playful pinch on his arm. "Oh, hush."

"I want to build a house behind the pond."

Everyone stared at Dalton. "Are you serious?" Levi asked him.

"Yeah. It's quiet back there. I figure the winnings from tonight will be more than enough to pay for it."

"That's some confidence," Chance said. "I like it."

Laney reached across the table and put her hand on top of Dalton's. "You want to live there with Winona?"

Dalton hesitated. "Uh, I hope to when the time is right."

Laney smiled. "I think that would be wonderful, and I'm sure your father will be happy to help. Isn't that right Levi?"

"Sure, whatever you need, Dalton. You bet. For now, though, let's all focus on tonight, okay?"

Everyone nodded. "First," Levi said, "we make sure everyone who comes into The Silo is patted down. No weapons are allowed inside–no exceptions. You'll be in charge of that, Chance. We'll have that big fella Riley helping out. Bennett, you'll be behind the bar with Laney. Dylan, I want you at the back of the room keeping an eye on everything–the door, the bar, the office, the poker table. You see any trouble, let me know. I'll be dealing the cards and keeping the money box next to me. As for you, Dalton–are you ready? There'll be some strong players showing up tonight."

Dalton shifted in his chair. "I'll be fine. It's just poker."

"Hold on now," Bennett said with a smirk. "Didn't you just say you were going to build a house with your winnings? Seems to me you're playing for your entire future tonight. That's a hell of a lot of pressure. I don't think I could handle it. I'd be more nervous than a whore sitting down for Sunday tea with the Pope."

Dylan threw his head back and laughed. Dalton sighed. "I said I'm fine."

"I'm sure you are, big brother," Bennett said. "I'm sure you are."

There was a knock at the kitchen door. Chance stood with his gun drawn and opened it. "Who are you?" he asked.

"My name's Cridert. This the Bowman place?"

Levi got up and went to the door. He told Chance to let him in.

"Mr. Cridert, what are you doing here?"

Cridert's hands and face were covered in fresh scratches. "I thought I should see you, given who came to see me yesterday."

Levi introduced Cridert to the others and then had him sit down. "How did you get here?" he asked.

"I walked."

Levi's eyes widened. "From the top of the Basin? Down the hill through all that brush?"

Cridert nodded. "I did. It wasn't so bad."

"But why?"

"Like I said, on account of who visited me yesterday."

"And who was that?"

Laney interrupted to ask Cridert if he would like a cup of coffee. He beamed at her and said he would like that very much. Then he continued. "There were two men at first. One of them about my age. The other might have been a little older. He said he was a sheriff. Went by the name of Blight. The other fella had a funny name. Said it was Quick. He didn't talk much. His hand stayed close to that fancy gun of his. I've never seen a gun quite like it. The handle was a soft white–like ivory."

"It *is* ivory," Levi said. "Tell me what they wanted from you."

Laney handed Cridert his coffee. He said thank you, took a sip, and told her how good it was. "They knew about the whiskey in the cave. The sheriff ordered me to show it to him. So, I did."

"And then what?"

"They took it. Every bottle. The sheriff left and then came back with three more fellas and they marched it all out of there over several trips. Took them most the afternoon. I thought about trying to stop them, but the one with the fancy gun, there was something about the way he looked at me that let me know if I tried, they'd be leaving me dead in that cave. The sheriff warned me I wasn't to make any more liquor. Said he'd haul me off to jail if I did. Then they left with the last of it. We had our deal, so I thought I needed to come here and let you know in person what happened. I didn't want you to make the trip all that way to my place only to find out I no longer had anything to give you."

"Those sons a bitches," Bennett hissed.

"Did they happen to mention who sent them to your place?" Levi asked.

Cridert shook his head. "No. I'm very sorry to have let you down, Mr. Bowman. I know how much you wanted those bottles."

Levi lit a cigarette. "It's not your fault. You were robbed. It'd be nice to know who was behind it though."

"I wish I could give you the answer. I honestly don't have a clue. First you show up and then those two. That's the most visitors I've had in years."

"It's got to be Noretta," Bennett said.

"I say it's Admiral," Laney added. "He was the only other one who knew about where Cridert lived."

"For now, it doesn't matter," Levi remarked. "We focus on the poker tournament going on tonight. That's it."

"Are you still going to save Admiral a seat at the table?" Dylan asked.

Levi shrugged. "I don't see why not."

Laney scowled. "You don't? And what if his two goons show up with him? Or Noretta? What then?"

"I already assumed Noretta would be there. Look, we're running a high stakes poker game. After that is when I'll focus on trying to figure out who took our hooch from Mr. Cridert."

"You say the sheriff came back to your place with three other guys?" Chance asked.

Cridert nodded. "That's right."

Chance leaned forward. "Catch any of their names?"

"No. One of them walked with a pretty bad limp, though. He was complaining about his foot. The others kept telling him to shut up about it."

"Might be the guy whose toe Pa shot off," Bennett said. "The same one who was working for Admiral clearing trees on Haystack. I think his name was West."

Levi got up. "You need a ride back to the top of the Basin, Mr. Cridert?"

"No, that's okay. I'll walk."

"You sure? That's at least two miles uphill."

"I'll be fine. Thank you. Feel free to stop by anytime, Mr. Bowman. I forgot how nice it is to speak to a friendly face. And thank you again for the coffee ma'am. It was delicious."

"My pleasure," Laney said. "It was nice to meet you."

Cridert left. Levi sat down and lit another cigarette. Laney pushed the ashtray closer to him. "I know how hard it is for you to have to admit Admiral can't be trusted."

Levi pursed his lips. "And I know how easy it is for you to want me to believe that."

Laney started to respond, but Levi cut her off. "How many times do I have to say it? We focus on the tournament. After that, we deal with this other stuff."

Laney put her coffee cup in the sink and started to leave the room. Levi said her name. She turned around.

"What?"

"I need everyone's help tonight, Laney—including yours."

"I know. I'll be there. I always am. We'll do it your way, Levi. We always do." She walked out.

"I don't think she's too happy," Chance said.

Bennett rolled his eyes. "Your powers of observation are really something, you know that?"

"Kiss my ass," Chance replied.

Levi slammed the table. "Enough. Shut up the both of you." He smashed his cigarette out in the ashtray. "We all need to be focused for tonight, understood?"

Chance and Bennett nodded. "Good," Levi said. "Now everyone, get out of here."

Levi's sons did something they knew he didn't really want.

They left him alone.

32.

The Silo's big night started smoothly. Chance carefully checked everyone for weapons on their way in. He would sometimes have to issue a stern reminder that no guns or knives were allowed. The few times someone complained about the rule, Riley would step forward, look down at the unhappy customer, and ask if there was a problem. The customer would shake their head, give up their weapons, and walk inside while avoiding getting too close to Riley.

Laney worked furiously to get all the drink orders out in a timely manner. Bennett helped. He was in a good mood–all smiles and happy nods. Whether it was the Index swill or the much finer Basin whiskey, it didn't seem to matter. Everyone who came in was drinking and asking for more.

Dylan sat in the back near the office door. He scanned the room looking for any sign of trouble.

Dalton was at the poker table. He had a drink in front of him and a scowl on his face. "When do we start?" he asked.

Levi shuffled the cards and shrugged. "Still waiting on Admiral and Mr. Lemkee. They should be here soon."

A red-faced and thick-fingered man extended his hand across the table toward Dalton. "Name's Jack Taub of Taub's Wheels and Deals, the top car dealer in the county."

Dalton didn't shake. "Aren't you the *only* car dealer in the county?"

Taub chuckled as he withdrew his hand. "Yes, I am. Hope to keep it that way too. Your brother Dylan is always stopping by my place to check out the new inventory, but I haven't seen you yet. Hope to remedy that soon."

"Remedy?"

"I just mean to say I'd appreciate a chance to earn your business, Mr. Bowman."

Dalton pointed at Levi. "*That's* Mr. Bowman. I'm just Dalton."

Taub sipped from his whiskey glass. "Oh, I know all about you Bowman boys. I hear you play a decent game of poker, Dalton."

The man who sat to Taub's right cleared his throat. He was dressed in a suit and tie and his face was lean and lined. Dark eyes looked out from behind a pair of round-framed glasses.

"I suppose I should introduce myself to the table as well then."

Taub smiled. "We all know who you are, Mr. Probst!"

"I don't," Dalton murmured.

"I'm Denver Probst. I deal in properties, and when the opportunity presents itself, in cards as well."

Taub nudged Probst with his elbow. "Don't be so damn modest. Mr. Probst doesn't merely deal in properties. He likely owns half the Seattle boardwalk! He has more money than he knows what to do with which is why he's soon to give some of it to me here tonight."

Levi lit a cigarette and then looked up as Noretta Saul entered The Silo with Robert. She nodded at Levi. Chance moved by her and leaned down so he could whisper to his father.

"I wasn't sure I should let her in. Give the word, and she's out of here."

"She's fine," Levi said. "We're associates now. Can I get you two something to drink?"

Noretta smiled. "That's quite all right, Mr. Bowman. You must be quite pleased with the turnout."

Levi raised his whiskey glass. "I am."

Robert stepped toward the poker table. "I'd like to sit in on the game."

Levi frowned. "I'm sorry. You should have come sooner."

Robert held up an envelope. "I have money."

"It's not about the money."

"There are two empty chairs at the table."

"Yes, and those chairs are spoken for."

"But I'm here now. They're not. Let me play. Isn't my money good enough for you?"

Noretta put a hand on Robert's arm. "You're being rude."

Robert dropped the envelope on the table and glanced at Dalton. "I brought my own money here. A thousand dollars. That's the buy-in, right? Tell me, Mr. Bowman, did your son bring his own money, or do you have him playing with yours? If that's the case, I don't think you should be the one dealing the cards. I'm pretty sure most around here would call that a conflict of interest."

Dylan stood with his hand on his gun. "Everything okay, Pa?"

"It's fine, Dylan. Isn't that right, Mr. Saul?"

Robert reached for his envelope. Dalton's hand slammed down on top of it. "Wait," he said. "We can play for my seat—you and me."

Robert's eyes widened. "Really?"

Levi's eyes were nearly as wide as Robert's. "What?"

Dalton nodded. "Yeah. We'll both cut the deck. High card wins. If it's you, I give up my seat. If it's me then your envelope is mine."

"You want me to wager a thousand dollars on *one card*? There's no skill in that. It's just dumb luck."

"You in or out?"

The room went quiet as the crowd circled around the table. Dalton leaned back and motioned for another drink. "I guess he's out," he said.

"Wait," Robert hissed. "Give me a little more time to think."

"What's going on here?" The crowd parted as Admiral approached the table. He handed Levi his money.

"Just a possible side bet," Levi answered as he dropped Admiral's thousand dollars into the money box next to him and pushed stacks of chips in front of Admiral's chair.

"Is that right? What's the bet?"

Laney delivered Dalton another shot of whiskey, gave Admiral a disapproving look, and returned to her place behind the bar. "Dalton's seat for the tournament," Levi said.

Admiral pointed to Robert. "He's the one who wants in?"

Levi nodded. "Yeah."

"Well, make up your mind," Admiral barked. "None of us are getting any younger."

"He's scared," someone whispered from the back of the room.

"I'm not scared!" Robert snarled. "It's just, well, a thousand dollars, one bet, that's a lot of goddamn money."

A voice repeated Robert's words but in a high-pitched, squeaky tone. Robert stuck his chest out. "I dare you to say that to my face. Go ahead. I dare you."

"We're all waiting, Mr. Saul," Levi said.

Dalton took the top card off the deck and pulled it toward him face-down. "There. I went first. Now it's your turn."

Robert's hand trembled as he reached for the deck. His eyes narrowed. "Maybe you already knew what that top card was."

Dalton returned his card to the deck. "Fine. I'll shuffle the deck again, and you can pick first. That okay with you, Pa?"

"Sure."

Dalton shuffled the cards and pushed them toward Robert. "Cut the deck. The bottom card is yours."

Robert's hand hovered over the deck then drew back like the tips of his fingers had been burnt. He pointed at Dalton. "You're crazy. Keep your damn seat. I'm gonna enjoy watching you lose."

Dalton gave the deck back to Levi and then looked up at Robert. "You say there was no skill in what just happened. That it was all luck. You're wrong about that. I knew you'd chicken out. Could read it off you a mile away. You have no business sitting at this table. You're a stuffed shirt."

Admiral chuckled. "Dalton's right about that. You were pissin' in your own shoes. Poker is a man's business. You should run along."

"You son of a bitch." Robert reached for a gun that wasn't there while Dylan and Bennett pointed theirs at him.

"Give the order, Pa," Bennett said, "and I'll happily blow his head clean off."

Noretta grabbed hold of Robert. "Sit down over there before they take a knife to you again."

Robert jerked his arm away. "I don't have listen to--"

"The lady said sit." Titus Lemkee stepped in front of Robert. Lemkee was the shorter of the two but just as wide in the shoulders and broad of chest.

The color drained from Robert's face. "Yes, sir, Mr. Lemkee." He backed away until he bumped into a chair against the wall and then promptly sat down.

Lemkee turned around and extended a hand toward Levi. "You must be Mr. Bowman. It's a privilege to finally meet you."

Levi stood and shook hands. "Likewise, Mr. Lemkee. Happy to see you were able to make the long drive down from Bellingham. Please have a seat."

Lemkee smiled as he sat. "I didn't drive so the trip wasn't so long. I'd introduce you to my pilot, but it seems she's preoccupied with the young man keeping watch outside. Apparently, they know each other. Small world, huh?"

"Can I get you something to drink?" Levi asked.

"Please just call me Titus. This is poker, and it's your establishment. No need for formalities. That said, I'm dying for a whiskey. I hear you have some that's quite good."

Admiral nodded. "It is good–brewed local."

"And who might you be?"

"Call me Admiral. I'm just a used up old cutter is all."

"You worked trees?"

"I did. Made my name in the woods around these parts. By the looks of you, I'd guess you've done the same. I'm too tired and broken to do it myself these days, so I hire it out. That is, until Levi started taking my workers from me."

Admiral looked at Levi. "What? You thought I wouldn't notice how you have one of my logging crew watching the door for you?"

Levi shrugged. "It wasn't that I didn't think you'd notice. I just don't care."

The bar went quiet. Lemkee's head swiveled from side to side as he glanced at Admiral and Levi. "Clearly, you two have some history. Hope it don't get in the way of the poker."

Admiral propped his meaty elbows on the table. "I practically raised him as my own. Just about everything he knows he learned from me. Ain't that right, Levi?"

Levi shuffled the cards. "Whatever you say, Admiral. You all ready? I'll ask that those of you watching to keep the noise down. If you can't do that, you'll be told to leave–no exceptions. We'll take a break every hour on the hour until we have a final winner. Good luck, gentlemen."

The first hand was dealt.

Everyone folded quickly the first few times. The pots were small as the players felt out the other's nuances. The fourth game was the beginning of something different. Dalton went all in against Jack Taub.

Taub stared at his cards and then looked at Dalton. "The old Bowman bluff, eh? Yeah, that's what I think this is. Thought you'd push me around? I'm sitting on two pair over here, Dalton. That's no lie. I call you, I win. That's how I figure it."

Dalton locked eyes with Taub. "Then stop talking and do it."

"If I fold, will you show me your cards?"

Dalton didn't answer.

"Shit," Taub muttered. He folded. "C'mon, let me see what you got."

Dalton turned his cards over. Taub's mouth fell open.

"You don't even have pair."

Admiral laughed. "A stone-cold bluff. Dalton's got a pair all right. Big brass ones."

The first hour of play passed quickly. Levi announced a ten-minute break. Bennett brought fresh shots of whiskey for all the players. Everyone drank but Admiral. He stared down at the amber liquid while swirling it in its glass.

"You're not thirsty?" Levi asked.

Admiral pushed the whiskey away. "Want to keep my head clear. Someone's gonna get bumped this next hour. I aim to make sure it isn't me."

Lemkee grabbed the whiskey and downed it. "Where'd you get this stuff, Mr. Bowman?"

Admiral grunted. "He won't tell you. Levi likes his secrets. He always has. If you're interested, I might get you some–for the right price. After we're done here tonight, you just let me know."

Dalton clenched his jaw. "You have something that don't belong to you, Admiral?"

Admiral wagged a finger. "Uh, uh, uh, Dalton, that's between your pa and me. You just worry about your cards."

Lemkee took out a cigar, bit off the tip, and lit it. "Anything I should know about?"

Levi shuffled the deck. "Nope. Second hour. Here we go."

It was during the seventh hand of the second hour that Denver Probst went all in and was quickly called by Lemkee. Probst showed three queens. Lemkee had a flush.

"Well played, sir," Probst said. He shook hands with each player. "This is a skilled table. If you host another match, I do hope you let me know."

Levi nodded. "You're welcome to stay and watch. Enjoy another whiskey on the house."

"I'd like that," Probst said with a smile. "Thank you." He left the table.

Lemkee had the most chips followed by Dalton. Admiral and Taub had the shortest stacks. Admiral let out a long sigh.

"Shit, I might as well drink. Maybe it'll change my luck." He snapped his fingers. Laney arrived at the table scowling. She slammed a shot glass down in front of him.

"That's the last time you snap your fingers at me."

"What? I didn't mean nothin' by it. Jeez."

Laney returned to the bar. Admiral took a sip and wrinkled his nose. "What's this shit?"

"That's what you get," Laney yelled back. "Take it or leave it."

Admiral looked like he might throw the glass at Laney. "Don't even think about it," Levi warned him.

Admiral took another sip and grimaced. "I wasn't going to do anything. There's no need for threats. I'm just hurt that you don't think enough of me to give me the good stuff is all."

"How would you know what the good stuff tastes like?"

Admiral waved off the question. "I'm here to play poker."

Levi glanced at his pocket watch. "It's break time. We'll start up again in five."

Admiral walked out the front door. Levi went into his office holding the money box under his arm. Bennett and Dylan followed him while Dalton remained seated at the table.

Levi put the box in the safe and then stepped outside. He took a deep breath while looking up at the moon and stars.

"Dalton's doing well," Bennett said from inside the office.

"Yeah," Levi replied. "He's on his game. That Lemkee has some skill as well."

"Was Admiral the one who took the Basin whiskey?" Dylan asked.

Levi turned around. "He's sure talking that way. Why the hell he'd be so blatant about it seems odd. He's got to know I'll take it back from him."

"It's a sign of disrespect," Bennett said. "That's how I see it. He's putting it right in your face, so everyone knows he stole from you. He doesn't give a damn."

Levi leaned against the hood of his car. "But why?"

Bennett shrugged. "He's old. He's crazy. Who knows?"

Dylan stuck his head outside. "We should probably be getting back. They're already lined up four-deep around the table, and they all want drinks. Laney says we might run out by the end of the night."

Levi cocked his head. "You hear something?"

Bennett nodded. "Yeah, what is it?"

The angry cries of several women rang out up and down Main Street. They were shouting over and over about how gambling was the devil and that everyone should say no to The Silo.

Levi closed his eyes and sighed. "That," he said, "is a pain in my ass."

33.

Jack Taub was eliminated by Dalton during the second hour of play. Taub cursed under his breath as Dalton took what remained of his chips. The win gave Dalton the money lead, followed closely by Lemkee and then Admiral.

Taub finished his whiskey, pushed away from the table, and stood. "You should do something about that racket. Makes it awful hard to focus on the cards."

"I agree," Admiral said. "Can't you get Fenton to run them off?"

Levi shuffled the cards as his gaze leveled on Admiral. "I was wondering if you might be the one who put them up to it."

"Now why in the hell would you think that? I have no say in what those church ladies will or won't do. Their way of thinking will forever be a mystery to the likes of me."

"I go out there, and this poker game stops. I'd be giving them what they want."

As if they somehow sensed the conversation going on inside The Silo, the women's shouting intensified. "Hey, Pa,"

Chance called out as he poked his head inside. "I think they're planning to storm the place."

Levi put the cards down. "You have Riley out front?"

Chance nodded. "Yup."

"Good. The both of you make sure to keep them out–but no violence."

Laney refilled each player's whiskey glass. Admiral's eyes twinkled as he gave her a big smile. "Thank you, darling." Laney walked away.

Admiral shook his head. "I'd sure like to know what I did to piss her off so much."

"She doesn't like you," Levi said. "Never has."

"I know, but why not?"

"I suppose by reputation."

"What reputation? I'm just an old man hoping to win some money at poker."

Levi shuffled the cards. "Uh-huh. So, let's play."

Right before the first card was dealt, the walls shook from the pounding of fists. Chance yelled at the women to step back from the door.

Levi stood up so fast he knocked his chair over. "Goddammit." He used his foot to shove the money box next to Dalton. "Keep an eye on that."

Dylan walked behind Levi as they both headed for the front door.

"It's getting ugly out here," Chance said. "These women– they're crazy. And they're not afraid of Riley. Not even a little."

Levi pushed the door open and went outside. He was met by the fierce stares of nine women as he calmly lit a cigarette, took a deep draw, and then exhaled. He pointed to the oldest among them.

"Bonnie Brown, you mind telling me what this is all about? I'm trying to run a business here."

The one named Bonnie stepped forward. Her red hair was streaked with silver, and her thin-lipped mouth was framed by deep lines that ran from the corners of her eyes to the top of her chin.

"Don't sass me, Levi Bowman. You know why we're here. It's our spiritual duty to put a stop to the drinking, gambling, and fornication that makes up what you call *business*."

Levi used his thumb to point behind him. "I assure you ladies there are only *two* out of those three accusations taking place inside there, so that makes me only two-thirds guilty. That's gotta count for something."

"It's just like a Bowman to act smart about sin," Bonnie said. "Know this. We're not leaving. Not until that poker game is halted and the people inside return to their homes and families where they belong."

"Where's Pastor Jim? Does he know what you all are up to?"

Bonnie poked Levi in the chest. "The pastor has nothing to do with *your* sins, Levi Bowman. This place is a dark and horrible stain upon our community. We're here to see it closed. Now. Tonight. For good."

Chance went to grab Bonnie's wrist. "Don't touch my pa."

Levi stopped him. "It's all right. She *wants* you to do something, so she can play the victim. Leave her be."

"You want me to move them back onto the street, Mr. Bowman?" Riley asked.

"Yeah, that'll work." He looked at Bonnie. "You're on my property. That's trespassing."

"And you're selling alcohol. That's illegal."

"Fine. Turn me in. Until then, get your bony ass back on the street. You can scream and shout, bark at the moon, whatever you want. I don't give a shit, so long as you do it from over there."

"And if we refuse to move?"

"Then I'll have Officer Fenner come down here and arrest you all for trespassing."

Bonnie stuck her chin out. "That won't be necessary. We aren't leaving. You won't get rid of us. We'll be right over there."

Levi smiled. "Enjoy the rest of your evening then. Goodnight, ladies."

The women returned to the street and resumed chanting. Levi told Riley to make sure they didn't come back to The Silo.

"But what if they *do* come back?"

"Have Chance come get me, and we'll figure it out then."

Riley nodded. "You got it."

Levi turned around just as Dylan pointed out a vehicle parked along the side of the building. "Hey, isn't that the car we saw driving by here real slow the night Laney blew that fella's head off?"

Levi took out his gun. "Yeah." He walked slowly toward the white car but found it empty. "You see who parked it here?" he asked.

"No," Chance replied. "I just noticed it. Think there'll be trouble?"

"Maybe. Anyone sneak inside?"

Chance glanced at The Silo's door. "I don't think so. Then again, I was watching things between you and those women, so I guess it's possible."

"You sure you weren't too busy talking it up with Lemkee's pilot? Where is she by the way? I was hoping to meet the mysterious lady of the sky."

"She drove back to Monroe to work on her plane. Noretta is supposed to drop Mr. Lemkee off at the barn when the poker tournament is over, and they'll fly back to Bellingham from there."

Levi double-checked that his gun was fully loaded and then went inside. Dylan followed close behind.

"There you are, Mr. Bowman. I told you I'd be back."

Levi recognized the voice but couldn't see the face until enough people stepped aside and Calwin Quick filled the void like Moses parting the Red Sea. "I'm not here to interrupt the game. That wouldn't be fair to the players. You go on and finish up. Our business can wait."

Levi's eyes narrowed. "What business is that?"

"Nothing you need concern yourself with just yet. Go on and deal your cards. I'll be sitting at the bar with a drink watching like everyone else."

"You took something of mine, Mr. Quick. I intend to get it back."

Quick stuck both thumbs inside his gun belt. "That's right. I *did* take something from you. And before the next sun rises, I aim to take a whole lot more."

Bennett pointed his gun at Quick as Quick kept his eyes locked onto Levi's. "I gave you my word," he said. "I won't do anything to interrupt the poker match."

"Your word?" Levi shook his head. "That isn't worth the spit it took you to say it."

"I haven't lied to you yet, Mr. Bowman."

"Do I have to take your word on that too?"

"I suppose you do."

"Now that there is a problem. I just explained how your word isn't worth anything to me."

"How about I give up my gun?"

"That would help."

Quick took out his pistol and slid it down the bar toward Laney. "That better?"

Levi nodded. "Yeah, that's better."

"Your boy behind the bar still looks like he wants to shoot me."

Levi took his seat at the poker table. "That's because he does. Now shut up or get out. Bennett, you keep on pointing your shooter at Mr. Quick. He makes one wrong move, you drop him."

Quick went quiet. The people around him backed away, including Noretta Saul.

Levi dealt the cards.

The third hour of the poker tournament was underway.

34.

"You don't have shit."

Lemkee grinned. "Then call me."

Admiral gritted his teeth. "Is that what you want?"

"Not if I don't have anything."

"So, which is it?"

Lemkee took a sip of whiskey. "You'll have to pay to find out."

The crowd edged closer around the poker table. Admiral stuck out his elbows.

"Give me some goddamned room, you bunch of mouth-breathers."

"We're waiting on you, Admiral," Levi said.

"You think I don't know that?"

Dalton stood and pointed toward the door. "Hey, let her through. Go on, step back."

Winona walked to the table and gave Dalton a quick hug.

"Oh, isn't that nice?" Admiral said. "Dalton got himself a pretty little Indian girl to play with."

Dalton's eyes shot Admiral a warning. "Fold or call," he said, "and be quick about it."

Admiral looked Winona up and down. "Mmmm, she's a tasty little thing."

Lemkee cleared his throat. "The man said fold or call. It'd be awful nice if you'd pick one or the other and stop trying to buy more time by pissing off a player who isn't even in the hand."

Admiral spit on the floor. "Don't tell me how to play poker. You're not even from around here."

"What's it gonna be, Admiral?" Levi said. "Are you calling Mr. Lemkee or not?"

Admiral pushed his chips into the center of the table. "Yeah, I'll call the bluffing son of a bitch. Let's see what he's got."

Lemkee had a sip of whiskey. "You first."

The room went still. Admiral turned his cards over and showed three nines. People murmured to each other as more side bets were hastily made.

Lemkee leaned back. "That's a decent hand. Decent don't mean winning though." He flipped a queen over, then another, and then another.

Admiral was eliminated. "Damn." He got up. "I needed to go outside for a piss anyways. These days that's about all I do right–pissing and sleeping." He left without looking back.

Levi shuffled the cards. "You two need a break?"

Lemkee shook his head. "I'm good if he is."

"Let's play," Dalton said.

"Good luck to you," Lemkee offered.

"Yeah," Dalton answered.

Winona squeezed Dalton's shoulder. He looked up at her and winked.

The first three head-to-head rounds were uneventful. Dalton folded early each time. Lemkee grew frustrated.

"I thought you said we were gonna play? We can't do that if you keep folding on me."

Dalton went all-in on the next hand. Lemkee folded and then rubbed his eyes. It was nearly midnight.

"Maybe I should have taken that break."

"I can brew up a fresh pot of coffee," Laney said.

Lemkee nodded. "That'd be nice. Thank you."

"I never got no coffee," Admiral called out from the back of the room.

"That's because I never offered it to you," Laney replied. After three more hands were played, she set cups of coffee in front of Lemkee, Dalton, and Levi.

Lemkee brought his cup to his nose and breathed deep. "Smells good." He took a sip. "Tastes good."

Levi dealt another hand. Dalton took two new cards. Lemkee took just one. Dalton raised. Lemkee went all in. Dalton called. Everyone in the room except the players and Levi leaned forward.

"You better have something good," Lemkee said. He grinned as he turned his cards over and showed three kings.

Dalton showed three nines. Lemkee's grin grew into a wide, toothy smile. He reached out to take the pot. Then Dalton turned over a pair of fours. "Full house," he said. Lemkee's chin dropped toward his chest. Winona clapped.

Admiral pushed his way forward and pointed at her. "You tell that squaw she shouldn't be celebrating like that. It isn't right to push a man's face in his own loss especially when it's a savage doing the pushing. When did you start letting just anyone into this place, Levi? She's subhuman. Might as well let a gaggle of baboons pull up a chair at the bar. It's a goddamn circus in here."

"Shut your mouth, Admiral," Levi said. "I mean it. I don't know what you're up to with that kind of talk, but it stops now."

Dalton gripped the sides of the poker table so tightly while he glared at Admiral that the wood started to crack. Winona put a hand over his. He looked up. She smiled. He took a deep breath and smiled back.

Admiral shook his head. "Now hold on. Did that little squaw cheat for you Bowmans? Is that what just happened? She comes in here and looks over our shoulders and then Dalton wins the tournament?"

All eyes turned to Levi as Admiral continued to outline his accusations. "Maybe Laney helped out too. She walks up with the drinks, peeks at our cards, then signals to Levi or Dalton or both. The whole thing could have been fixed from beginning to end."

Dalton got up. "I don't cheat. I won fair and square."

Admiral grunted. "What else are you gonna say? Of course, you'll deny it. Didn't someone else accuse you of cheating at cards not so long ago? Your brothers attacked the poor bastard, right?"

A few heads nodded. Levi pushed the deck of cards to the side. "It's time you go home, Admiral. You keep talking like this, it won't be in one piece."

"Ha!" Admiral shouted. "See? Now they resort to threats. Just more proof something stinks here. I want my goddamn money back."

Dylan, Chance, and Bennett watched Levi for any sign he wanted them to do something. Levi rose from his chair with the money box tucked under his arm.

"Do *you* think we cheated you, Mr. Lemkee?"

"No, I don't. I lost fair and square. Dalton is a hell of a player."

"How about you, Mr. Probst?" Levi asked. "Or you, Mr. Taub? Either of you think you were cheated tonight?"

Both men said no. Levi downed the last of his whiskey. "There you go, Admiral. Seems you're the only one trying to spread this conspiracy. Go on home. Get some rest. You're tired."

"There might have been some cheating," a voice called out. It was Quick. He pointed at Winona.

"Those dark, savage eyes of hers were staring real hard at Admiral's cards when she walked by right before she had that hug with Dalton."

"But me and Admiral were the only ones in that hand," Lemkee said. "Are you saying I was in on the cheating too?"

Quick stood with his feet shoulder-width apart. "Maybe you were, and maybe you weren't. I just know what I saw. She shows up, and Dalton starts winning big. Coincidence? Is that proof of a crooked game? Guess that's for everyone else in here to decide. We all know what we saw."

"He makes a fair point," Admiral said. "The timing of Dalton's good fortune is suspect at best. Seems the Bowmans might have cheated all of us."

Levi glared at Quick. "Who are you working for?" He pointed at Admiral. "Is it him?"

"Nah," Quick said smirking.

"Then who?"

Quick looked around the room. "These people don't give a damn about that, Mr. Bowman. They want to know if you've been running a crooked card game. They want what's in that locked box under your arm."

"That's right!" someone in the crowd shouted.

Levi pointed his gun at Quick. "Then come and take it."

Quick shrugged. "Sure, I'll shoot you for it. Just follow me outside. We can do it in the street fair and square. Let's see if you're really as fast as some folks around here seem to think you are. I'm man enough to find out. Are you?"

"I got twenty on Quick!" Admiral bellowed. "Any takers?"

Several bets were made. Laney grabbed Levi by the arm. "Tell me you're not actually thinking of meeting that man in the street."

"Bennett," Levi said, "I need you to go to the house and get my pistol. The one hanging inside my closet."

Laney's eyes were fire. "Levi Bowman, I won't be made a widow. You stop this nonsense now."

"We're not married, Laney. Win or lose you won't be a widow either way."

Laney appeared ready to slap Levi across his face. "Don't play word games with me. And don't insult me and all the years we've shared together."

"I'm sorry. I didn't mean to offend."

"And yet you really do aim to go up against that killer?"

"He called me out–called me out in front of everybody."

"So?" Laney hissed. "Is that any reason to risk dying?"

"I can handle myself. You know that."

"What I know is that until now, despite all our bickering, our disagreements, I never considered you a stupid man." Laney wiped away tears. "This is stupid. Stupid, stupid, stupid. You heard what Quick said when he came in here. His plan was to fight you in the street all along. The accusation of cheating is just the lie he's using to make that happen. Why would you go and fall for it?"

Admiral laughed. "Looks like old Levi is gonna back down. His boss won't let him come out and play. Ain't that right, Levi?"

331

Levi's jaw clenched. "Just waiting on my pistol, Admiral. It'll be here soon enough."

Quick appeared disappointed. "Why not just use the gun you already have, Mr. Bowman?"

"This gun is for self-defense. My boy went to fetch the one I use for putting down grinning halfwits like you."

"There's a difference?"

"Yeah."

Quick shook his head and grinned. "I like you, Mr. Bowman. I mean that. You're one of the most interesting dead men I've ever met."

"You come across a lot of dead men in your time?"

Quick's smile widened. "That I have. I'm almost sorry to be adding you to the list."

"You sure about this, Pa?" Dylan whispered. "Laney's right. That man's a killer."

Levi glanced at Dylan and shrugged. "Aren't we all?"

35.

Admiral jammed a wad of chewing tobacco into his cheek as he watched Levi. "Why do you keep looking at your pocket watch?"

"I like to know the time," Levi replied.

Cars lined both sides of the street with their headlights on. Rows of people stood between the cars jostling to get a better view of the gunfight.

"It's not too late to back out. Nobody would blame you if you did."

Levi adjusted the pistol and gun belt Bennett had brought back from the house that now hung off his hips. "You and I both know that's not true. These people aren't gathered here to see me back down. They want a show. They want blood, and I'm pretty sure they don't really care whose blood it is. I also find it unlikely that you're suddenly concerned about my well-being."

Admiral spit and then wiped his nose with the back of his hand. "It's been a while since you shot with that thing is all. I know you were fast, but there's been a lot of years come and go since then."

"How much you aim to make off my dying tonight?"

"I'm not betting against you, Levi. I put up that twenty to get people to jump in is all. I have another hundred floating out there that says you'll be the one to walk away from this. I hope to collect on that other fella being the one to end up face down–not you."

"I don't need any convincing about how much you love money. You have your doubts about my walking away from this?"

"Of course, I do."

Levi looked at his watch again. "Well, we'll all know soon enough. I'd like some time with my family. Go tell your boy Quick I'll be ready in five minutes."

"He's not my boy. I'm not lying about that. I wasn't the one who brought him here."

"But you knew he was coming, didn't you? Just like you knew that what's playing out now was likely to happen the moment he stepped foot in Sultan."

Admiral avoided Levi's stare.

"And I'm also sure you know where Quick is keeping Cridert's stash that he stole from me."

"Dammit, Levi, how'd things get so sideways between us? The last thing I want is to see you dead. I swear that's the truth of it. I need you to believe that."

"And I want you to tell me who brought Quick here."

"You survive this night, and I'll do just that. I promise. Come find me, and I'll tell you everything I know–every bit of it."

Levi cinched his gun belt tighter. "Oh, I'll find you, Admiral. No worries there. Now leave me be."

Admiral retreated into the crowd. Laney stepped forward while Dalton, Dylan, Bennett, Chance, and Winona stood directly behind her.

"Why are you doing this?" Laney asked. "It doesn't make any sense."

Levi pulled Laney toward him. "Sometimes the things a man has to do don't need a reason."

"Pa," Chance said, "I can just walk over there right now and put a bullet in him. I'd be happy to do it."

"No. You'd just be making a liar of me. I agreed to settle it this way. I gave my word."

"What if he pulls before you?" Bennett asked. "Can we take him out then?"

"If that happens, you boys need to find out what Quick did with the whiskey he took from us. It belongs to this family. We can't have everyone around here thinking they can steal from a Bowman without paying a price. Beyond that, it doesn't much matter to me. I won't be around to care."

Dylan shook his head. "You're not dying, Pa."

"We're all dying, son. It's just a matter of when."

"Well you're not dying tonight. I know that much. You're gonna kill that sonofabitch, and then we're all going back into The Silo for a drink like we always do."

Laney nodded. "Dylan's right. That's *exactly* what's going to happen, you stubborn old fool." She turned away.

Levi looked down at his watch and then up at his sons. "It's time." He hugged Chance, Bennett, and Dylan before pausing in front of Dalton who reached out and squeezed his father's shoulders.

"I get it," Dalton said. "I understand why you have to do this."

"I figured you would."

"You saved me, Pa. I came back a broken thing, and you helped to put me back together. I'd like to be able to return the favor. I owe you that. I owe you everything. What do you say? Will you let me pay you back?"

"I plan to do my best to see you get that chance. If this goes wrong, though, you watch over your brothers and Laney, okay?"

"You got it. And win or lose, Quick won't leave Sultan alive. I promise to settle that account one way or the other."

"I don't doubt you, son. I never have."

Quick was already in the middle of the street with his hand resting on the butt of his gun. He locked eyes with Levi. "We gonna do this or not, Mr. Bowman?"

Levi checked his watch yet again. He was almost smiling. "I'm ready when you are."

The two men stood forty paces apart. A final few bets were made before silence descended over the crowd. Quick spit. Levi took in a slow breath and held it.

Laney walked into The Silo mumbling how she couldn't watch any longer. Winona followed her. Down the road, a dog barked while in the distance a faint rumble grew louder.

"That sneaky little shit," Admiral said.

"What do you mean?" Bennett asked.

Both men drew. The crowd gasped. A thunderous shriek echoed across the town.

Two shots were fired—one a fraction of a second sooner than the other.

Levi Bowman fell.

Calwin Quick did not.

36.

"You said to come find you. Here I am."

Admiral turned around. He stood in the shadows that stretched out over the river where it ran underneath the Sultan bridge.

"Any bites?"

Admiral shook his head. "No. Seems the fish have been waiting on you as well. You want to try a few casts?"

"I'm not here to fish."

"No, I suppose you're not," Admiral said as he set his pole down in the grass. "Glad you're up and about. When I saw you go down the other night, I was sure Quick had lived up to his namesake."

"He did."

Admiral wagged a finger. "He might have been a touch faster, but you sure as hell were the better shot. Then again, you made certain to give yourself a little help with that didn't you? It took me a while to catch on to why you kept checking your watch. You knew that train and its whistle blast were coming. Just like you knew it might be just enough to knock

Quick off his game. His shot was a touch wide. Yours wasn't. That was the difference between you living and him dying."

"Been hearing that whistle most my life, but there were no guarantees. I'm damn lucky it worked out. Still took a bullet."

"How's it healing?"

"Finnicus was able to get it out. My shoulder hurts like hell, but he says it'll heal fine–just another scar."

"Men like us, we carry plenty of those."

"Yeah, I suppose we do."

Admiral poked the middle of his forehead with the tip of his finger. "You put your shot right between Quick's eyes. Pretty sure I knew it before he did. He stood there for a second or two looking around. Even managed to take a step back before dropping to his knees and then bouncing his face off the street."

Levi didn't reply. Admiral cleared his throat. "You gonna kill me too?"

"Thought about it."

"Can't blame you for that. I never lied to you, but I'll admit to being less than honest."

"Where's my whiskey?"

"Not sure, but I know who should have the answer."

"Who?"

Admiral plucked out a long strand of grass and stuck it between his teeth. "You sure you want me to tell you? It's the kind of information that'll force your hand."

"So?"

"So, it'll likely make things even more complicated for you than they already are."

"Just tell me who it is."

"You really don't know?"

Levi reached for his gun. "Dammit Admiral, I don't have time for this shit."

Admiral shuffled to where Levi stood. The effort left him struggling for breath. He wiped his brow with a handkerchief as he looked up at the sunlit sky.

"Getting warmer. Figure this'll be the last summer I get. Suppose that's for the best. Things are changing around here and not for the better."

"The only thing I see changing is the subject. Stop stalling and give me a name. You promised to tell me everything. Remember?"

"And I will Levi. I will. Word is, you're going into business with that Lemkee fella from Bellingham. That true?"

"Could be. We'll see how it all shakes out."

"He seemed mighty impressed with how you handled Quick."

"That right?"

"Hell, yes. He didn't say much, but I could tell. He strikes me as the kind of man who wants to go big, and I guess it's your plan to be a part of that. How much money you aim to make off him?"

"Admiral, where's my whiskey?"

"Been to church lately?"

"What?"

"I said have you been to church lately?"

"What's that got to do with who's keeping my whiskey?"

Admiral grinned. His eyes narrowed until he looked like a clever pig.

"Pastor Jim?"

"The good pastor has taken to thinking himself the fearless defender of our community's moral fabric. I fear it's twisted him some. Caused a series of rash decisions."

"What decisions?"

"Hiring Quick to shoot you dead for one. I'm pretty sure he hired that other fella too. The sloppy job at The Silo. The one whose head Laney plastered on the wall."

"Bullshit."

"Whether you choose to believe me or not, it's the truth. The pastor was the one to bring Quick here. Quick openly advertised his services, but he wasn't cheap. My guess is Pastor Jim was gonna pay him out of the proceeds from selling all that whiskey."

"Were you the one buying?"

"What? The whiskey? No, no, not me. I don't have that kind of cash these days. Hell, I had to cut down and sell off a whole slew of trees just to be able to afford a chair at your poker tournament. If cash is king, I'm its pauper."

Levi lit a cigarette. "Does Pastor Jim still have it?"

"I'm not sure. He might. He might not."

"You're not giving me much to go on. How about you tell me what you know instead of what you don't? Start with who the pastor thinks he could sell my whiskey to."

Admiral pulled out a flask from inside his jacket, unscrewed the cap, took a sip, and then offered some to Levi, but Levi declined.

"I just want a name."

"That was a lot of booze. Who do you know has access to that kind of money and a place to store it? I see your wheels turning now. Yes, sir, first place I'd look if I were you would be your new business partners. Might be the Noretta woman, Lemkee, or just as likely both. Pastor Jim already knew Noretta right? There you go. It's the only answer that makes any sense."

Levi took in and then let out a deep breath. "I have one big problem with that version, Admiral."

"What's that?"

"It's missing the part you played. Outside of my family, you were the only one I told about Cridert's stash up on the Basin."

Admiral frowned. "Well, shit, Levi, I was just a messenger is all. I had no idea the pastor would actually act on the information I gave him."

"So, you admit to telling him. Why would you do that? I'd already agreed to cut you in for five percent."

Admiral turned away. "You wouldn't understand."

"You best try me before I do to you what I did to Quick."

"You'd really take it that far?"

"I don't see how you've left me much choice."

Admiral coughed into his hand and then spit. "I'm the one without a choice, not you. I'm living in a body that's betrayed me. *That's* why you wouldn't understand. I needed to try and be right with God, and around here the pastor is the quickest way to get there."

"You stabbed me in the back. Now explain why. I don't want to hear your poor old man crying bullshit. That's no reason to do what you did."

"Levi, I don't have to tell you fuck all about the whys of my ways. That's the answer you get. Do with it what you will."

"Why were you pitting the pastor against me, my business, my family?"

"He needed no convincing of that. Pastor Jim says you've been a plague on the town for far too long."

"And you agreed with him?"

"Of course not."

"But you still worked with him."

"Yeah, but that was just business."

"Go to hell."

Admiral shook his head. "I'm dying. Congestive heart failure."

Levi flicked his cigarette away. "What are you talking about?"

"It's true. My ticker's about done, like a broken old watch winding down to its last second. A fancy Seattle doctor said I have a few more months. Six at most if I'm lucky."

"And I'm supposed to feel sorry for you?"

"I didn't say anything about feeling sorry for me. You're the only one I've told. Now if you want to put some lead into me, go right ahead because I really don't give a shit. Living is a young man's business, and I haven't seen young for a very long time."

"You poor thing."

Admiral stood up straight. "Go on then. Take out your shooter and pull the trigger. You said it yourself. I deserve it. Besides, you'd be doing me a favor."

"Right now, you're the last one I want to be doing any favors for. You sure Pastor Jim has my whiskey?"

"He should, unless he sold it already."

"You better hope he hasn't."

"Or what? You gonna kill me? I told you already. I'm dying. There's nothing you can do to me now that isn't done already."

"There are worse things than dying, Admiral."

"Yeah? Like what?"

"Dying slow."

Admiral dropped his head again. When he looked up, his eyes were wet. "I miss the way things used to be around here."

"How's that?"

"It's like I said. Things are changing, and not for the better. The train, the paved roads, the telephone, electricity, it all adds up to interference against the people of this town to be who or what they want to be. The county sticks its nose into our business. Then the state. And now the feds. They don't ever aim to give that power back. It'll be one stack of rules and regulations followed by another and then another."

Levi arched a brow. "You've turned from town boss to philosopher in your old age."

"Maybe so. I'm right, though. You'll see. Soon there won't be any room in this world for men like us. The way of the gun and the fist is going to be replaced by faceless bureaucrats behind a desk with their boot heels pressing down on all our necks."

"You paint a mighty bleak picture."

"I paint the truth."

"I hope not, for my children's sake."

Admiral sighed. "Yeah, well, that'll be their problem and your problem—not mine."

"Never took you for a man who gives up."

"Isn't about giving up. It's just reality. I'm tired. I'm done."

Levi turned around. Admiral called out to him.

"Where you off to now?"

Levi kept walking. "I'm doing what you told me to do."

"What was that?"

"Going back to church."

37.

Pastor Jim held the Bible high as his voice rang off the church walls. "Never again drink the wine for which you have toiled." He smiled at the congregation. "That is from the Book of Isiah and remains so applicable to our lives today. They are words of sadness and of hope–of troubled times but also a promise of better times to come. Please bow your heads and let us pray."

Levi got up from his seat at the back of the church. "No need for that, Pastor. The sermon's over. Everyone out."

Pastor Jim clutched the Bible to his chest. "Excuse me?"

"No, I don't think I will." Levi raised his gun over his head and fired a shot into the ceiling. "I won't ask again. I said everyone out–*now*. And close the door behind you."

People scrambled through the church doors until only Levi and Pastor Jim remained.

"Mr. Bowman, even for you this behavior is unacceptable."

Levi pointed the pistol at the pastor. "Come here and sit down. You and I are going to have a conversation. A *real* one, not that preaching bullshit."

The pastor's stutter returned. "I'm not moving until you put that gun away. This is God's house, Mr. Bowman."

Levi looked up at all the stained glass that surrounded them. "God sure as hell didn't pay for those windows. I did. You remember that? I welcomed you here, Pastor Jim. Helped get you started. And what have you given me in return?"

The muscles in the pastor's face showed the strain it took for him to form the words. "I really have no idea what you're talking about."

"Yeah, you do. You're a lying, stuttering piece of shit hiding behind a book you clearly don't live by."

"Mr. Bowman, if I've done something to offend, I am truly sorry."

"I said come here and sit down." Levi pointed at the pew in front of him.

"And I told you I wasn't moving until you put the gun away."

Levi shot out one of the stained-glass windows. "Stop it!" Pastor Jim cried. "What are you doing?"

Levi took aim at a second window. The pastor scrambled to the pew and sat down.

"Mr. Bowman, please tell me what this is all about."

Levi holstered his pistol inside his jacket. "I intend to, but where to begin? How about you taking something that didn't belong to you? Something of mine. Let's start there."

"What?"

The back of Levi's hand crashed against the pastor's cheek. "Don't."

"Don't *what*?" The pastor's mouth trembled.

Levi leaned forward. "Don't lie to me."

The pastor opened his mouth. Levi cut him off.

"I said don't lie to me. Now tell me where my booze is. I know it was you who had Quick take it from Cridert's place on the Basin."

Pastor Jim rubbed the side of his face. "Who told you that?"

"Don't ask me questions you already know the answer to. That just tells me you're trying to buy yourself time which means you're lying–*again*. Where's my goddamn whiskey?"

Both men turned at the sound of a knock on the door. "Pa, it's Bennett. Fenner's out here asking to be let in. We got a mighty big crowd gathered out front, and it's getting bigger by the minute."

"Go ahead and let him in. You and your brothers keep everyone else out. This'll be over soon."

Fenner stepped inside the church and closed the door. He looked at the pastor and then at Levi. His hand rested on the butt of his gun.

"I can't have you shooting the pastor, Mr. Bowman. You'd be forcing my hand."

"You can take that same hand and shove it up your ass. Go back outside and keep everyone in line. I won't be long."

Fenner looked every bit as old and tired as he likely felt. "I mean it, Levi. I won't abide bloodshed in here. Think of all the witnesses not more than a few feet beyond the front door."

Levi's eyes flared. "You won't *abide*? Really? That's cute. Now get out, or I'll call my boys in to drag you out. Don't think I won't."

The pastor tried to stand. Levi reached over and pressed the business-end of his pistol against the side of the pastor's head.

"Sit."

"Don't leave me alone with him," Pastor Jim said. "He's clearly lost his mind."

"What's this about, Mr. Bowman?" Fenner asked.

"He stole from me. That's all you need to know."

"Stole *what*?"

"My fucking livelihood. Now get out."

"Are you really gonna kill him?"

"Don't know yet. That's up to him."

"How so?"

"All he has to do is tell me the truth."

"And if he does that, you'll let him go?"

"Maybe."

"*Maybe*? I'm sorry, but I can't leave this room on a maybe."

Levi aimed his gun at Fenner's face. "That isn't your choice to make. Get the fuck out. NOW."

"Jesus, Mr. Bowman. You're threatening to shoot me? All these years we've known each other, and you've never done that. First Admiral leaves Sultan for good and now this."

Levi lowered his pistol. "What did you say?"

"What?"

"About Admiral leaving town."

"You didn't know?"

"If I knew I wouldn't be asking."

"He up and left. Saw him late yesterday with this other fella, the real big one from his logging crew I think, driving a pair of transport trucks out of town. Admiral stopped and told me good luck. I asked him what he meant by that, and he smiled and said it was time for a change of scenery. He put the truck in gear, honked, waved, and was gone with the other one following right behind him. I went by his place an hour or so later and had a look. It was pretty much cleaned out."

"Empty?"

Fenner nodded. "That's what I said. Admiral's gone. And don't ask me where to because I have no idea."

Pastor Jim groaned. "That decrepit snake."

Both Levi and Fenner looked at the pastor. Levi arched a brow.

"Is there something you'd like to tell me?"

"Yes, there is, Mr. Bowman, but I'd prefer to keep it between us."

Levi looked at Fenner as he tilted his head toward the door. "It's time you get going."

Fenner shrugged. "Sure. I'll go after you promise not to do any harm to the good pastor here. That's the deal. You may be a lot of things, Mr. Bowman, but everyone knows your word is good. Always has been. That way I can go back outside and let everyone know you two are just having a talk. Shake on it?"

Fenner stuck out his hand. Levi shook it. Fenner turned to leave.

"Hey," Levi said.

Fenner looked back. "Yeah?"

"You happen to see what Admiral had in those trucks?"

"Nope. The backs had canvas covers on them. I'd guess it was stuff from his house. A lot of it too, piled high. Those trucks were loaded down heavy–sittin' real low."

Pastor Jim closed his eyes and shook his head.

"Thanks," Levi said.

Fenner left. The pastor sighed. "Follow me."

He led Levi to a door at the back of the church and unlocked it with a key from his pocket. He carefully made his way down a narrow staircase and then opened another door. It was pitch black beyond the door's threshold.

"Hold on," the pastor said. "There's a light." He flicked on the switch and walked into the basement. The space was full of furniture, old clothes, and a few pieces of framed art.

The pastor looked around stunned. "What the hell is all *this*?"

"This," Levi said, "used to be inside Admiral's place. That painting, the dresser, the rugs, those boots, it's all his stuff."

"But what's it doing here?"

"How about we start with you telling me what *isn't* here? As soon as you heard Admiral left town in those trucks, you knew it was likely gone, didn't you? I'd guess you weren't around here yesterday. Am I right?"

"I was at a seminar in Portland. Admiral knew about it. I didn't get back until late last night. Still, for him to swap out the alcohol for his personal belongings strikes me as bizarre."

Levi chuckled. "Then you don't know Admiral. What's that bit of light coming from the back of the cellar?"

"That would be the door to the outside."

"If you had it locked, it's likely broken. That's how they got in."

The pastor ran a hand over his face. "Yeah."

Levi pointed. "Look there. Is that a note on top the dresser?"

Pastor Jim picked up the piece of paper. Levi watched him read it.

"Is it from Admiral?"

The pastor nodded.

"What's it say?"

"He asks that I accept his donation to the church. Says some of these things are actually worth a few bucks."

"I imagine so, but I don't think it's worth anything close to what all that whiskey was." Levi levelled his eyes on the pastor. "The whiskey you stole from me."

"Are you going to kill me down here, Mr. Bowman?"

"You heard me promise Fenner I wouldn't. I don't go back on my word–ever."

"I appreciate that."

Levi lit a cigarette. "Might want to hold off on thanking me. This is your last day in Sultan."

The pastor's stutter was getting worse. "I'm sorry?"

"You heard me. You leave–today. And don't ever come back."

"But my church. My flock. They need me."

"Like hell they do. This was never *your* church. It's Sultan's church. Always has been. Always will be. You're just a face. Like a portrait hanging on the wall that can easily be replaced."

Pastor Jim's features tightened. "You can't force me to leave. The people would never allow it."

"No? You sure about that?"

"I am."

Levi blew a thick, rolling cloud of tobacco toward the pastor. "I heard you say something today during your sermon about wine and toil. You remember that?"

"I do– from the Book of Isiah."

"Yeah, that's right. I've read that passage before and I think you know where."

"I don't know how I would."

Levi flicked ashes onto the pastor's shoes. "It was written down on a piece of paper stuck onto a knife that was buried hilt-deep in a dead body."

"And?"

"And you were the one who put it there."

Despite the cool, damp chill of the basement, Pastor Jim was sweating. He wiped his forehead. "That's ridiculous. No one would ever believe I had anything to do with Chan's death."

"I didn't mention a name. How'd you know I was talking about Chan?"

Pastor Jim's mouth closed like a trap. Levi nodded.

"Uh-huh, it's probably best you shut up and listen. I know you did it. Chan was a big man. You're even bigger. Big enough to wrap a rope around his neck and hang him from his ceiling. You saw me sitting at the back of the church this morning. That's why you said that verse. You know how my son Dylan likes words? One of the ones he uses from time to time is hubris. You know what hubris is, Pastor Jim?"

"Yes, I do."

Levi pointed at the pastor with the cigarette lodged between his two fingers. "I figured you might. Well, hubris is exactly what motivated you to speak the same Bible verse you left stuck in Chan's body. That's how arrogant and confident you are. You're not so confident now, though, are you?"

When the pastor kept quiet Levi repeated the question and then waited for an answer.

"No," Pastor Jim mumbled.

"You'll hang for what you did to Chan. Dylan would call that irony. Me? I'd call it justice for a lying, murdering fuck like you."

"There's no evidence. It would be your word against mine–the word of a poison peddler, a criminal."

Levi clicked his tongue. "You're not listening, Pastor. I still have the note you left. The one you wrote in Chan's blood. Oh, and there's something else you left behind that day. Something you don't know about."

The pastor squinted. "What?"

Levi blew smoke into the pastor's face. "A witness."

"You lie. There's no--"

Pastor's Jim's eyes widened. "The little savage girl. The one I've seen with Dalton. She was there? She was one of Chan's whores?"

"You mean the whores you burned alive? No, Winona was never a whore. That was some real Old Testament shit you did there. I always figured you for more of a New Testament kind of preacher–all smiles and nods and pass the collection plate."

The pastor's stuttering words escaped through clenched teeth. "Don't talk about God to *me*, Mr. Bowman."

"You do see why you have to leave Sultan for good, right? You're a murderer, Pastor Jim–a killer of women. I gave my word I wouldn't harm you... today. What you did to Chan and those women might compel you to try the same to others. People I care about. People under my protection. I'd have no choice but to put you down like the mad dog you are. The booze you stole from me that Admiral then stole from you? That'll be a funny story I get to tell my grandkids. Life goes on. But murdering a business associate of mine? No, that demands retribution, and you and I both know that would be messy. It's a mess I'd rather avoid by you doing the right thing and getting the hell out of town."

"And if I refuse?"

"Then I kill you. Won't be today–but soon. Real soon."

"Go ahead. I'd rather die than be forced to leave what I've spent years building up. Surely you understand that?"

Levi stomped out his cigarette. "You serious? You really care that much about this place? Your reputation? Or is it you don't have anywhere else to go?" He took out his gun.

"I thought you weren't going to kill me? You gave your word."

Levi pointed the pistol at the floor. "I'm not. You said you'd rather die than be forced out. How about we explore that option further? I leave the gun. You pick it up, put it against your skull, and pull the trigger. That'd be a whole lot better death than the ones you gave Chan and his whores. Speaking of which, why'd you do it? Taking a stash of booze, I understand. There's easy money to be made. But murder? That must be weighing awful heavy on your conscience, you being a man of God and all."

"Don't mock me, Mr. Bowman. It's unseemly."

"Unseemly? Me? You're the one who killed a bunch of innocent people."

"They were far from innocent. They had abandoned God long ago. You know that."

"What I know is that Chan was an honest businessman who provided a service. That's it. Him and his whores didn't deserve to die."

Pastor Jim closed his eyes, pinched the space just above his nose with his fingers, and shook his head. "He sold poison to the people of this town and forced women to lie down with men for money. That isn't a service. That's a scourge. I didn't murder those women. I freed them. As protector of this community's eternal soul it is my duty to do battle with such things. To do battle with *you,* Mr. Bowman."

"You're some small-town version of the righteous hand of God, huh?"

The pastor's eyes smoldered. "Something like that, and as such, I fear neither death nor you."

"Good. That'll make blowing your own head off easier."

"Killing oneself is a sin."

"But killing others isn't? What kind of fucked up religious backdoor logic is that?"

"You wouldn't understand. You're not a man of faith."

"If being a man of faith also means being a murderer of innocents, you can keep that kind of faith for yourself. I want nothing to do with it."

"What of all the killing *you've* done, Mr. Bowman? Do you mean to tell me they've all deserved it?"

"Something like that."

The two men stood quietly staring at each other until Levi took a step back. "I'm going outside and report to Fenner and everyone else that it was you who killed Chan and those women. I have the note you left using the same words you just spoke to the congregation this morning. I have a witness. Fenner will come in and arrest you. He'll hand you over to the county boys. The papers are sure to pick it up. It'll make for quite a story. There'll be a trial. It'll be quick, and after that, you'll hang. Your reputation will be ruined. I know you did it. Just like I know it was you who tried to pit Noretta Saul against me. You were willing to bring war to Sultan, put lives at risk, just to get your way."

"It would have been a blessing to have you two poison peddlers kill each other. She thought she was manipulating me when actually I was the one manipulating her."

"I wonder," Levi said.

The pastor's bottom lip trembled. "You wonder what?"

"I wonder how much Noretta has on you as well. How easy it would be for a smart woman like her to spread that knowledge to the others in your congregation including how you stole alcohol with the intent to sell. Seems you were very interested in becoming a poison peddler yourself. Then there's the hiring of Quick to kill me, and you likely hired that other fella, too. The one who shot at Dalton before Laney blew his head off. How much of the church's money did you use for that? You pay them to snuff Chan out as well? It couldn't have been cheap. Murder never is. What will the town say when they find the church coffers were cleaned out by your schemes? Is that why you turned to stealing my booze? Nothing you did before will matter. The only thing you'll be remembered for is being a murdering thief. The law is going to string you up high for all the world to see. I won't lie. It'll be brutal. You won't have any say in what they do to you or how they do it. You're going to suffer more pain and humiliation than you ever thought was possible. You'll piss and shit yourself as the rope squeezes the life from you and many of the same people outside the church this morning, your congregation, will be there to watch it."

The pastor turned away. His entire body shook. His stuttering voice was that of a frightened child. "Shut up-- *please.*"

"I tell you what, Pastor Jim. I'm gonna make my way upstairs. I'll leave my gun on the floor. You take some time to decide how you want to use it. Take all the time you need."

"What if I choose to use it to come outside and start shooting?"

Levi shrugged. "Either way the people of this town will see you for what you really are, and you'll be dead."

"Wait."

"Yeah?"

"If I decide to stay down here, will you promise to keep what I did a secret?"

Levi nodded. "Sure. I won't tell a soul. Your reputation will remain intact, and in the eyes of Sultan, you'll die a saint by suicide. That's what you want isn't it? You really do care what others think of you. Hell, I'll even see to it there's a plaque over a door of the church with your name on it."

The pastor started to cry. "You would do that for me? You promise?"

"I give you my word. If you leave Sultan, though, I'll tell everyone everything I know. You'll be caught, and the people of this town will curse your name for generations to come. If you want to avoid that outcome all you have to do is pull the trigger and you'll have purchased my silence. All that pain, the shame and guilt that you've been bottling up for the things you've done, it all ends today. You'll finally be at peace. The choice is yours."

Pastor Jim licked his lips. His face was grim and his eyes haunted, a man broken from the inside out. He wiped away tears.

"Thank you. I know having a choice is more than I deserve."

"You're right. It is."

Levi backed away and then placed his pistol on the floor. "You take care, Pastor."

"You too, Mr. Bowman."

Levi went upstairs and walked outside. It seemed the entire town had gathered at the bottom of the church steps. Fenner grabbed Levi's arm.

"Where's the pastor?"

Levi looked down. Fenner quickly pulled his hand away.

"I didn't hurt a single hair on his head. He's weighing his options."

"Options? What options?"

Everyone but Levi flinched at the sound of a single gunshot from inside the church.

"Mr. Bowman," Fenner said, "what the hell did you do?"

Levi struck a match against the side of the church and lit a cigarette. He took a couple long, slow drags.

"I didn't do anything. I'm standing here with you and all these other fine people. Whatever happened in there was the pastor's doing–not mine."

"Where's your gun?"

"Sounds like the pastor decided to borrow it."

"Jesus Christ, Levi."

"Hey, hey, not in front of the church. Watch the language."

"What kind of mess am I gonna find in there?"

"Trust me. This went as clean as it could. You should be thanking me."

Fenner leaned forward until his face was inches from Levi's. "Thank you? For contributing to the death of the town pastor?"

Levi pushed Fenner away. "That's the last time you take that tone with me. As for what you find in the church basement, I'll just say this one time, and then you don't ever bring the subject up to me again. Good riddance."

"Good riddance? That's it?"

"Yeah. That's it."

Fenner started to say something more. Levi cut him off. "Not another fucking word. Now get in there and do your job."

The crowd parted as Levi went down the church steps. Dalton, Dylan, Bennett, and Chance joined him.

"Where are you going?" Fenner asked.

Levi stopped and turned around. The sun was in his eyes. A cloud of smoke hovered above his head.

"Back to work. Somebody needs to make sure this town gets what it wants. Stop by The Silo later today with my gun. The pastor won't be needing it anymore. One last thing. I want a little plaque made up with the pastor's name on it. Hang it above the door of the church outhouse."

The Bowmans left. Fenner cursed under his breath as he and the rest of Sultan watched them go.

38.

Nearly three months had passed since Pastor Jim put his mouth around Levi's gun and pulled the trigger. It was summer and one of the Bowman boys was hard at work building a house.

"One more nail in, and a thousand more to go," Dalton said. He was uncharacteristically cheerful as he kept hammering. Winona watched him intently.

Dalton glanced over his shoulder. "This look right?"

Levi closed one eye and cocked his head. "It's level. Keep going. Your brothers should be here soon to help. At this rate, you'll be finished long before the October rains arrive."

Dalton grinned. "That's the plan."

Levi noticed Winona staring at something behind him. He turned and saw an older man walking across the field toward them. A few seconds later, Dalton noticed him as well and stopped hammering.

"Who's that?"

Levi shook his head. "No idea."

"Come over here," Dalton said to Winona. "Get behind me."

The man stopped some forty yards away and held up both hands. His white hair was cut short and a long mustache of the same color framed his mouth. He wore spectacles and a dark suit and tie.

"I come in peace, Mr. Bowman. My name is Silas Moore. I'm an attorney."

"State your business, Mr. Moore."

"I'm here to deliver you some legal papers."

"Papers?"

"I was hired by Larson Kohl a few years ago to put his estate in order."

"You mean Admiral?"

Moore nodded. "That's right."

"What does that have to do with me?"

Moore's eyes widened. "Oh, you didn't know?"

"Know what?"

"Mr. Kohl passed on last month while convalescing at a resort in Tucson. His heart failed. Died in his sleep."

If the news saddened him, Levi didn't show it. He shrugged. "That it?"

"No, Mr. Bowman, that's not it. Far from it." The lawyer's hand went into his jacket.

"Don't move." Levi pointed his gun at Moore.

"It's just an envelope."

Dalton walked over to Moore, reached into his jacket, and pulled out a manila envelope that was folded in half. He held it up, so Levi could see it.

"It's like he said--just an envelope."

Levi put his gun away. "Bring it here."

Dalton dropped the envelope into Levi's hand. Levi opened it and withdrew a stack of papers.

"There's a personal letter from Mr. Kohl in there for you as well," Moore said. "He wrote it just a week before his passing."

Levi found the letter and started to read.

Levi,

If you have this, that means I made good on my promise that I didn't have long to live. Truth be told, I wish that could have been one promise I couldn't keep. It was a good run, and I've managed to make these final weeks enjoyable ones. The women are pretty, the days long, the sun warm, and the drinks plentiful. I just wish the time hadn't passed so quickly.

In addition to this letter, there are nine deeds representing the entirety of my remaining property holdings in Sultan. Each one has been signed over to you. The town is yours Levi–nearly all of it. That should more than make up for the alcohol I stole. I hope you can find it in yourself to forgive me. I just needed one more adventure. One more deal. One more run at a worthy opponent. If you don't yet understand that kind of motivation, give it time. One day you will.

I heard about what happened to Pastor Jim. How you managed to have him off himself I'll never know. You possess a talent for that sort of thing that escapes my comprehension. I quietly tried to run that man out of town for years. You finally did and without having to pull the trigger yourself. Take care in choosing his replacement, and don't think he was your only source of trouble. More is sure to come starting with your new business partners Mr. Lemkee and Ms. Saul. I understand you're doing well, that business is booming. Enjoy it, but always keep one eye on those two while you do. Sooner or later, people like them always try to take more, especially when what they want belongs to someone else. Relationships are a lot like the weather–both can change quickly. You must always be prepared to change as well. I learned that lesson much too late in life. Don't repeat my mistake. Protect yourself, protect those you love, and protect Sultan.

I'm tired. As tired as I've ever been. I just want to sleep now, so I guess this is goodbye.

You did good. I'm proud of you. I mean that. Keep doing it for as long as you can and try to enjoy every second of it.

Always your friend,

-Admiral

"That concludes our business, Mr. Bowman. I'll be on my way."

Levi shook Moore's hand. "Is that it?"

"Yes, sir. Enjoy your properties." Moore turned around and left.

Levi stuffed the papers into his jacket. "Guess we can get back to framing this wall."

Dalton pointed toward the pond behind them. "Not yet-- more company coming this way."

Laney, Dylan, Bennett, and Chance were walking with Fenton Fenner. "What does *he* want?" Levi mumbled.

Fenner smiled. "Finally getting around to putting up the house eh, Dalton?"

Dalton didn't smile back. "Yup."

"What can I do for you, Officer Fenner?" Levi asked.

Fenner shook his head. "Just call me Fenton. That's the reason I came out here. I wanted to tell you in person. I'm retired, Mr. Bowman–as of this morning. Getting too old for this shit. Please don't try and talk me out of it. My mind is made up, and there'll be no changing it."

Levi frowned. "Is it the salary? You want another raise?"

"No sir," Fenner said. "It isn't about money. Not this time. It's about me. I'm not up to the job. Sultan is growing. The town needs a younger man to keep the peace around here. Of course, I figure you'll have a lot of say in who that might be. I've already posted the job opening."

"We still haven't filled the pastor position yet. Can't you stay on until we have your replacement ready to go?"

Fenner shook his head. "Sorry, Mr. Bowman. I don't want to be stuck here waiting for that to happen."

"Fair enough. Let me know when you have a potential candidate. We'll want to make sure it's someone who fully understands how the job requires they look the other way regarding certain business practices."

"Of course, Mr. Bowman. Nice to see you all again."

After Fenner was gone, Laney stood next to Levi. "Is his leaving going to be a problem for us?"

Levi lit a cigarette. "No more a problem than what passes for normal around here. We'll be fine. Crooked cops are like assholes. Every town has at least one. We'll find ours."

Dalton picked up a hammer. "Until then, how about we get back to work?"

Bennett gave Dalton a playful shove. "Listen to you, big brother. You sound awful anxious to move out of the big house."

"If it means not having to share space with you, you're goddamn right I am."

"Gee," Bennett said, "pretty soon it'll just be Dylan and me."

Levi arched a brow. "How's that?"

Bennett plopped a cigarette into his mouth and fired it up. "Dalton and Winona will be married soon, and with how much time Chance has been spending with his pilot girl, I'm guessing he's not far behind."

Levi glanced at Chance. "That situation getting serious?"

Chance looked down at his boots. "Maybe."

Bennett chuckled. "See? I told you. He's a goner! There'll be just two of us to carry on the proud Bowman bachelor tradition."

"Leave me out of this," Dylan said.

Bennett's face went pretend-serious. "What are you talking about? There's a whole stash of pretty girls out there waiting to be discovered. I'll even give you first chance at my throwaways."

Dylan grimaced. "Ugh."

Dalton slammed another nail into a piece of wood. "Will you two shut up, and lend me a hand?"

Levi watched as his four sons grabbed hold of the framed wall and pushed it up. "Should we help?" Laney asked.

"Nah," Levi said. "They're plenty old enough to do it on their own."

With arms trembling, Dylan, Bennett, and Chance held the wall while Dalton nailed it in place. The brothers stepped back and admired their work.

Dalton's eyes softened as he looked at his three younger siblings. "Thanks for the help."

"Our pleasure big brother," Dylan said. "It's going to be a beautiful home. Winona and you will be very happy here."

Winona slid her arm around Dalton's waist. Dalton gave her a warm smile, pulled her close, and then looked at Levi.

"How do you think it's coming along, Pa?"

"You're building it on solid ground. The kind of ground a man can raise a family on. Dylan's right. It's already a beautiful home. We're all happy to see you smiling again."

"I have a lot to smile about these days. We all do."

Laney nodded. "That's right. We've had our struggles, but we're still here. Still have our health and the ability to make a living. That's all that matters. When this family sets its mind to it, we can do anything."

Bennett lifted his cigarette high like he was making a toast. "Here, here."

The noon train's whistle carried on the wind to where the Bowman family stood. A faint smile flittered across Levi's face when he heard the sound.

"Anyone else hungry?" Laney asked. "I can make us up some sandwiches back at the house."

Chance grinned. "Hell, yeah. I'm starving."

Laney looked at Levi. "How about you?"

"You all go on ahead," he said. "Gonna finish my smoke. I'll catch up. Just save me a bite."

Laney squeezed Levi's hand. "Okay. Don't be too long. You know how tough it is to keep those boys from eating everything in sight."

Levi watched them go. Dalton and Winona walked arm in arm as Laney complimented Winona on her dress. Bennett was giving Chance a hard time about his new girlfriend. Chance threatened to kick Bennett's ass if he didn't shut up about it. Dylan was a few paces behind the others with his hands stuffed into his back pockets, part of the group but also the perpetual loner intent on doing his own thing.

A dark line dissected the otherwise blue sky above. It was a far-off summer storm that moved so slow it was hard to tell it was moving at all. A gentle breeze pushed it toward Sultan. Levi took out Admiral's letter and re-read part of it.

Relationships are a lot like the weather—both can change quickly. You must always be prepared to change as well. I learned that lesson much too late in life. Don't repeat my mistake. Protect yourself, protect those you love, and protect Sultan.

Levi put the letter away and finished the last of his cigarette just as a drop of rain struck the side of his face. He looked up. The storm was closer. Admiral had been right. Eventually everything was bound to change.

"Let it come," Levi whispered to no one and everyone. "I'll be here waiting."

It was time for lunch.

Time for family.

Time to go home.

End.

Your feedback is always appreciated. Please remember to leave a quick review for The Bowman Boys on its Amazon page. Thank you!

And while you're there, check out these other novels by D.W. Ulsterman HERE

ABOUT THE AUTHOR

D.W. Ulsterman is the writer of the Kindle Scout-winning San Juan Islands Mystery & Romance series published by Kindle Press as well as the bestselling family drama, The Irish Cowboy.

He lives with his wife of twenty-six years in the Pacific Northwest. During the summer months you can find him navigating the waters of his beloved San Juan Islands. He is the father of two children who are now both attending university and he is also best friends with Dublin the Dobe.

Made in United States
Troutdale, OR
12/05/2023

15327268R00216